CW00410509

Shoot the Breeze

Kate Rosetti, Volume 1

Gina LaManna

Published by LaManna Books, 2020.

SHOOT THE BREEZE

First edition. March 27, 2020.

Written by Gina LaManna.

To everyone quarantined at the moment... hang in there! ;)

Special Thanks:

To Alex and Leo—for being the best quarantine buddies I could ask for! я тебя люблю!

To my family—for being the best virtual quarantine buddies I could ask for! ;)

To Stacia—for being the best friend a girl could ask for (and editor, of course!)

To my family, friends, and LaManna's Ladies, thank you for coming along on another ride with me!

1

Blurb

Welcome to St. Paul, Minnesota—home to strong coffee, deadly winters, and Detective Kate Rosetti—a rising star in the local homicide department. When a young woman turns up dead along the Mississippi River in her latest assignment, Detective Rosetti quickly realizes it's the work of a notorious cross-country serial killer.

To complicate matters, Kate's troublemaking sister turns up out of the blue in need of a place to live. A strikingly handsome FBI agent appears at the crime scene, convinced this case belongs to him. And a certain British billionaire is a little too interested in the murder... and in Kate.

As she begins to close in on the killer, the investigation takes a turn for the personal. It's one riddle after the next, and if Kate can't sort out the murderer's identity before his next kill, she'll be up next on the autopsy table.

Chapter 1

"This is black coffee." I frowned into the mug, then looked up at my mother. "I didn't order this."

My mother peered into the cup she'd just poured. "Will you look at that," she said. "I guess I made some adjustments to your usual order, seeing as otherwise, it would kill you. The amount of sugar and caffeine you consume is alarming."

"A caramel latte with extra whip is not a bad way to go out," I said. "But I might agree to a compromise."

"Skinny latte, half-caff. Final offer."

"Make it full-caff, and you've got a deal."

My mother eyed me warily before she extended a hand to shake mine. I returned her handshake solemnly.

"By the way," I said, "Jimmy asked me to pick up his order too."

My mother, Annie Rosetti, wrinkled her nose and wiped her hands on her apron. "If Jimmy can't walk over here himself, how can he be expected to protect you? I'm not trying to be judgmental, but the man hasn't run in over twenty years."

I reached around the counter, grabbed my mom's wrist, and dragged her into the back room of Seventh Street Café—a little coffee shop that had become her life's passion and sole source of income after my parents divorced when I was five.

It was, as the name suggested, located on West Seventh Street in St. Paul, right next to the precinct where I was employed as a homicide detective. I inhaled the familiar scent of frosting, icing sugar, and freshly brewed coffee before cornering my mother. Then I crossed my arms and waited until she looked me in the eye.

"We talked about this, ma," I warned. "Please don't interfere. You promised."

"I'm not interfering with anything. I just love you, is all. And speaking of love, have you heard from your sister?"

"No, why? I thought she was staying with you."

"She was. Until two days ago."

"Where'd she go?"

My mother just stared at me, her brown eyes the exact same shade as mine. People said we could be sisters. I didn't see it, though the resemblance between us was there. We'd both inherited the Italian nose that was about three times too big, along with the dark hair, the big smile, and far too much sarcasm.

I was taller than my mother by a good six inches, and where I'd grown taller and leaner throughout high school, my mother had gone shorter and wider as the years had slipped by. She wore a bright red apron with the name of her café embroidered on the front and just a hint of makeup that had several of the single, older cops from the station next door slipping their digits into the tip jar on the counter.

Along with the nose and the sarcasm, I'd inherited a family that was too loud and too big, and just a little too Italian. My father, Angelo Rosetti, had been a cop until it'd been gently recommended that he retire. It just so happened he left the force under a cloud of suspicion that involved some mob-involved payoffs. Judging by the ensuing newspaper articles, along with my parents' split, I took his early retirement for what it was: involuntary.

"I haven't known where your sister disappears to since she got her license," my mother said. "You know that. And it's not for lack of trying."

"Are we sure she's not adopted?"

"Can you look into it for me?"

"You want me to abuse my job resources to check up on my sister?" I gave a wry smile at my mother. "Come on, don't worry. She's probably just shacked up with her latest boyfriend. Give it a few days."

"I thought you might say that."

"I say that every time she takes off for days on end. She missed work?"

"Yesterday."

"Ma—"

My mother heaved a huge sigh, pulled out her phone and slid it across the counter toward me. "She's at the station; she spent the night."

I stepped closer, glanced at the phone. "What did she do this time?"

My mother shrugged. "I have no clue. She didn't use her phone call on me. I told her last time that it was the *real* last time I'd bail her out."

"It's been the last time since college." I squinted at the app my mother had pulled up on her phone. "Are you tracking her location?"

My mother's face split into a huge grin. "Yes."

"Last time I checked, you had difficulty turning your phone on. How'd you get a tracking device installed on Jane's phone?"

"You know that mommy blog I love? Well, the woman who writes the tech column recommended it. It's an app! Free! It tells me exactly where your sister is at all times. I just had to sneak it on there one night while she was sleeping, but the article had an idiot-proof, step-by-step guide that made it easy. It's meant for husbands, but since I don't have one of them, I thought I could use it for my daughter."

"Don't you think that's a bit invasive, seeing as Jane's thirty-two?"

"My house, my rules. And she doesn't know about the app, so don't spoil it."

"I'll see what I can do," I said. "But—"

My phone buzzed, interrupting our conversation. I pulled out my cell and saw a familiar number.

"Rosetti," I said into the receiver. After a few moments, I nodded and added, "I'll be right there."

My mother looked on eagerly. "You caught a case?"

"I'll look into Jane later," I said. "She's not going anywhere. Can I get that mocha for Jimmy now? And my latte?"

My mother returned to the front of the shop and punched in the order, dictating to Elizabeth Walker, the young college student who worked part-time at the shop. With a grin, Elizabeth slid my latte across to me.

"Skinny latte," she said with a wink. "And here's Jimmy's mocha."

I picked up the mocha and took a sip of the skinny latte which wasn't skinny at all. It was a whole milk caramel latte with extra whipped cream. I slid an extra tip across the counter to Elizabeth.

My mother watched the exchange. "Let me smell your cup."

"Ma—"

"Kate."

"I was married to your father for over ten years," she said. "I know a payoff when I see one."

"This is a coffee shop," I said. "Not a drug bust."

"Could've fooled me," she muttered.

I found Jimmy waiting for me next door at the police station on West Seventh off 35E in St. Paul, hovering against his coat. Jimmy was a large, dark-skinned man who was counting down the days to retirement like a kid counts down to Christmas. And while we both joked about it often, I was already dreading the day he turned in his badge. Though I'd die before I told him so.

I tucked my chin deeper into my jacket, fighting off the deep winter chill. A solid six inches of snow stuck on the ground from a storm a few days back, and my toes froze during the short walk between my mother's bakery and the station's parking lot.

I'd only been based on West Seventh for a short time. At twenty-six years old, I'd been the youngest female to make detective this side of the Mississippi. That year, the TC Task Force had been created by the mayor, and Jimmy and I had been the first recruits to the team. Two years later, we were still going strong covering the grisly, high-profile murders across the Twin Cities.

"My mom misses you," I said as a greeting when I neared Jimmy. "She was asking about you."

Jimmy grunted. "Mayor's already on us about this one—get in."

Jimmy was short and wide, his time on the force having added pounds along with wisdom. He had just under a year left until retirement. The paper-linked chain surrounding his desk that notated his remaining days of service had grown steadily shorter in our time as partners.

"Why? High profile vic?"

Jimmy gave one of his big shoulders a shrug as he climbed into the driver's seat of his car. I climbed in the other door and deposited his Styrofoam cup into the holder.

"I don't think it's high profile," he said. "But when a young girl ends up dead in a college town, it freaks everyone out. Parents suddenly want to pull their kids out of school... it's a mess."

"You're such a softie."

Jimmy's face cracked into a grin. He was quick-witted and good cop by all accounts. "By the way, how is your mom doing?"

"She's worried about my sister. Nothing new there; Jane took off again."

"Sorry to hear it."

I raised a shoulder, took a sip of my foamy latte and inhaled a few marshmallows straight down my throat. "You know how it goes."

"Did your mom ask you to hunt her down?"

"No hunting necessary. A little birdie told me she might be sweating it out in a cell overnight."

"Sounds like some party." Jimmy cackled, switching the lights on above the cruiser and shooting us through a stop sign. "I don't know how the two of you came from the same parents."

"You and me both," I said. "Let her sweat for a bit longer—she'll still be there after we finish up here. It's good for her."

"Tough bird."

"Jane brings out the best in me."

Jimmy screeched through the St. Paul streets, hopping up Montreal and squealing past the old, expensive homes in Highland Park, buzzing through the college zone and continuing another mile or so down to the expensive properties that lined the river's edge. He threw the car into park outside of the crime scene tape.

I climbed out of the car and took another sip of coffee, letting the extra hot latte slide down my throat in the early morning freeze. Christmas was a week away and Mother Nature had decided to hit us hard with snow this week to make up for a mild fall. Flurries were already swirling in the air, and the gray clouds above threatened to dump loads more as the day continued.

"Three hundred and twenty-four more days of this mess," Jimmy said with a shiver. "Three hundred and twenty-four."

I glanced over at my partner. "What are you going to do with your time after that?"

"Not stand outside in a snowstorm."

"Touché."

We checked in with the officer and gloved up. I took in the scene, a crystalline winter wonderland marred only by the body sprawled on the ground. I exhaled, glanced across the river.

This morning's murder was on the St. Paul bank. A stone's throw away, just across the Ford Parkway bridge, sat the trendier half of the Twin Cities—Minneapolis. The close proximity of the two cities was one of the reasons the TC Task Force had been created. Less jurisdictional red tape, more solving of actual murders. The mayor was happy, the cops were happy, the citizens were happy. Wins all around, except for our victims.

"Aw, man," Jimmy said. "She's young and pretty. I hate that."

"They're all too young."

"Where's mine?" Melinda Brooks, the uber smart medical examiner stood up, nodded toward my coffee. "I'm freezing."

I extended my drink to her. "Flat white."

"You're lying."

I shrugged, pulled it back toward me. "Fine, I'll keep it. What've we got here?"

Melinda smiled, her cheeks red against the wind. Her lipstick was perfect as usual, her blonde curls somehow shiny and picturesque and dotted with snow flurries beneath her pale pink hat. It even had a single pom pom on top. The hat alone probably cost more than my entire outfit.

Melinda wasn't only the smartest person I knew—she was also the richest. And most beautiful. And best dressed. It was amazing we maintained a friendship outside of work.

Where she wore designer duds from head to toe, I had donned my customary dark jeans with heeled boots that I'd gotten from Nordstrom Rack with a gift card and a coupon. My mother had purchased a few blazers for me so that I could trade off colors over my standard black tank tops. That constituted my uniform.

I'd swept my dark hair into a low ponytail and added an ear band to battle the cold. I completed the look with a swipe of mascara and medicated lip balm. Winter was hell on my lips. Not that any of it mattered—I didn't have many people to impress, seeing as all my victims were already dead.

"We've got a female," Melinda said. "I found a passport on the body that puts her name as Alison Newton, twenty-three years old."

"Cause of death?"

"I can't be certain until I get her back to the table."

"Guess?" I asked.

"I don't guess," she said briskly. "But we've got markings here and here."

I followed Melinda's pointed finger to our victim's neck. I studied her for a long moment noting, as Jimmy already had, that she was young and quite beautiful, her features marred only by the cruelty of her death.

Bleached blonde curls spread from either side of her head, matted by snow and blood. Her eyes were closed, her lips blue from the cold. Her skin was a ghastly pale, visible beneath the short red party dress she wore beneath a faux fur black coat. Makeup and attire signaled that she'd likely been out for a night on the town, or maybe a date.

"Strangled," I said as Jimmy joined my side. Melinda frowned at my assessment, and I raised my eyebrows. "Don't worry, you can confirm it for me at the autopsy."

"I plan on it," she said. "Estimated time of death is a bit tricky—she's been out here for a while but is preserved incredibly well thanks to the cold. My best guess is between eleven p.m. and two a.m. I'll narrow it down tomorrow morning."

"Great," I said. "What about robbery? Is this her purse?"

Melinda nodded toward the purse that was scattered next to the dead woman's hand. "Can't rule out robbery. Her wallet was left but there was no cash in it. Passport, lip gloss, tampons. No keys, either. No driver's license."

"That's odd," I said. "Who carries their passport but not a license?"

Melinda shrugged. "That's your job to find out."

I glanced at Jimmy. "Thoughts?"

"I don't think we've got an experienced killer," Jimmy said. "Scene's a bit messy for a professional—looks like she was hit over the head before she was strangled. I'm assuming she was dumped here, since we don't have any blood spatter."

"Not to mention the fact it's a bit hard to strangle someone in plain sight." I crossed my arms over my chest, closed my eyes. "So, our girl Alison dolls herself up last night. She's got someplace to be. Someone she wants to impress."

Melinda leaned back on her Jimmy Choos and waited.

Jimmy cleared his throat. "What makes you say that?"

"Because most women don't look like they're going to Cinderella's ball on an otherwise average Wednesday night," I said. "For me to put on that sort of makeup—"

"You've never put on that much makeup," Melinda said.

"Bad example," I agreed. "But if I'm squeezing into a dress, it's for a man who's buying me dinner."

"You should really raise your standards when it comes to men," Melinda said. "Red Lobster doesn't constitute a fancy date."

"Bear with me. I think it's safe to assume Alison had someplace to be. Where? A date? Was she meeting girl-friends? I'm tempted to say no as this isn't a girlfriend sort of dress. This is an 'I'm getting laid' dress."

"How would you know anything about that?" Jimmy asked with a wry smile. "The last time you took a guy home was a year ago."

"Shut up, Jimmy," I said. "You should talk."

"I'm married."

"Exactly."

He shrugged in agreement. "So, she's got herself a hot date. Where does it go wrong?"

"That's what we need to find out," I said. "Have any wit-nesses come forward?"

"Nothing yet," Jimmy said. "Officers knocked on all the doors with a view of the river road. Nada. At least, nobody's talking."

"They'd talk if they saw something," I said. "You know how much these houses go for? A three-bedroom rambler fetches an easy million around here. People forking over that sort of money on a mortgage don't want murders happening in their front yards."

Jimmy nodded along. "You think she's a student from around here?"

"Maybe," I said. "But I can't get past the fact she's got her passport instead of a license. No school ID?"

Melinda shook her head. "That's all for identification until we can pull her prints."

"I don't get the impression she's a student, but I could be wrong," I said. "So she goes out, probably meets a guy. Definitely a man."

Jimmy raised his eyebrows.

"Strangling ain't easy," I said in explanation. "But he didn't go straight down to business. He hit her over the head first—why? Maybe it was an accident? He got upset at her, hit her, then got carried away?"

"That would make this personal," Jimmy said.

Melinda nodded in agreement. "We do have blunt force trauma to the back of the skull. I'll try to match the impression for what instrument might've been used."

"If it was an accident, he might have panicked—hauled Alison into the car and drove around, wondering what to do about it."

"When she starts to wake up," Jimmy continued, "he panics worse."

"He decides to finish the job," I said dimly. "Turns down the darkest street he can find, which lead him to the river. He could've come from the St. Paul or the Minneapolis side—hard to say."

I paused, glanced across the river then back to the victim, wishing she could talk to me. She might have known her killer. Recognized him. Trusted him, even.

"We'll find him," I said, as much to myself as to Alison. "Are you all good here, Melinda?"

"I'll be wrapping things up shortly. I'll do the autopsy in the morning if you want to join," she said. "In the meantime, I'll call you if we find anything else."

I reached for the passport with my gloved hand, snapped a quick picture of it. The photo matched the image of the dead woman as far as I could tell. It looked real, felt real. If it was a fake, it was a good one. The crime lab would test to be sure.

"Where are you off to?" Melinda asked. "You've got that look in your eye."

"I've got some digging to do on Alison," I said. "But I have to stop at the precinct first."

Melinda frowned. "Another case?"

"A nutcase," I said dryly. "It's Jane."

Melinda stood, shook the snow off her furry boots. "Oh. I'm so sorry, Kate. Can I buy you a drink tonight?"

"A big one," I said. "Bellini's at seven?"

"It's a date," Melinda said, then gave me a wry smirk. "Wear a dress."

I laughed and spun away on a heel. "Is that your offer to buy me dinner and take me home?"

Jimmy coughed so hard he just about lost a lung.

I thwaked him on the back. "Easy, big boy. She's not my type."

Chapter 2

Jimmy dropped me off at the station. I hopped into my car and headed downtown to where Jane was being held. I didn't recognize the cop working the desk when I signed in, which was probably for the best.

After completing the logistical rigamarole to bail my sister out, I found her waiting for me in a slinky black dress hiked up to her thighs and boots that inched above her knees. Her eyeliner was smudged, but it didn't mask her obvious physical beauty. While I'd gotten the tall, plain, and slender genes in the family, my sister had inherited the Betty Boop build that had been attracting attention from boys since she'd bloomed in the sixth grade.

"Kate!" She waved, grinning from ear to ear. "Thank you for picking me up. I thought I'd be stuck here another day. I've been waiting on you *forever*."

"Get your things," I said. "I caught a case this morning. We can talk in the car."

Jane sighed and grabbed a glittery silver clutch. "Don't be mad. It's not what you think."

"It never is." I led the way to my department-issued car and beeped the doors open. "Where am I dropping you?"

"About that." Jane shivered against the cold wind and fumbled with her bag as she slid into the passenger's seat. She popped the mirror down and pulled out some gloss, swiping it across her lips before turning her hazel eyes on me. She looked as innocent as a child, even with her current attire. "I was hoping I could stay with you?"

I was mid-sip of my quickly-cooling latte when she asked, and I spluttered half of it back into the cup as I glanced at her. "You can't be serious. We haven't lived under the same roof since you turned eighteen and fled the nest."

"I know. Maybe it would be fun?"

I squinted. "Are you in trouble?"

"Why do I have to be in trouble to want to stay with my sister? I'll contribute to rent. You won't even know I'm there. I'll find a job."

"What happened to your job at the real estate office?"

"It didn't work out."

"Ah." I lifted my eyebrows. "Mom said you didn't show up for your shift at the café, either."

"I was busy," she said. "Anyway, please?"

"I'll drop you at mom's."

"No! You can't. Please, Kate." Jane's lips turned into a pout, her eyes filling with tears. "I don't have anywhere to go. Mom—she's got a new boyfriend. I don't want to stay there. It's too hard to see her with another man."

"It's been over twenty years since the divorce."

"Please, Kate. I'm your sister."

"And us living together is about the worst idea ever. We're as opposite as they come."

"I swear, you'll barely know I'm there."

"Jane..." I shook my head. "Where can I drop you? Who were you with when you got picked up last night?"

"A complete and utter jerk. We're over. His name was Yanis, and he was an asshole. He's the one who got me in trouble, and guess what? His *girlfriend* bailed him out! Can you believe it? He told me he was single!"

I didn't comment. Going solely off my sister's track record, it wasn't exactly a stretch to believe she'd been duped by a man. Yet again. Frankly, this wasn't the worst one, as far as I could tell.

"So, obviously I can't stay with him," Jane said. "Mom's house is out. I don't have any close girlfriends..."

I tapped my fingers on the steering wheel. Jane reached over, cranked the key on in the ignition and turned the heat up to full blast.

"It's freezing," she said.

I just stared at her bare legs.

"Beauty is pain," she said. "So, what do you say, little sis? Are you going to leave me to fend for myself on the streets? At least give me your pants if you do. I'll get frostbitten and die otherwise."

"I'm not giving you my pants," I growled. "I'll bring you to my house for the day. You can shower and get cleaned up. You've got twenty-four hours to figure out a plan that doesn't involve surfing my couch. Got it?"

"Oh, thank you, Kate!" she squealed. "Can you take me home first to grab a few things?"

"I've got a case to work," I said. "I'll take you tonight. Unless you have someplace you need to be today?"

"Well, I was thinking of meeting this guy—" Jane turned to look at me, her lips fading into a thin line as she said meekly, "No, I'm all good."

I DROPPED MY SISTER off at home after laying down the ground rules: no alcohol, no boys, no staying out all night without letting me know first. Why would I need kids when I had my sister? I glanced back as I pulled away from the little house that I called quaint and my mom called a "work-in-progress".

My house was tucked in a small neighborhood near Mancini's, a west side staple. When I was little, the area had been a booming little Italian hub of eateries and pool halls. We'd ridden our bikes up and down the alleys, straying only as far as we could go and still make it home by the time the streetlights flickered on in warning.

Unfortunately, the homes in the area hadn't progressed with the times. While some of West Seventh was going through a hipster-esque re-vamp, the rest of it hadn't aged for the last thirty years—leaving a strange mixture of new bars and peeling front porches, organic eateries and crumbling fences, flashy cars and foreclosed houses.

It took me six minutes to get to the precinct, four minutes to get to downtown St. Paul, and thirteen minutes to get to Minneapolis if I flashed my lights and dodged traffic. Until the roof collapsed on me, I wasn't planning on moving anywhere.

I pulled up my cell, dialed Jimmy. "Is it okay with you if I do next of kin notification? I've got the address from Alison's passport. Has anyone been to see her parents yet?"

"We've been saving that task for you."

"How sweet. I'll take care of it, then I'll be in after."

"We're holding down the fort here. No rush. Let me know if you want company."

"I'm good. Thanks, Jimmy."

I plugged the address into my GPS and took a quick trip out toward Mendota Heights to a residential neighborhood much more manicured than mine. The car wound along the slippery narrow streets flanking the river, and I finally managed to uncurl my knuckles from the steering wheel when I turned onto the wide, tree-lined streets where security stickers sat on every fence and fancy cars dotted the driveways.

I stopped in front of one of the more intimidating-sized homes and parked along the curb, sliding my feet out onto the freshly plowed street. I made my way to the front door and knocked, scanning the neighborhood while I waited. At least two drapes twitched across the street from curious neighbors.

When the door finally opened, it revealed a woman somewhere in her late fifties with salon-perfect brown hair. She wore black yoga pants and an expensive sweatshirt, and her lips cracked with just a hint of pale pink lipstick.

"Yes?" she asked, glancing at my car. "May I help you?"

"Mrs. Newton?"

"Yes," she said. "That's me."

"Is your husband home?"

"He's not. He's at work," she said with a frown. "Is he in trouble?"

"No, ma'am, it's not that. I'm Detective Rosetti." I pulled out my badge and let her examine it. "Do you have a minute to talk?"

"I, um—sure," she said. "Is this about Alison?"

"It is," I said. "But it might be best to talk inside."

"Have you found her?"

I blinked. "Excuse me?"

"We've been waiting to hear for ages."

"You have?" I hesitated. "Mrs. Newton... is this your daughter?"

I pulled out my phone and flashed the image of the passport I'd snapped at the crime scene.

"That's my address, yes. And my daughter's name." She glanced up at me, then pointed a manicured nail at the picture in the small booklet. "But that's not my daughter."

AFTER LEAVING ALISON'S mother—her heartbroken, me confused—I pulled into the precinct and parked. I tossed my coffee cup as I made my way inside, stopping by the breakroom to pour a cup of tar masquerading as coffee. Taking a sip, I wrinkled my nose and made my way to my desk.

Jimmy was sitting at the desk next to mine, clicking at his computer screen and cursing a blue streak.

I raised an eyebrow. "Everything okay?"

"Jerks," Jimmy said, sitting back in his seat. He wiped his forehead off with a napkin. "All of them. These stupid online auctions. I'm trying to get a new pair of kicks for my grandson, and they're sold out everywhere."

"Kicks?"

"That's what they're called," Jimmy said. "Ain't called shoes anymore. Anyway, how's your sister?"

"Sobering up in my shower," I said. "She decided she's going to live at my house for now."

Jimmy winced.

"I don't want to talk about it," I said. "Did anything else come in on the case?"

"We're just waiting for the lab results on a bunch of stuff. I got a copy of the passport to Asha—she's going to call when she finds something."

"I'm going to go hound her," I said. "Do you want to come with?"

A new countdown flashed on Jimmy's screen. "Oh, these mother—"

"I'll leave you to your kicks," I said. "Good luck."

Jimmy didn't bother with a goodbye. His trigger finger was already busy on the mouse.

Asha West was the sort of woman I'd avoid if I ran into her on the street. Half her head was shaved, and the other half was covered in a hundred tiny braids. She had a ring under her nose that made her look a bit like a bull, and the only reason the chief hadn't kicked her out of the precinct for her smart mouth was because she was a wizard on the computer.

She grinned, flicked her braids over one shoulder. Asha had a Chinese mother and an African-American father, and somehow that combination had given her the best skin and prettiest black hair of anyone on the globe. If not for the ring in her nose and the fact she was missing half of her hair, she could have had a career starring in shampoo commercials. Luckily for us, she'd chosen a career in hacking, and after one too many juvie pickups, she'd turned straight for the right price.

"I was just about to call you," she said without looking back as I approached from behind. "I've got something for you."

I came around to the side of her desk and paused. "That was fast."

"I didn't promise you'd like it."

"I rarely like what you have to tell me," I said. "And I suspect I know what's coming. Tell me about Alison Newton."

"I think you've got a Jane Doe, at least until they pull the prints and try to match dental." Asha raised an eyebrow. "The passport you gave me is crap. Alison Newton went missing two years ago. She's never been found."

"I figured," I said. "I followed the passport's address to try to notify her parents. Right address, right name, wrong picture."

"This is the real Alison Newton." Asha clicked through a few screens that showed a plump young girl at least six inches shorter than our victim. "Any resemblance to your vic?"

I glanced at the screen and sighed. "I should have known it was too easy. I can't help but think our prints are going to be useless. Same for dental."

"She could be a foreigner," Asha said. "Trafficking vic?"

"It's definitely possible. Young, beautiful, some European features."

"I'll keep digging with facial recognition, but don't get your hopes up. It can be next to impossible getting a name for these girls. No ID, no family in the country, no medical history of any sort." Asha shook her head. "As for the real Alison Newton, the poor girl's probably long dead. Someone browsed missing persons records and used her name. Easy enough to do."

"The only thing I can't get over," I said, "is the fake passport. These girls that've been trafficked in from Europe have legit passports—they just get taken away by their pimps so they can't leave."

"Assholes."

"So why would she have a fake passport? It seems to me we've got a college girl caught up in something, but then I can't figure why she wouldn't just have a fake driver's license. What sort of sorority girl uses her passport to get into bars?"

"What sort of girl joins a sorority?" Asha smirked. "Don't tell me you were kappa delta bullshit, Rosetti."

I winked at her. "I have no doubt you could find out if I was, but I'll spare you the research. No, I wasn't what you'd call 'sorority material' in college."

"I'll keep digging," Asha said. "I'll call you when I find anything. Oh, and detective, there's one more thing."

I waited. "Yeah?"

"It's not about the case." Asha shifted in her seat, flicked a stray braid off her shoulder. "Your sister's name pinged. You asked me to keep an eye on her..."

"I know. I picked her up this morning."

"Wild party?"

"What other kind of party is there when Jane Rosetti is involved?"

Asha grinned. "Your sister knows how to have a good time."

"Speaking of a good time, Melinda's buying me a drink tonight. Bellini's at seven, are you in?"

"And Lassie?"

"I'm sure she'll be calling the second she catches wind of the case."

"Ah. See you then."

I left Asha to her work and headed downstairs. The elevator doors opened, and I made my way to the morgue. I strolled down the hallway, glanced through the windows, and saw Melinda perched over her table in her scrubs.

"Anything?"

She glanced up as I entered the room, gave me a half smile. "Where's that flat white?"

"It's freezing outside," I said. "I didn't have time to stop."

"You did this morning."

"If I walk over there this second, will you expedite those prints?"

"You already talked to Asha, I see?"

"I did," I said. "I also tried to notify the family. The *wrong* family."

Melinda winced. "Did you get to the part—"

"No, thank God. I figured it was a fake ID before I explained about their daughter—or her imposter—being found dead this morning." I shook my head. "That poor woman. Her daughter's been missing for two years."

"I know that tone of voice," Melinda said. "Don't get sucked into the Alison Newton missing person's case—you have your plate full with one already."

"I know." I shook off the questions creeping into my mind from my glance into the files of the real missing Alison Newton. I focused instead on the body before us. "Find anything?"

"See here?" Melinda switched tracks seamlessly, turning a gloved hand toward Jane Doe's wrists. "Restraint marks."

"She was tied up?" I frowned, trying to fit that in with my first guesses of the way the murder had gone down. "So maybe the guy conks her on the head, hauls her to the car, ties her up when she starts to move?"

"Maybe. But these restraints weren't incredibly tight. She was conscious when she was bound; the marks are clear signs of a struggle."

I leaned closer, peered at the pinkish lacerations around the wrists. "Maybe Asha was right. Could this be a sex trafficking situation?"

"It very well could be," Melinda said. "But I'll know more after the full autopsy tomorrow. I'm running the prints through the system today, but if she was incognito, I doubt we'll get a hit. Ditto on dental records."

"Maybe we'll get lucky. She could've been picked up for solicitation, something like that. Fat chance, but let's run 'em as fast as we can anyway. I'd like to get this one closed up by the holidays."

"Merry Christmas to you too." Melinda looked at the body, shook her head. "Her poor family. I can't imagine having to do notifications this time of year."

"It's not fun," I said. "Then again, if we could only get a memo to the murderers to take a break from their work between Christmas and the New Year, it'd get a lot cheerier around here."

Melinda shooed me away. "Let me work. You owe me a coffee."

"Better yet, I'll buy your drink tonight."

Melinda waved her finger at me. "Tomorrow morning. Coffee if you want entrance to the autopsy."

"You drive a hard bargain."

I left Melinda alone with Jane Doe and returned to the bullpen. The TC Task Force was set up inside one of the local St. Paul stations with a special room for the team. There were four detectives—me and Jimmy made up half the team. Two other detectives completed the gang, but they were currently working a case in Minneapolis and had been scarce around the office this week.

Our team shared resources with the regular precinct, though Asha worked almost exclusively with the TC Task Force. Melinda covered autopsies for all of St. Paul, but often ours rose to the top of her priority list because of their high-profile nature.

This particular case had fallen into our jurisdiction for two main reasons. The first—location. Not only had the body been found on the border of the two cities, but it'd been found in a renowned neighborhood. Million-dollar homes. Manicured lawns. Old money. It hadn't taken long for the mayor to dispatch the task force to the scene. Rich people don't like dead people turning up too close to home.

Besides location, the victim's young age promised publicity. Nobody liked to see a pretty dead girl. But everyone wanted to read about the gory, morbid details. It was tragic, a life lost so young. This case would catch a lot more publicity than, say, the suspicious death of a seventy-year-old overweight male with high blood pressure.

"Did you get the shoes?" I asked Jimmy.

Judging by the growling sounds coming from him, I figured that was a negative.

"Jerks," I said.

He burst out laughing. "What'd Melinda have to say?"

"The victim's hands were tied—literally. Can't quite figure how that plays into everything."

"Huh."

"Unless the victim began to regain consciousness in the car," I mused, "and the killer panicked? Maybe he was trying to stage a robbery."

"I suppose we'll know more after the autopsy tomorrow," Jimmy said. "What's next?"

I blew out a breath. "We'll have to start asking around. Door to door in the neighborhood."

"Officers already did that."

"I'm all ears if you have a better idea?"

He heaved himself out of his seat. "Your mom needs to start doing delivery."

"Your mom—" I hesitated. "Dang, I can't think of anything."

"Good thing you're a cop, not a comedian."

Chapter 3

The neighborhood canvass lasted three hours and turned up zilch.

"My nuts are freezing," Jimmy said as we made our way back to the car after another door closed in our faces with the *'Sorry, I can't help you'* response we'd been getting all morning.

"Buck up, buttercup," I told him. "This is Minnesota."

"My circulation isn't the same since I turned fifty. Someday, you'll know what I mean."

"If I ever tell you my nuts are freezing, take my gun and shoot me between the eyes."

Jimmy's eyes crinkled when he grinned. "I'm going to miss you when I retire."

"At what age did you turn soft?"

"Watch your mouth, grasshopper."

I frowned as I glanced at the former crime scene. The techs had long-since cleaned up the evidence of the tragedy, but there were still plenty of footprints in the snow, scuff marks around the scene, and tire tracks where cop cars had squealed to a stop. More importantly, there was a man standing right where our victim had lain, his arms crossed, staring at the ground.

I nodded to Jimmy. "Get the car warmed. I'd like to say hello to our little friend."

"Right," Jimmy said. "I'm coming with you."

We crossed the street and left the expansive front yards behind us. The river stretched before us, icy and frigid, but not entirely frozen over. It was the Mississippi—it never froze entirely.

The early darkness was beginning to set—the shortest day of the year was coming upon us quickly, and the only positive about the winter solstice was the fact that the days could only get longer after it.

The river was lined by a hundred feet of steep embankment dotted by dead trees. During the fall months, the trees lit on fire with reds and yellows and oranges, coloring a stretch of city as if by magic. All throughout autumn, lovers walked hand in hand along the sidewalks and groups of college students jogged along the path with a level of excitement only possible by kids of a certain age. Dogs loped along with their owners and children screeched with delight as they pedaled bikes and dinged bells up and down the street.

This time of year, the path was deserted save for hardcore runners decked out in lemon-lime colored vests and flashlights strapped to their heads, Vaseline slathered over their faces to prevent the wind from cracking their skin. Today, not even the hard-core runners were out. I had to admit Jimmy had a point. If I had nuts, they'd be freezing, too.

As it was, I stamped my feet, rubbed my hands together, and tried not to let my hand stray too close to the gun strapped to my hip as I approached our looky-loo.

"Can I help you?" I asked.

The man looked up and gave a smile that burned hot against the cool air. A five o'clock shadow decorated his chin beneath a set of brown eyes that were worthy of movie star status. I wasn't sure I understood the word smoldering, but if I did, I might say his gaze smoldered. A shock of dark hair sat touched by snowflakes, ruffled from the gloved hand that raked through his locks. His eyes twinkled with curiosity as I moved to stand in front of him.

"Is this your property?" he asked. "I thought sidewalks were city property."

I ignored his particularly nice-looking smile and returned my finest scowl. "Is there any reason in particular you've come out to this spot today?"

"Rumor on the streets is that a girl was killed here recently."

"Can I see some identification?"

He watched me carefully, his gaze not faltering as he sized me up. I returned the favor, taking in his broad shoulders and tall figure, imagining the body beneath his winter clothes matched the chiseled lines of his face. He wore a suit and gloves, and by all accounts, he should have been freezing his privates off. But aside from his slightly red—and very soft looking—lips, he showed zero signs of being cold.

"My name's Jack," he said finally. "And you are?"

"Detective Rosetti," I said. "Do you have a last name?"

He shifted, gave a thin smile. "I've heard great things about you, detective."

I frowned. Jimmy stiffened beside me.

Jack nudged snow out of the way with a polished shoe as he shifted his weight and reached into his pocket. I reached for my gun, rested my hand on it. The weight of it was comforting, especially seeing as this guy was throwing me all sorts of off balance. Jimmy stepped closer. He fixed his gaze on Jack, too.

"Let me pull out some ID before you shoot me." Jack withdrew his hand from his pocket, and with it, a badge. He flashed it toward us. "Jack Russo, FBI."

I exhaled a breath as Jimmy cursed.

"Why didn't you say something sooner, man?" Jimmy groaned. "What are the feds doing here?"

"Checking out a case."

"This is my case," I said, then corrected myself. "Our case. There's absolutely no reason we need federal help. At least, not yet."

"Tell me, did you find a young girl dead by the river with a fake passport left on her body?" He studied me, not backing down. "I would imagine she was strangled. And the autopsy will turn up signs of a struggle—markings on her wrists."

"Have you talked to Dr. Brooks?" I asked.

"I don't need to," he said. "We've had four similar cases across the country."

"When? How'd you catch wind of this one?"

"I flagged it. We've been chasing this guy for years. The Riverbank Killer," he said. "Three years. One body per year until this last year. He's picking up the pace—we've only got a limited time before this guy disappears again. And if he goes back underground, we'll have to wait until he resurfaces... along with another dead body in the middle of nowhere."

"Um," I drawled, gesturing to the city skyline. "The middle of nowhere? St. Paul is a great city. It's a big metropolis.

Not to mention the fact that Minneapolis is a huge hub... just across the street."

"Sure."

"Okay," I said. "Well, if you're not a fan of our city, why don't you let us handle the case and head back to DC?"

Jack laughed, then raised his hands before slipping his badge back into his pocket. "I didn't mean to offend. I'm sure your little town is very quaint."

I rolled my eyes. "And you wonder why feds get a bad rap."

"I'm hoping we'll be able to work together, detectives," Russo said, glancing first at me, then at Jimmy. "You must be Detective Jones."

"That's right," Jimmy said.

"Would you like to go somewhere else to talk?" Russo asked. "It's freezing out here."

"Nah," I said, ignoring the fact that I couldn't feel nine of my toes and my fingers had long since stopped tingling. I was fairly certain I had icicles hanging from my nose, and I sensed that any second, my eyelashes might freeze shut. "I think it's pretty balmy out here. Plus, I don't have anything else to say to you."

"The FBI is hoping for your full cooperation on the case."

"You never leave us much of a choice," I said dryly. "Don't worry, if you want the credit once we solve it, I'll happily hand it over. We don't need the pat on the back; we just want justice for our vics."

"How noble of you." Jack nodded, glanced out toward the river. "I'd heard Minnesotans were nice. I didn't know y'all were angels."

Jimmy snorted. "Give her a few days. If anyone can change your mind, it's Rosetti."

I glared at my partner. "You're not helping anything."

Jack's eyes followed our exchange, then landed keenly on me. "Who do I have to sleep with to get a cup of coffee around here and an internet connection?"

"Her mom," Jimmy said, thumbing toward me. When Jack stared at him, Jimmy shrugged. "It's true. She makes the best coffee in town over at Seventh Street Café—it's next door to the precinct. I'm sure Kate will be happy to escort you there and give you the rundown."

"Jimmy," I said. "A quick word?"

"If we can go in the car," he said. "I can no longer feel my nuts."

Jack Russo burst out in laughter, the sound all too attractive and all too unwelcome. His eyes crinkled, and I caught a glimpse of laugh-lines around his eyes that signaled just maybe, he wasn't always the stuck-up prick he presented to the world when on the job. Unfortunately for him, first impressions lasted a long time in my world, and his wasn't all that great.

Jimmy led the way to his car, and I climbed inside along with him. He cranked the heat. "Come on, Rosetti. Swallow your pride. Dance with the devil. Keep Russo in the loop—fighting the feds is only going to make things worse."

"He's an asshole. Did you hear him talking?"

"Not really," Jimmy admitted. "When feds talk, it goes in one ear and out the next. We know how this works. Play nice. We catch our killer, everyone's happy."

"Not if I have to work with a stuck-up pain in the ass like Russo."

"Tell me how you really feel about him."

"He's—" I hesitated. "You're hilarious. I hate it when they swoop in like this, thinking the case is theirs. Plenty of girls are killed each year, unfortunately. How does he know this one is the same guy?"

"I expect that's what he's here to find out. Sort of handsome fellow, don't you think?"

I ignored Jimmy's side-eye. "Your nuts really must be gone if you think so."

Jimmy barked a laugh. "Come on, Kate. Entertain him for the day. Let him sit in on the autopsy. Maybe it'll loosen the stick in his ass."

"Nah," I said. "That's wedged up there for good—I think they get implanted when anyone joins the FBI."

Jimmy shook his head, his eyes gleaming. "Take the advice of an old dog. It will only make things harder for you if you fight him on this. It's the holiday season. Consider it your Christmas gift to the bureau."

"I'm not really feeling like Santa at the moment."

"If nothing else, it's a good incentive to close this case quick," Jimmy said. "Now, pull up your big girl panties, buy him a coffee, and show him what Minnesota's all about."

"What *is* it about?"

Jimmy shook his head. "Fifty-plus years living here, and I still haven't figured it out. I have to think that anyone with half a brain would move somewhere warmer. Now, get out of the car before it gets dark, and we get snowed in here."

"Let me call it in," I said. "Make sure he's kosher."

Jimmy warmed his hands by the heater while I made a few quick calls and confirmed that Jack Russo was, in fact, exactly who he said he was. My last call was to the chief.

"I hear it in your voice," the chief said, the second he picked up. "I know why you're calling."

"Can't you call off the dogs?" I asked. "Russo is a—"

"Can it, detective," he interrupted. "Do me a Christmas solid. Take Russo out for coffee. Make amends. I assume you got off on the wrong foot judging by the fact that my other line is ringing, and it's a number from the bureau I don't feel like answering."

"In my defense, it's not completely my fault."

"Why don't I believe you?" the chief snapped. "You can make it up to me by taking Russo out for a bite to eat. Show him the ropes. That's an order."

"Yes, sir."

"And Rosetti?"

I groaned. "Yeah?"

"Tie this up with a nice bow," he said. "I want it gift-wrapped and under my tree by Christmas."

"Good one, sir."

"I've been working on it for a while," he said. "While you're with Jimmy, tell him to stop using work computers for his freaking eBay auctions."

"Of course."

I hung up. "No more eBay auctions."

Jimmy rolled his eyes. "He's just jealous I outbid his wife on the shoes."

"I thought you didn't win the shoes?"

"I didn't," he said. "But I lost less badly than the chief."

"I'll get you your shoes if you agree to take Russo out for coffee."

"Get out of my car." Jimmy unlocked the door. "Don't come back until Russo's eating out of your palm."

Chapter 4

Russo drove a sleek black rental with heated seats that just about set my ass on fire.

"Cripes," I said, shifting as we cruised away from the river and toward the precinct. "Can't you control these things?"

Russo glanced over, took a look at my seat, which felt just a little too invasive, then reached over and clicked a few buttons that significantly reduced my rate of perspiration.

I shot him a grudging nod. "Thanks."

"My pleasure. Though I thought you might welcome the heated seats after stomping around outside all day."

"I was born in the ice," I said. "I'm not a pansy."

Russo's eyebrows raised. "That's what you think of me?"

I shrugged, glanced out the window.

"I assume you talked to your bosses in the car," he said. "They probably gave you instructions to cooperate with the bureau. Specifically, me."

I shrugged again.

"Is this you trying to play nice?"

"Look, Russo—I'll cooperate because I have to, but don't expect me to be happy about it. I'm still not convinced your case has anything to do with mine."

"It's better to be safe than sorry, isn't it? If nothing else, we can both agree that we don't want this guy to strike again. Related or not. And if he is the same guy I've been after, he'll be back. Sooner rather than later. Then he'll bug out and move on to the next city. Selfishly, I don't want to chase him to another city. The chances I'll be working with people as charming as yourself are slim."

"What can I say? I'm one of a kind."

"In the interest of collaboration, I'll start talking," Jack said. "As soon as we get a coffee. But first, what's this about your mom having the best coffee in the Twin Cities?"

I sighed. "Long story."

"I've got nothing but time."

I gritted my lips, remembering the orders from the chief. "My mom divorced my dad when I was five. He was a cop. Long story short—she needed to figure out something to do with her life when she kicked him out. She'd always loved to bake. A café was a natural fit for her."

"She was a stay-at-home mom before that?"

"Got married straight out of high school, pregnant at twenty, no college degree. She found herself approaching thirty with two little girls to raise on her own and an ex-husband serving jail time."

"Yikes."

"It wasn't easy for her," I said. "But she made it work. Now she's making it work right next door to the precinct. She's always had a soft spot for cops."

"Despite your father?"

"He made bad choices because he was acting stupid. Not because he was a cop."

"Touché." Russo glanced over at me. "Thanks for sharing."

I lapsed into silence, surprised I had shared as much as I had. For a first-class jerk, there was something about Russo that made him easy to talk to. My last boyfriend hadn't known all those details about me.

"Don't get used to it," I said finally. "You caught me by surprise."

"You got it, sweetheart."

"Say that again, and I'll shoot you."

"That's not very cooperative." Russo hid a smile, flicked on the blinker. "Is this it?"

I gestured for him to park near the café in one of the spaces my mother had reserved for officers on duty. We climbed out of the car. I didn't wait for Russo before I stomped through the front doors and let them close behind me.

I was still caught off guard by how Russo's simple questions had gotten me to open up so quickly. It was no wonder Russo had climbed the ranks and made for a good agent. If he could get me—a frozen, experienced detective—to spill my guts for a cup of coffee, there was no saying what he could do to an unsuspecting criminal.

I stomped up to the counter. "I'd like one latte, please."

My mother glanced up, frowning at my snippy tone. Before she could respond, the bell above the door tinkled. She caught sight of Russo, and her eyebrows crept all the way up to her hairline. "And what will he have?"

"I don't know," I growled. "We're on separate tabs. I'm sure he's expensing his entire trip. I have to foot my own bill."

Russo joined me at the counter. His sheer presence would have been intimidating for anyone who didn't have a gun at their hip. He stood a good six inches taller than me, and when he extended a hand toward my mother and brushed against me, I could feel the hard muscles beneath his coat. I shifted away, putting a more comfortable distance between us.

He offered a charming smile that had my mother turning into a puddle of feminine goop behind the counter. "Jack Russo, FBI. You must be Mrs. Rosetti."

"It's *Miss*," she offered with a hiccup and a giggle. "I'm single."

My eyes twitched, wanting to roll again. "And you're over fifty."

"Kate!" She snapped her gaze to me. "Where are your manners?"

"They're frozen," I said. "How about that latte?"

"I've heard wonderful things about your café, Ms. Rosetti." Russo swooped in to save the day. "Please put your daughter's order on my tab."

My mother giggled again. She raised a hand, fanned at her face despite the fresh burst of frigid air and gust of flurries that brushed in when the front door opened and closed behind me. "What can I get you? On the house for the FBI."

She whispered the last part as if his status as an agent was top secret.

Jack leaned forward, lowering his voice conspiratorially. "I'll take whatever the house specialty is. I trust you."

Another hiccup.

"Just give him a latte," I said. "Please, Ma. We've got to get back to work, and I'm sure Agent Russo wants to check into his hotel."

"On the house for Agent Russo," my mother said pointedly, typing at some keys on the cash register. "That'll be four dollars to you, Detective Rosetti."

"Ma!"

She glowered at me. "What?"

"Please, I insist." Russo fished out a credit card and handed it over. "Kate was right—I am expensing it."

My mother's eyes gleamed with hope at the gentlemanly gesture. Her eyes flicked upward at the mistletoe she'd hung over the door, and I could practically read her mind. She hadn't given up on hopes for grandchildren, though her optimism had dwindled lately. Between Jane's dedication to partying and my marriage to the job, she'd begun to doubt real romance would ever be a thing in either of our futures.

"Any friend of Kate's is a friend of the café's," my mother said.

"I appreciate that, ma'am."

I put my hand on Jack's arm and tensed, startled to feel the firmness there. I'd caught hints of muscle during our quick brushes of movement, but he was fitter than I anticipated. Everywhere.

"She'll bring it to our table." I directed him to the corner of the café, ignoring the fact my mother was watching our every movement. "Sit down and tell me: What the hell was that?"

"What?"

"The Charming Jack show. Why are you trying to win over my mother? You'll just get her hopes up."

"Hope for what?"

My gaze was pulled like a magnet toward the mistletoe. Jack followed my line of sight, his lips curving into a smile.

"Ah," he said. "I see. You're single?"

"That's irrelevant to the case, Agent Russo," I said, easing into the chair opposite him. "Start talking. And if you try to suck up to my mother again—"

"You'll shoot me, I know." Jack seemed entirely uninterested by the fact that I was more than willing to pull a loaded weapon on him. "I was just waiting for our drinks. Wasn't sure if your mom planned to stare at us for a while longer, or..."

He trailed off, and I glanced over my shoulder. My mother leaned against the counter, completely ignoring the other customers in line as she watched us like her favorite soap. I waved a hand, and she snapped to attention, shoving the milk under the frother as her cheeks turned pink.

When our lattes arrived, I passed Jack's to him, then noticed the note on the side. It said *Come back soon*! I quickly switched our cups. For this, I'd suffer through a regular latte instead of my typical order.

Jack took a sip, flinched. "What is this? I haven't had this much sugar since Halloween 1995."

"You're welcome. Now, dish."

Jack's eyes fixed on the note on my cup. He watched as I took a sip of the regular latte and tried not to wince. Reaching over, he pulled a pen from his pocket and scratched out the note on the cup so it was illegible. Then he switched our beverages.

"Better?"

I brushed his hand off my cup and switched our lids. "Can't have FBI germs."

"Wouldn't want that." Jack smirked, took a sip of his latte, and answered his own question. "Much better. Now, where were we?"

"The case. What makes you so certain this is your guy?"

"I can't say for sure, but my gut instinct tells me I'm on the right track. The timeline works out, the similarities are there, and I don't believe in coincidences. I'd like to sit in on the autopsy tomorrow."

"Fine," I said. "Tell me about your vics."

"Four women, three years," he started. "First two were a year and a half apart in two different cities. The first one... we think the killer botched the job and had to take off, hence the long wait in between. He was relocating, practicing, planning."

"Where was that?"

"Buffalo," he said. "The second was in Tennessee. Nashville. He was a little cleaner there, but DNA from one scene linked him to the next. No hits in the database."

"DNA?"

"There were defensive wounds on both vics. DNA, presumably from our killer, under their fingernails."

"Was there DNA found on the third and fourth victims?"

"The third but not the fourth," he said. "Both were in DC. That was when I came on the case—last year after the third victim. At that time, he only waited six months between killings. He's getting better and opted to stayed in the same city."

"A sign of confidence. He's getting more daring," I said. "He's sticking around longer and picking off local women."

"Exactly. By the time he got to victim number four, there was no DNA under the fingernails. There was a head wound and evidence the woman's wrists had been restrained. She was strangled by a thin, smooth material—likely a tie or something similar. I am expecting the results will be much the same from the autopsy tomorrow."

"So, I shouldn't get my hopes up for DNA?"

"I wouldn't. And if I'm correct, he'll have been even more practiced than his last attack in DC. I'll bet he sticks around for a while."

"If he's into sticking around places, then why'd he leave DC? You obviously didn't catch him while he was there."

"We were close."

"What do you have on him?"

"Him in particular? Not much. But we linked both women to a nightclub and started sniffing around there."

"Do you think the killer worked at the club? Seems like it shouldn't be too hard to check if they have any employees turning over around the time of murders."

"Have you ever worked in a club?"

My blank stare probably told him that I'd barely stepped foot in a club, let alone worked in one.

"They've got under the table shenanigans up the wazoo, and that's not to mention legal turnover. He might have worked there, but there's no record of anyone quitting or getting fired that works within our timeline. He could have been a regular patron. One of the security guards copped to seeing our second vic leave with a male."

"Description?"

"Too dark. Couldn't see. He drove a black car."

I could hear the chagrin in Russo's voice. "Ah. Not very cooperative?"

"He offered us the bare minimum to keep from getting charged with possession."

"I see. So, we've got a potential serial killer."

"The markings around the neck are consistent from case to case. I think there's a very good possibility we're looking at one murderer."

"He's using the same tie, or whatever, to kill these girls."

"I'd put money on it."

"Are there any similarities between the girls aside from the fact they went to the same club?"

"All of them had fake passports left on the scene with them, and we haven't found any real identities."

"That's strange in and of itself. How do four girls go missing and nobody knows who they are?"

"We're thinking trafficking of some sort because we see that sort of thing there, but..."

"It's not quite adding up."

He spared me a small smile. "Glad we agree on something. Other than that, we've got a fairly common set of characteristics that we find in many serial killer cases. Young women in high risk situations. Young, attractive. All of them were dressed for a 'night on the town' if you will. Each had some alcohol in their systems, though none of them were over the limit, suggesting they were out for a date, or an evening with friends, dancing, whatever it is young women do these days."

"Don't look at me," I said, raising an eyebrow. "I've no clue. Though you could ask my sister."

"I thought she was older than you."

"She is."

"Ah." Russo glanced at my face and took the hint that the subject was closed. "You know, touching base with your sister might not be a bad idea if she's as tuned in to the party scene as you say. The club in DC was a local place, brand new and flashy. Big money, best women and cocktails."

"You would know?"

"I heard rumors."

"Aha," I said, then I gave a huge sigh. "Well, I'll ask. If anyone will know the hot place to be these days, it's Jane."

"Look, I'm sorry if I brought up something sensitive." Russo gave me a surprisingly curious look that was filled with more understanding than I'd expected to see from an FBI suit. "I understand families are complicated. Leave your sister out of this—we'll figure it out without involving her."

I gave him a thin smile. "Speaking of family, I've got some obligations and have to finish up my day before I head out. Can I walk you over to the office?"

"How about I drive you?"

"It's next door."

"I enjoy your company."

I grabbed both of our cups and tossed them in the trash. One look outside told me the flurries had turned into a full-on snowstorm. Walking a single block in this weather would have my eyeballs freezing.

"About that ride," I said as Russo joined my side. "I think it's the least you can do for me."

Russo stifled a smile. "I can't agree more."

From behind us came the clearing of a throat. I glanced back at the same time as Russo and turned right into his chest. We stumbled together, his arms reaching out to steady me as I collapsed against him.

My mother's eyes traveled upward.

The mistletoe above us beckoned.

"You give that even a second of thought," I said to Russo, "and I'll—"

"You'll shoot me," he finished with a grin. "I know."

Chapter 5

I finished up at the precinct by six. I'd gotten Agent Russo introduced around the office and settled him at a spare desk in the TC Task Force room. When I said my rounds of goodbyes for the day, I grudgingly stopped before his desk.

"Need anything?" I asked gruffly. I'd mostly refused to speak to him all day, leaving Jimmy to field the agent's questions on the case.

"Got any recommendations for a dinner place?" Russo glanced up at me. "I'm assuming you've got plans, or else I'd invite you out with me."

"What gave you the impression that Rosetti has plans?" Jimmy called across the room. "Surely, it's not her packed social calendar. Kate hasn't gone on a date in over a year."

I ignored the quirk in Russo's eyebrow. "Jimmy's full of it. I do have plans tonight, actually."

"By plans," Russo said, "I assume you mean anything, so long as it's not dinner with me?"

"Believe it or not," I said, "I have plans with real people tonight."

"The delivery man doesn't count," Russo said. "Neither does the fast food order window at LeeAnn Chin's."

Jimmy laughed from behind his desk.

I gave Russo a smirk. "You think you're funny."

He sat back in his chair, hands folded behind his head, and glanced at Jimmy with raised eyebrows. "Maybe she does have a hot date. Little Ben and Jerry action?"

Jimmy cackled. "A ménage is a bit exotic for our girl Kate. Even in a pint of ice cream."

"Maybe," I said, raising my eyebrow. "Maybe not. You've no idea if I'm exotic or not, Jimmy."

"I'm intrigued," Russo said. "Have dinner with me? I'll put it on the FBI's tab. You can join if you like, Jimmy."

"The wife cooked," Jimmy said. "I've got plans at home. Kate, though..."

"I have plans," I insisted. "Why is that so hard to believe?"

Silence fell in the room.

"Goodnight," I said and stomped out.

I didn't have time to change before my dinner date at Bellini's. It wasn't important that the only date I'd had in over a year was my standing get together with Asha, Melinda, and Lassie. I wasn't interested in romance. I'd tried it before, hadn't found success, thought it was overrated.

My body, however, was telling me different. I was feeling fired up on all cylinders as I drove across town at a snail's pace, struggling to see through the windshield as the snow pelted down with fury. Somehow, I suspected it wasn't the pair of lattes I'd had. My body was accustomed to caffeine. My body wasn't accustomed to Jack Russo, and the man had an effect on me that I preferred not to think about.

He was handsome, obviously intelligent, and ultimately infuriating. My brain wandered into restricted territory as I came to a dead stop in the middle of a traffic jam. It'd take me forever to get to Bellini's, but I didn't care. I had nowhere else to be, and I needed a margarita.

I found Lassie waiting for me at the bar. She had a glass of red wine sitting before her and a phone out, her glitterized nails clicking away on the screen as I sat down next to her and ordered a pitcher of margaritas.

She didn't say a word, but her eyebrows pinched together at the sound of my voice. "Rough day?"

"A bit. But then again, you probably already know that."

"I heard from Asha," Lassie admitted, finally looking up from her phone. "I figured I'd badger you about your day after you'd had a drink. You're much more likely to talk about a case with tequila swirling through that pretty head of yours."

I snorted a laugh and clasped an arm around Erin Lassiter—a long-time friend and short-time reporter. Erin Lassiter was a big girl with bigger dreams. Her hair stood out in a bob that belonged on a sixties housewife. You didn't want to sit behind Erin Lassiter in a movie theater.

For a long while, Lassie had dreamed of being on Broadway. Then she'd experimented with an acting stint in Hollywood. Next had been a short career as a stand-up comic in New York. She'd flirted with fashion design before diving head first into a singing career that had been cut short due to the fact that she was tone-deaf.

Eventually, her experiments had brought her back to Minnesota where she was currently a blogger focused on local entertainment, news, food, and crime. Pretty much, she wrote about whatever tickled her fancy.

The real kicker was that she'd found quite an audience doing so and had somehow managed to squeak a full-time living out from her blog. If nothing else, the woman was determined. And ambitious.

"So, should I get you a straw?" The bartender chomped on a huge wad of bubble gum and stopped before the counter with my vat of margarita. "Or do you actually have a date tonight and need a real glass?"

"You're hilarious, Angela." I nodded at Lassie. "We're meeting the girls tonight."

"Ah," she said. "That's cute."

My cousin, Angela Bellini, looked a bit like she belonged in a Soprano episode as Hot Chick #1. Her hair was held together in a helmet with about five pounds of spray and her chest had been propped up by a bra so sturdy I wondered if it had a steel support system. She wore skin tight jeans and a hot pink tank top that was just a shade less bright than the orange aura radiating from her spray tan.

"Does your mother know you're drinking on a school night?" Angela snickered. "You know, I heard your sister had a little fun last night. Wouldn't kill you to take a few lessons from Jane. Fun never killed anyone."

"I actually doubt that's true."

"Not with that attitude." Angela harrumphed. "I heard your sister's bunking with you for a while."

"If by awhile, you mean twenty-four hours."

"Yeah, okay." Angela raised her painted on eyebrows. "Good luck with that. Tell her to stop by sometime. I want to hear about Yanis."

"No, you don't," I said. "And she's not allowed to drink while she's at my house."

"That's exactly why she should come here to drink," Angela said. "Plus, I need her help. She's got this new guy she's seeing, and apparently he's pretty rich. I need a little help with this one Christmas present. I think he has connections."

"I'll let her know," I said. "Thanks, Angela."

We left Angela snapping her gum as Lassie and I shuffled over to our typical corner booth. I slid into the L-shaped bench first and Lassie followed. A new waitress I didn't recognize brought over two margarita glasses rimmed with salt, and I filled them both before Lassie let loose.

"You aren't going to tell your sister a thing, are you?" Lassie asked.

"What, you mean about Angela's request? No," I said. "I'm not. Jane needs to be associated with Angela's *'connections'* like she needs a hole in the head."

"Aw, but Kate, it's Christmas."

"And knowing Angela, she's looking for a handgun with the serial number scratched off for a new boyfriend," I said, shaking my head. "Angela's a Bellini through and through."

"You're related to her."

"Hence the reason I know all her tricks."

"Was your dad close with the Bellinis?"

I flicked my gaze up at her. "Why?"

She heaved a sigh. "I'm not going to write about your family drama on my blog. I'm just curious. Plus, you already warned me that if I spill secrets on the blog before you say I can, you'll shoot me."

I grunted an agreement, realizing I probably needed to stop telling people I would shoot them before someone took it a little too seriously. HR would probably not be amused.

"Yes, he was. My dad's sister is Angela's mom. She married Bobby Bellini. Which means Angela's got mobster blood passed down on both sides. Poor thing didn't stand a chance."

"Is that what set you on the straight and narrow?" Lassie asked. "Your mom?"

I shrugged. "I'm the black swan of the family."

"What do you mean? You're the opposite of a black swan. You're a cop."

"And not a dirty one," I said with a pointed look at Lassie. "That's exactly my point. In my family, *I'm* the weird one. Go figure."

"Drink up, will you?" Lassie pushed my margarita closer to me. "I want to talk about the dead girl you found today."

"Have a little tact!"

"I mean, she was a girl, and she was dead, right?" Lassie shrugged. "That's all I'm saying. Is it a big thing?"

"All murder is a big thing." I licked salt off the rim of my glass and watched Lassie. She stared with her huge eyes back at me until I relented. "This is off the record."

"Of course," she said. "I won't print a word until you tell me."

"The FBI thinks this might not be the first time our murderer has killed."

"You mean, like, a serial killer?"

"Not a word."

Lassie's eyes were the size of quarters. "My lips are zipped. How did she die?"

"Let's ask the professional," I said as the door to the restaurant opened and a snow-covered pair of women entered.

I gestured to the waitress for another two margarita glasses, then watched as Dr. Melinda Brooks and Asha West—the most opposite of women—stomped their boots against the welcome mat.

Bellini's was a bar and restaurant and deli all in one go. A girl could get a fresh prosciutto sub and wash it down with an authentic negroni at one stop. Rumor had it this bar had been standing for over a hundred years.

It'd made it through the Prohibition, the Great Depression, and the seventies without changing hands from the original family business. I was just thankful it wasn't my job to audit the books on Bobby Bellini.

Melinda led the way through the dimly lit restaurant while unraveling a scarf that appeared to be pure cashmere. She took off a dainty pair of gloves and slipped them into her Louis Vuitton bag as she slid in next to Lassie.

Asha took the other side next to me. She wore no scarf, no hat, and fingerless gloves that showed off a smattering of tattoos on the back of her hands. She reached for my glass and took a sip of my drink while I poured one for her.

Melinda wrinkled her nose at the exchange but refrained from commenting. Once she finally had her own glass, Lassie pounced on her.

"It's just the super-smart woman I wanted to talk to," Lassie said. "How'd Kate's vic end up dead?"

Melinda didn't look surprised. We'd all been on the receiving end of Lassie's inquisitions. I stared down into my drink and pretended I wasn't responsible for the attack.

"Nothing I say is on record," Melinda said grudgingly. "Though it's looking like the official cause of death will be asphyxiation by a smooth fabric, unless I find a surprise. Oh, and Kate, Agent Russo and I discussed the similarities between his cases and this one. I had the files sent over and will be reviewing them thoroughly tonight. But a quick glimpse at the autopsy reports indicate that the MO is quite similar."

"Agent Russo?" Lassie waggled her eyebrows. "Oh, now he's a hunk."

We all swiveled to face her.

"How do you know that?" I blurted. "Or rather, how do you know who he is?"

"So, you do think he's a studmuffin!" Lassie winked one eye at me and wiggled her pointer finger in my direction. "I knew it. Your mom texted me a picture of the two of you."

"She didn't."

"There are no secrets in this town," Lassie said. "Not from me, at least. Anyway, is this guy here for your case?"

"He thinks so," I said. "Though he's a colossal prick."

The table fell silent. Lassie's eyes went over my shoulder first, then Asha's, and finally Melinda's. Asha slunk back in her seat and downed the rest of the margarita, refusing to make eye contact with me.

"What?" I said. "It's just a fact."

"I'm sorry to hear you think that." A deep voice sounded from behind me. "But I can't say I'm surprised."

I slid around in my seat, the back of my neck burning up. "Agent Russo—I, uh, didn't realize..."

"I didn't realize you actually *did* have plans tonight." Jack smiled wanly at the rest of the women. "Here, I thought you were turning down my invitation to dinner because of my status as a colossal prick."

"I had plans; I wasn't avoiding you." The blush on my neck had moved up to my ears. "I didn't mean what I said about—"

"You meant it," Jack said, resting a hand on my shoulder. "It's fine. We got off on the wrong foot. Maybe I can buy you lunch tomorrow so we can set the record straight. And discuss business."

"Er," I hesitated, but the way Melinda was glaring at me, there was only one answer I could give him without feeling like the world's most awful person. "Sure, that'd be great. Thanks."

"Anytime." Jack's hand squeezed, then released from my shoulder, leaving behind a chilly void. "Sorry to intrude on your dinner, ladies. I hope you don't mind I stopped by to drop off the last file for Dr. Brooks. Jimmy thought I might find you here."

Melinda gave a pretty little smile and accepted the file. "Thank you very much, Agent Russo. I'll have this reviewed by tomorrow morning. Like I mentioned, you're welcome to sit in on the autopsy. We'll begin at eight."

"For the price of a flat white, if I remember correctly," Jack said with a wink.

Melinda's cheeks blushed pink. "Oh, there's no need—"

"Great," Jack said. "I'll see you tomorrow, doctor, detective."

I felt like a human made of slime as he turned to leave. My back was stuck to the booth and my limbs felt a bit wobbly as I wiggled lower in hopes that I would just disappear into the upholstery.

"*That's* Agent Russo in the flesh?" Lassie remarked. She smacked her lips. "I saw a photo, but it was sort of a weird angle due to the sneak attack nature of your mom trying to take a photo without a detective finding out. He's way hotter in person. Even Melinda blushed when he talked to her."

"I didn't," Melinda retorted.

"You're still blushing," Asha said. "You're a doctor. You should be able to diagnose yourself for blushing."

"I was just embarrassed for Kate's sake!" Melinda fixed her gaze on me. "What's the beef between the two of you anyway?"

"You heard him," I mumbled. "We got off on the wrong foot."

"Well, I'd work on getting onto the right foot as quickly as you can," Lassie said. "Then maybe you can just get on him in general. It's not really a workplace romance if the two of you work for different agencies, right? So, dating him is allowed?"

"That's not an option, and anyway, I'm not interested. Can we focus on our ladies' night please?"

"What do you think ladies are supposed to talk about when they're out for drinks?" Lassie shot me a mystified stare. "I mean, most women don't discuss dead bodies and blood and guts. They talk about cute guys and love lives."

"She's got a point." Asha raised one pierced eyebrow. "I mean, would it kill you to let your hair down for the night? Take a page out of your sister's book."

"Too soon," I said.

"You didn't tell us he asked you out to dinner tonight," Lassie said. "That's important information."

"I had plans," I said. "And again, I'm not interested."

"I like a man who's persistent." Lassie fanned herself dreamily. "You know, in a not-stalker way. You were busy tonight, so he asked about lunch tomorrow."

"It's a business lunch," I said. "Back to the case. Melinda, you really think these murders are all related?"

"I will let you know tomorrow," she said, "once the autopsy is complete."

"Let's say you've got a serial killer on your hands," Lassie said. "When they make a movie out of this, can I play you?"

"Me?" I glanced at Asha and Melinda. "Why would you want to play me?"

"Dude, Hollywood loves a badass woman," Lassie said. "I want to be the fictional you. I mean, we don't look alike, but it's fine—artistic license. However, I want someone who looks exactly like Agent Russo to play the love interest. And I'd like three sex scenes written into the script. Do you think they'd televise the wedding if fake Agent Russo and I fell in love and got married?"

I pushed my margarita glass toward the center of the table. "This has been fun and all, but I really have to get home."

"We just got here," Melinda said, frowning at the half-full pitcher of margarita. "How are we supposed to finish all this without you?"

"Be creative. I'm sure you can find a lonely FBI Agent looking for a dinner invitation."

"Oh, no," Lassie said. "I don't want to step on those toes. He's all yours. I'm waiting for the Hollywood version of my agent to sweep me off my feet."

"I've got an early morning," I said. "And I need to get home and talk to my sister. Who knows what she's gotten into while I've been away. If my house is destroyed..."

"You'll shoot her," all three women finished in unison.

"I really need a new line," I said, climbing over Asha while shoving my arms into my jacket. "See you later."

I headed up to the bar, credit card in hand. I waved Angela over and handed her the plastic. I was surprised when she shoved it back toward me.

"You never turn down money," I said. "What's the deal? I've got a tab to settle."

"It's settled."

"But—"

"It's taken care of," she said, more urgently. Then she nodded toward the opposite end of the room. "*He* settled it. And left a very handsome tip. Seriously, cuz—if you don't jump on that, I will. Literally. And no man has ever been known to resist the Angela Bellini charm."

I pasted on a fake smile. "I'd like to see him try."

"Is that permission?" She chomped her gum. "You wouldn't be upset if I asked him out?"

"Be my guest."

As I turned, following Angela's gaze toward the deli counter, I felt the sinking sensation in my stomach before I saw him. Once I made the full circle, I kept the smile pasted on my face and gave Agent Russo a nod of thanks.

His eyes were fixed on me. If he'd noticed Angela's blatant attempts to wink at him, he didn't show it. Instead, he raised a foot-long sub in salute. Then he turned and made his way out of the bar, letting in a whoosh of frozen air as the door snapped shut behind him.

"Aw, how sad," Angela chomped. "He likes you, but you abandoned him. Now, all he's got to look forward to is a night alone in his hotel room with his footlong."

"What more does any man need?"

"You have a point there," Angela said. "They do like their footlongs. And their sandwiches. Anyway, I think you should give him a chance."

"I didn't ask for your opinion."

"Nah, but I'm a wealth of great information," she said. "You're welcome. And remember, tell your sister I need her connections for some Christmas presents. I'll make sure she's compensated for it."

"I'm sure you will," I said. "But Jane can't afford to get in trouble."

"Since when do I get in trouble?"

"Since half your family is in the mob."

"My family is your family," she said. "We're cut from the same cloth, Kate. Like it or not."

I didn't like it all that much, but I flashed Angela a smile and headed outside before she could regale me with more unwanted advice. The second I made it outside, I realized I should have let her pound her knowledge into my head for a few seconds longer.

"Detective." Russo nodded at me. He leaned over his car, mid-scrape of his windshield. "Need a ride home?"

"You know how to drive in this stuff?"

"Is this your way of offering to show me the ropes?"

I shifted in my boots. "Look, I'm sorry about what I said in there."

"Tequila under the bridge." He winked. "Sorry to disrupt your ladies' night."

"I didn't mean it."

"Yes, you did."

"Okay, I did," I said. "But it was uncalled for. And probably unfair. I can be a colossal prick, too."

Russo just shrugged, which had me ruffling under the collar just a bit.

"You could have at least denied the part about me being a prick," I said. "Just a tiny little denial."

He broke out in a laugh. "Good night, detective. I'll see you tomorrow."

I strode past him and paused. "Thanks, by the way. For the drinks."

"On the bureau," he said. "Not a problem."

"Russo."

At my tone, he stopped, brushed the snow from his gloves, and waited patiently for me to continue.

"I really do want us to work together to solve this thing," I said. "Five young women dead is five too many. Let's catch the bastard before he kills again."

"I agree." Russo's eyes went dark. "Watch out, detective—keep agreeing with me, and we might just become friends."

It was my turn to laugh. "Goodnight, suit."

"Goodnight, Kate."

Chapter 6

The drive home was miserable. I could only imagine it was worse for Jack Russo. I'd grown up driving in sloppy messes. I was used to snowy roads, slippery exits, and black ice. Russo, probably not so much.

I pulled in front of my house and parked on the street. There was a single car garage at the rear of a long, skinny driveway that was so narrow if I drove my car inside, there was no chance of me getting out.

The sun had long since set, and the street was pitched into half-darkness, half Christmas cheer. My house was on the darker side of things. Though a suspicious light glinted through my front windows. Or rather, hundreds of suspicious multi-colored lights along with a star.

With a groan, I climbed up the front steps and slipped my key into the lock. Obviously, Jane had made herself quite at home already if the Christmas tree in my window was any evidence. Jane loved Christmas. She loved decorating things, and she had no sense of personal boundaries. She was the recipe for a frustrating roommate.

It wasn't that I hated Christmas. I wasn't a *Grinch*; I was just busy. I had holiday spirit. I looked at the Christmas tree the precinct had propped up in the front lobby. I was pretty sure I'd ordered a package on Amazon to drop in the Toys for Tots basket. I had scarfed down at least one green and red doughnut. I could be festive.

My thoughts of Christmas cheer were debunked by a loud thump coming from just outside my house. It was a human-sized *thump* which wasn't a good sign, seeing as I wasn't expecting any company. Especially not on the perimeter of my house.

I had my gun out as I slunk off the front steps. I left my keys in the lock so as not to jangle them and warn the intruder of my presence. I crept around the house, wincing as eight inches of fresh snow found a home inside my heeled boots.

I hesitated, listening. A male voice whispered through the darkness.

Why was there more than one person trying to break into my house? Was it a team effort? Kids goofing off? Something far more sinister?

I reached for my flashlight and flicked it on. "Hands up!" I bellowed, swiveling around the corner, my gun and flashlight pointed at the intruders. "Police! Drop your weapons!"

My last warning was quite unnecessary. The man before me wasn't armed. He wasn't much of anything, in fact—including clothed.

"Who the hell are you?" I called, averting my flashlight from his figure. "And why are you naked?"

"Don't shoot!" he said. "I'm—"

"For crying out loud, Kate! Put down your weapon." Jane's head poked out the window. "That's Wes. You need to relax."

"I need to relax?" My voice squeaked. "I have a naked male breaking into my house. And I need to *relax*?"

"Take a chill pill! He's my friend! And he's not breaking *in,* he's breaking out."

"Even better."

"Here, Wes. I'm sorry about all this." Jane disappeared from the window for a moment. When she returned, she was holding a fuzzy pink robe. "Take this, put it on, and come inside. Warm your poor... um... *toes* up by the fire."

"Yeah, I'm sure he's worried about frostbite on his *toes*," I said as Wes clutched the robe around him. I raised my flashlight so it beamed in his eyes and kept my own eyes well and firmly staring above the waist. "Why'd you climb out the window?"

"Because your sister told me to," Wes said. "She said that you told her not to have people over, and if you found me here, you would shoot me."

"For Pete's sake, I don't go around shooting people willy nilly!"

"Speaking of willy nilly." Jane eyed me, then eyed her naked friend. "Can we do this inside?"

I lowered my gun and flashed the light at the path around front. "Move it."

I marched Wes inside and immediately went to wash my hands. Then I found the open bottle of wine on the counter. I debated asking Jane why she had alcohol in my house when I'd specifically asked her to refrain, but then I decided against it. Instead, I poured myself a coffee mug full of the cabernet.

Holding my mug, I took a sip, appreciating the deep, warm trickle of wine into my stomach as I made my way to the living room. Upstairs, the shower in the guest bedroom clicked on as I curled onto the couch and pulled a fuzzy blanket over my legs. I closed my eyes. A few minutes later, the sound of cautious footsteps came from the bottom of the staircase.

"I'm sorry, Kate."

My sister appeared and tiptoed tentatively next to me. I sighed and slunk deeper into the sofa.

"Wes is just getting warmed up in the shower. Then I told him he has to go home."

"That's probably for the best."

"What's wrong?" The blanket over my lap shifted as Jane eased onto the couch and yanked a corner for herself. "You're not mad... and you should be. Did you get an ugly case?"

I gave her a dry smile. "How'd you guess?"

"We might be polar opposites, but you're still my sister."

"Well, you pegged it right," I admitted. "Someone called in the body of a young girl, and she might not be the only victim of this particular killer. On top of that, the feds are in town. One in particular—Jack Russo—is a gigantic pain in my ass. Worse, he heard me saying so tonight."

"He sounds hot."

"That's beside the point."

"So he is?" she pressed. "Attractive, I mean?"

"What does it matter if he is?" I retorted, unable to push the image of a five o'clock shadow, broad shoulders, and snow-flurried dark hair out of my mind. "We work together. He's only in town for the case."

Jane flopped backward, easing into a more comfortable position on the couch, crossing her legs as she let out a tiny squeal. "This is huge, Jane. You never admit to being interested in anyone."

"I'm not interested."

"But you could be. If the circumstances were different."

"Nope. Not a chance, Jane."

"Maybe this is just what you need! A quick fling. Great sex equals great endorphins. It's like running a marathon but more fun."

"I'd prefer to run the marathon."

"Just think about it, Kate. You need to loosen up."

"Like you?"

"Don't take your crappy work day out on me."

"I'm not. I'm taking my frustration with *you* out on you."

"Look, I'm sorry you saw Wes's wiener, but come on. I'm not a teenager anymore. You don't have to worry about me."

"I still asked—"

"I know what you asked, but Wes is different. Just give him a chance, please."

I gave a shake of my head. "I've already seen him naked. How am I supposed to look at him over the dinner table?"

My sister laughed. "That's the right attitude."

Upstairs, the shower clicked off.

"Well, I should get going," Jane said. "I'll show Wes out the proper way this time."

While she made her way upstairs, I inhaled a gulp of wine and turned my attention to the previously unused fireplace that, courtesy of Jane, had been cleaned out and stocked with wood. She'd even lit a real live fire.

I briefly wondered where she'd gotten the wood before my thoughts drifted toward naked lumberjack Wes, and I quickly gulped more wine to scrub my brain of the image. Next to the fire was a huge tree—real, I noted—and decorated with whatever the two lovebirds had found in my house. Random candy canes, paper snowflakes made from old parking tickets, a box of ornaments from my mother that I'd forgotten existed.

The lights glittered in all shades of red and blue and green, twinkling in a charming pattern. I stared at it, mesmerized by the flicker, the dancing lights, the swirling ornaments in my drafty old house. It'd never looked so festive.

I shuddered, whether from the drafty chill or the fact that my living room had turned into Santa's workshop was hard to say. I ignored the two sets of footsteps clunking downstairs and the chaste kiss at the front door. I looked up only when I heard my name called.

"Kate?" Wes stepped into the living room. "I'm sorry about tonight. Thanks for not shooting me."

I raised my wine-filled mug. "Thanks for getting dressed."

He laughed. "Anytime."

Fully dressed, Wes was actually quite attractive. Tallish and thin, dressed in a suit that made him look impeccably professional. His hair was still wet but combed neatly, and his face was handsome despite the sheepish expression lodged there.

"Well, goodnight, Wes." Jane put her hands on his back and steered him out toward the front door. "I'll call you."

The smack of another kiss sounded, followed soon after by the closing of the front door. The next second, a familiar set of footsteps shuffled into the living room as Jane dragged herself back to the couch.

"I'm sorry if we went overboard on the decorations," she said, gesturing toward the fire and the tree. "I just thought—I love Christmas. You used to love it, too. And Wes offered to help me get the tree, light the fire, all the rest. I couldn't say no."

"He seems like a nice guy."

"You seem surprised by that fact."

"Your last boyfriend was named Yanis. He had a girl-friend that wasn't you, and he left you sitting in jail."

"Fair point." Jane's eyes flicked to my mug. "Are you drinking—"

"It's wine. My wine. The wine you opened with your boyfriend."

She hesitated again.

"Help yourself," I said. "I'd hate to finish the bottle alone."

Jane went to the kitchen, poured the rest of the wine out in her own mug, and then returned to the living room. She sidled up next to me and snuck under my blanket. It'd been a long time since my sister and I had cuddled next to one another on a couch.

We sipped wine in silence while we stared at the Christmas tree. The exhaustion from the day caught up to me. The fresh outdoor air combined with the stress of a new case, a home intruder, my sister moving in, along with the hit of a decent cabernet, had me ready to sleep.

My eyes were closed when Jane spoke.

"Thanks for letting me stay with you," she whispered. "You are a good sister."

I peeled my eyes open and gave her a short smile. "How'd you meet Wes?"

"A club. But, like, a nice one. It's new. And Wes wasn't just there—he helps run the place. I was out with my girlfriends a few days ago, and we connected. But I was seeing someone at the time, so it didn't go anywhere. Now, I'm single."

"A club, Jane—really?"

"I know what you're thinking, but we really connected," she said. "He's not an idiot. He's not the typical guy that I end up dating, I promise. He's different."

"I hope so."

"Come on," Jane prompted. "You think the other idiots I dated would have helped me decorate a Christmas tree? And offer to make cookies?"

"Where are these cookies, anyway?"

"I told him that the cookies would have to wait." Jane reached a hand over and squeezed my knee. "I was thinking maybe you and I could decorate some cookies. You know, for old time's sake."

"I don't know. Your friend's probably better at baking than me. I didn't inherit those genes from mom."

"That's not the point," Jane said. "It's about us hanging out again. Like old times."

The wine was thoroughly spiraling through my head, and judging by the molasses-like quality to Jane's voice, she was feeling the alcohol too.

"Like old times," I echoed.

"Speaking of old times, I've always wondered," she drawled, "why you didn't ever pick me in Duck Duck Grey Duck?"

"What?" I squinted at her. "I picked you. At least once."

"Nope. Never once," she said. "Not at school, not at a family gathering, not in the neighborhood—nothing."

"I dunno."

"Sure you do." Jane looked over and winked. "Because you knew you could kick my ass, and you never wanted to tag me."

"I don't know."

"Wes is right, Kate. You're a good sister. He told me that tonight, just before he left." She set her glass of wine down, rolled onto her side and met my gaze. "I really appreciate—"

"Did you get a tattoo?"

"What?" Jane shot to a sitting position. "I was in the middle of a heart to heart, and *that's* what you're paying attention to?"

I reached for Jane's arm and pulled it toward me. On the inside of her wrist was a doodle that looked like a misshapen diamond.

"No, I didn't get a tattoo." She snatched her wrist back. "It's the stamp from last night at the club."

"Oh. What is it supposed to be?"

She rolled her eyes. "You can't see it properly; you need a black light for that. I just colored over it while I was waiting at the bar. It took forever to get drinks."

I was already picking up my phone and jotting a note to myself.

"What?" Jane asked. "It'll wash off."

I gave her a smile. "You're brilliant, do you know that? I owe you one."

"Um, okay." Jane shrugged and accepted my praise at face value. "Does that mean I can pick a Christmas movie and you have to watch it with me?"

"Jane—"

"Elf. Final answer."

Chapter 7

The credits to Elf rolled through for the millionth time. The movie must have gone on auto replay all night. I knew from experience the song would be stuck in my head for days.

The fire had burned to a low crumble in the hearth. I reached for an extra blanket, threw it around my shoulders as I stretched my stiff muscles. I wasn't yet thirty, but I felt about fifty this morning between the crick in my neck and an aching back.

I glanced over at my sister. Both Jane and I had fallen asleep on the couch, and somehow, she looked even more uncomfortable than I felt. Gently, I tipped her into a more natural looking position before I tiptoed upstairs to get ready for the day.

I took a longer-than-usual hot shower and let the bathroom fill with steam in an effort to relax. It'd prove to be another long day if yesterday was any indication.

By the time I was out of the shower and dressed, the smell of coffee had wound its way up the stairs. I trundled down and found Jane standing over the stove burning bread.

"What are you making?"

"I tried toast," she said. "But your toaster started sparking. So, I dunno, I'm just making something up."

"Where'd you find coffee filters?"

"I used toilet paper."

I winced.

"Leave me some money, and I'll get you some groceries, coffee filters, and a toaster that won't burn your house down."

"Really?" I asked. "You'd do that? Don't you have plans for the day?"

"I don't work until tonight."

"Work?"

"I might have a new job," she said slyly. "Cross your fingers. I think this one might finally be a good fit for me."

"Good luck," I said. "That's great."

I did a quick check—gun, badge, keys, wallet. Black slacks, blazer, blue shirt. A little higher heels on my boots, seeing as I'd be sitting at an autopsy today and hopefully heading out on a few interviews once Asha's data came back. Before I left, I tossed a few bills on the counter and snuck out so I didn't get roped into a cup of toilet paper coffee.

The snow had accumulated overnight, leaving a solid eight inches on the ground. Even worse, the plows had done a half-ass job clearing the streets while doing a full-ass job of blocking me in. There was a full snowbank surrounding my car.

It took fifteen minutes to get any sort of traction, and by then, the effects of my beauty routine from the morning were completely gone. My hair went flat and limp, my feet were wet, and my attitude had sunk to a new low.

Blasting the heat in my vehicle only went so far, seeing as my jaunt to the precinct didn't take more than a few minutes. I parked in the precinct's lot, then stomped through the snow to the bakery. I feared that once I parked my car, it would be stuck for good.

"Flat white, a regular latte, and a s'mores thing," I said. "All large, all extra hot."

"Good morning to you, too," my mother said. "You look like you drowned on your drive in."

"Pretty much."

"If you'd just hire someone to fix the garage like I suggested when you moved in, you wouldn't look like a drowned mouse at work. A cute drowned mouse."

"Cute?"

"I'm your mother," she said. "I have to say nice things about how you look."

Elizabeth snorted from behind the counter. She covered it up by flicking the steamer onto super high gear and drowning out all conversation.

"So," my mother wheedled after Elizabeth's racket quieted down, "did you see your sister yesterday?"

"She's staying at my place for right now."

"That's nice of you."

"She's my sister; what else could I do?"

"I've wondered the same thing."

"It's not so bad."

"Maybe not the first time, or the second, or the third, or when she takes your car and crashes it because her boyfriend needed cigarettes."

"She'll be okay, mom," I said. "Maybe this time will be different."

She smiled blandly back. "What about that nice man you were in here with yesterday? Will things be different this time?"

"I can't talk about work."

"What about men?"

"Not them either," I said. "Elizabeth, can I get those drinks rushed?"

Elizabeth smirked, shook her head, and dumped extra marshmallows into my cup. "I'm staying out of Rosetti family business."

"You're part of the family business," my mother barked happily. "No escaping us."

"Sorry," I whispered as I picked up a to-go tray and stocked it with drinks.

"Are you working that one case?" Elizabeth stopped me in my tracks. "With the girl down by the river?"

I turned slowly around. "How'd you know?"

"I read Lassie's blog," she said. "It's actually really funny. You know, not the murder case, but her other stuff."

"Oh, I'm going to kill her."

"It didn't say much," she said. "Just, you know, the basics. But she wondered why a young, college-age girl would be killed around here. If so, does that mean the rest of us are at risk?"

"I can't comment on an active investigation, I'm sorry. But we will find him, I promise."

"I know you will. You always do."

But I didn't miss the sideways look she gave my mother when she thought my back was turned, or the way she pulled up her phone and anxiously tapped a few buttons as I let my-self out of the shop.

Great, I thought. Just what we needed.

Panic in the city.

"WILL THIS BRIBE BE sufficient?" I handed Melinda her flat white as we strode into the lab.

She took a sip. "It'll do."

"You're a hard nut to crack, doctor."

Melinda opened the door to the hallway outside of her lab, and we came face to face with none other than Agent Russo who had been waiting on the other side. Presumably for us.

"Speaking of nuts," I said. "You're here early."

"Didn't want to miss anything." He grinned, then extended a coffee cup to me just as I extended one to him. We met halfway, our glasses touching. "Did you buy me a coffee, Rosetti?"

"Hold your shorts on. I get a discount from my mother."

"That hardly seems fair." He winked. "I paid full price, so you should probably drink mine first."

"Mine has extra marshmallows."

"So does mine. And whipped cream."

"Dang." I'd forgotten to ask Elizabeth for whip. Grudgingly, I accepted his proffered cup. "You win this time."

Melissa just watched us. "Shall we get started?"

Half an hour later, Melinda was kicking off her autopsy while Russo and I made small talk off to one side. The previous night hadn't produced any magical leads in our case.

With the fake ID and no hits on facial recognition for the girl, we still had a Jane Doe. No clue where she'd been the night she'd died, who she'd talked to, or who might be missing her.

I glanced at my phone as it pinged with a message from my mother: **DID CUTE AGENT GIVE YOU DRINK.**

I responded: **Is that a question or a statement? And why all caps? Are you shouting?**

Ma: **NOT SHOUTING. KEYBOARD STUCK LIKE THIS.**

Me: **Yes, he gave me the coffee.**

Ma: **DON'T DRINK BOTH CUPS. YOU WILL DIE OF HEART ATTACK.**

As I closed out of my messaging app, I caught sight of the note I'd made last night. My neck snapped upward so quickly I startled the others. Melinda raised her eyebrow in annoyance at the interruption.

"What is it?"

"Have you done the blacklight part yet? Do that now, please. If you can."

Melinda patiently stared me down. "Are you expecting to find something?"

"Can you shine it on her wrist? The right one."

Melinda took her sweet time setting down her tools, changing gloves, adjusting the wrist and pulling out the black light. My phone buzzed.

Ma: **DID YOU FIX YOUR HAIR? DROWNED MOUSE = NO DATE WITH CUTE AGENT.**

I closed my phone, saw Russo trying to glance over my shoulder at my screen. "Mind your own business," I snapped.

"Kate," Melinda interrupted. "How'd you know we'd get a hit?"

Russo's eyes switched over to the doctor. "A hit?"

I stepped closer, already knowing what we'd find on her arm. A tiny ink stamp that glowed ruby red in the shape of a gem under the black light. "Bingo."

Russo looked at me with renewed interest. "Care to explain?"

"Not really," I said. "Let me get a shot of it."

I snapped a cell phone photo and then texted it to Asha asking for a quick match. She called me back almost at once.

"You know, clubs don't make a habit of posting their entrance stamps online," she said. "That would be stupid."

"I know," I said. "But I figured you could work some magic and scour the internet, maybe find a match on social media. You are a wizard, aren't you?"

She blew out a huge sigh. "You expect so much of me."

"Call me when you find something."

I snapped my phone shut and glanced at Russo. He was watching me with a curious expression.

"Be right back," I muttered. "I need to make a personal call."

I stepped outside the lab and watched as Russo and Melissa exchanged words over the body. Russo bent closer, examined the stamp. Melissa pointed out something.

I hit dial. While Asha was a wizard on the computer, I happened to have an even better source than a social media profile.

"What color do you like better?" Jane answered the phone with a question. "Purple or super boring black?"

"I think you've already answered your own question."

"Pretty much," she said. "Just getting your approval. This new toaster is a beaut. By the way, you forgot coffee this morning!"

"Dang," I said. "Anyway, quick question for you. That gem on your wrist—what club was that from?"

"The one where Wes works," she said crossly. "I told you."

"I mean the name of it."

"Rubies."

"Ruby's?" I asked. "Like the girls name?"

"No." She expelled her breath. "Sometimes, I wonder about you being a detective."

"Jane."

"Rubies. Like, the precious stones. Hence the stamp," she said. "It's owned by Alastair Gem. The club's only been around a few weeks."

I waited. The name sounded familiar but was taking some time to click.

"*The* Alastair Gem," she said. "You know, the billionaire who owns half this city and plenty of others, too."

Suddenly, it clicked. The newest skyscraper. The hotel in downtown Minneapolis that had opened last year with a sparkling diamond restaurant on the top that twirled and lit up the entire city.

"Interesting," I said. "Thanks."

"Why? You're not thinking Wes is in trouble, are you?"

My heart just about stopped. Was there any coincidence that my sister had acquired a new boyfriend on the very same night our victim had been killed? *And* that he worked at the very same club where she'd last been seen before her untimely death?

"What time did you meet Wes?" I asked urgently.

"It was late. After two," she said. "I hadn't seen him earlier, or I'd have remembered. Some idiot was trying to feel me up at the bar during last call, and Wes came over and swooped in to save me."

"Modern day Rhett Butler," I mumbled. "Do me a favor and stay away from the club for the next few days. And Wes."

"But Wes and I were supposed to wrap presents today."

I pinched my forehead. What new boyfriend agreed to help his one-day-old girlfriend wrap Christmas presents? Unless he wanted something. And I had the ugly feeling that Wes wasn't after my sister's love. Was he trying to get close to Jane so he had access to me? Access to the case? If he was involved in the murder and wanted to stay one step ahead of the police...

"How long has Wes lived in town?"

"Not long," she said. "He moves around a lot."

"Do me a favor. Don't see him. Just for a few days. Please."

"What's going on?"

"I'll explain later," I said. "I have to go."

"But—"

"Get the purple toaster," I said. "It's my compromise. Final offer."

I clicked off before she could argue and returned to the lab. Russo was looking at something on his phone.

"What's that?" I asked, coming up beside him. I caught notes of spicy aftershave and expensive shampoo and took a step further away.

"Did you talk to a blogger?" He didn't look happy as he flipped his phone around. "I recognize this woman's face. She was with you last night at dinner."

I groaned. "I'll talk to her."

"This *Lassie* all but insinuated more young college girls might be murdered." Russo carefully managed the frustration in his voice. "We can't spook this guy."

"I know. I told her not to print anything."

"She *is* free to speculate," Melinda pointed out. "It's public news that a young girl got murdered."

"But she might not have speculated in that direction if it weren't for us," I said, turning to Russo. "I'll take care of it."

"Do that."

His pissy attitude undid all the goodwill his delicious coffee order had gained him. "I've got a few things to take care of this morning. Call me if you turn up anything huge."

"Need company?" Russo's jaw was set, his lips a firm line.

"Nah," I said. "Why don't you stay cozy and wait for the autopsy results? We'll keep you posted if we get anything."

"Is this related to the stamp?"

I was already halfway out the door and pretended not to hear Russo's question. I stomped upstairs, both coffees in hand, and halted in front of Jimmy's desk. "Jones, get up. We're going out."

"Double-fisting coffee, Rosetti? Are things that bad?"

"You don't want to know."

Jimmy hauled himself out of his seat. "You're driving."

"Your car is a decade newer than mine."

"And I'm two decades older than you. If your hands are full, I'll carry your keys."

Chapter 8

We pulled up outside Rubies, but at ten in the morning, there wasn't a blip of movement inside the building. We sat for ten minutes while I sipped my coffee and Jimmy reclined the passenger's seat and closed his eyes.

After listening to Jimmy's nose whistle for thirty minutes, I was relieved to find some action outside of my window when a truck pulled up to the side of the club entrance and wedged itself into the alley. A crew opened the doors to begin unloading. Before they could get started, a shiny black Maserati screeched to a stop at the curb out front.

I hardly recognized the man exiting the vehicle. Because today, he was fully clothed.

"I'm going out," I said to Jimmy. "Do me a favor and wait here for a second. It's personal."

"You know him?"

"Jane knows him *very* well."

"Ah." Jimmy nodded, rested his hand on his gun, and struggled to keep his eyes open.

I let myself out of the car with one of two coffee cups in hand. I picked my way through the snow in heels that were, in retrospect, a stupid choice. By the time I reached Wes, I was sweating under my coat and had lost sensation in three of my toes.

"Wes?" I asked, pulling out my badge. "Detective Rosetti."

Wes turned at the sound of my voice, his lips parted in surprise when he came to face me. "Yeah. We've met."

"I remember. Though it threw me off to see you wearing something besides a pink bathrobe."

He gave a wry smile. "I'm really sorry again about yesterday. I tried to tell Jane that you'd be reasonable and let me out through the front door, but she insisted on my trying to vanish through the window."

"Jane can be very persuasive."

"She can be."

"When did you meet her?"

"Is this..." He hesitated, glanced over my shoulder at the car. "Is this a business or personal question?"

I followed his gaze to find Jimmy staring down Wes like he wanted to eat him for lunch. I didn't doubt that he could. Where Wes was stretched tall and wiry, Jimmy was wide and round. Jimmy had the same look in his eyes as he surveyed Wes that he did when someone brought fresh doughnuts to the conference room.

I turned back to face Wes. "I haven't decided yet."

"Okay." Wes shifted from one foot to the next. "Well, I met your sister the night before last."

"Where?"

"A club."

"Which club?"

"This one."

"Wes, let me be honest with you," I said. "I don't think you're a shy guy, seeing as the first time we met, you weren't wearing any clothes. Now's not the time to clam up on me."

Wes ran a hand through his hair, then glanced back at a trio of big guys—each the size of my car—who were unloading liquor cartons from the truck. "Bring 'em all inside. Don't leave before I sign off."

One of the men grunted, and the other two ignored Wes entirely.

"Shall we go inside?" Wes asked. "You look cold."

"I think that sounds great."

Wes led me around through the back alley. Rubies was located in a fairly well-to-do neighborhood near Capitol Hill. The area had gone through rehab a few years back when the city had swooped in and turned derelict, century-old buildings into up-and-coming, trendy restaurants smooshed between kitschy shops and yoga studios. I had to give Alastair Gem credit—he'd chosen prime real estate for his new venture.

Wes led me through an employee entrance at the rear of the building. Out front, the only signifier that the club existed was a tiny, neon sign in the shape of a ruby that glowed red after dark. The same emblem that had been stamped onto the wrists of my sister and our Jane Doe.

Jane and Jane, I thought uncomfortably. How close had my sister come to meeting a serial killer? As I watched the back of Wes's head, I wondered if maybe she already had. From what I'd been able to turn up so far on Wes—job history, past home addresses, etc.—it didn't seem like he was our best bet as prime suspect, but I wasn't counting him out yet.

He took me straight to the second floor. Exposed beams and peeling brick on most walls gave the impression that while music might be pulsing downstairs, the execs on the second level were living a hundred years in the past.

Wes led me into a quite ordinary office. There was a large desk in the middle of the room, complete with a computer and chair. Two guest seats were on the other side of the room. A K-cup machine sat on a small table along with a few photos of Wes and friends.

"Coffee?" Wes asked.

I raised my cup to decline. "Were you here yesterday evening?"

"Can I please get coffee before we start this again? I had a late night."

I waited while the machine gurgled to life and spluttered. I sipped my own cold latte and debated asking for a refill when I saw a photo that distracted me from my frozen latte.

"Who's this?" I asked.

Wes just stared at me.

"What?" I looked pointedly at his cup. "You have coffee. I'm allowed to ask questions."

He gave a smile. "I see you and your sister share a biting sense of humor."

"Oh, I'm not funny," I said. "Who is this?"

I picked up the photo and looked closer. The man looked familiar, but it took a few moments for the name to click. I'd seen this man before. In a newspaper. On a magazine. Plastered across the television. The man looked familiar because he was the famous Alastair Gem.

In the photo, Gem stood even taller and broader than Wes. He filled out his suit like it was made for him. Then again, it probably had been custom tailored to his body, seeing as Gem probably owned the suit company too. His hair was dark and curled just slightly around his forehead, which made his eyes stand out in their stunning shade of slate gray. His lips tipped up, not quite in a smile, but in amusement.

"That's Alastair Gem, of course, on opening night at Rubies," Wes explained. "He didn't stay long. Never does, but he likes to pop in now and again to make sure things are running smoothly."

"You got a last name, Wes?" I set the photo back down.

"Wes Remington."

"How close are you with Gem?"

"We're friends."

"Good friends?"

"Look, I'm all about being open, but I want to know why I'm doing it." Wes sat, clinking his cup on the table. "I get the feeling you don't like me, which is understandable. What I'm trying to figure out is if you're here because you're afraid of me dating your sister... or if you're here to investigate a murder."

I crossed my arms over my chest. "I don't think I need to say much on the subject of my sister. It goes without saying that I expect you'll treat her nicely. Buy her a flower now and again."

He met my gaze evenly. "You've got it."

"Now, we can put the personal business behind us and focus on what's important." I pulled out my badge and set it on his desk. Then, I pulled out my phone and pulled up the picture of the ruby stamp on Jane Doe's wrist. "Let's make this official. I'm Detective Kate Rosetti, and I've got a few questions about a murder investigation. Let's start with your alibi. Where were you the night before last?"

"Kate—"

"If you'd rather start with the second question, why don't you tell me if you recognize this woman?"

Wes leaned forward and studied the image of the tattoo under the black light. His face went pale. My instincts told me that he was genuinely shocked.

"Are you saying that the woman killed near the river, the one who was on the news," he said slowly, "was *here* before she died?"

"Judging by the fresh stamp on her wrist, I think it's pretty obvious. Where were you that night?"

"I was here, upstairs—alone," Wes said. "In my office. Working."

"Any security footage that can confirm that?"

He winced. "We're still getting the cameras working. We had security guards and bouncers on the clock, obviously. They all saw me arrive. But that's it. I didn't have any visitors."

"What's your job title?"

"I'm the manager for Rubies. Gem owns this place, but I'm the one who runs it. I oversee everything from inventory to staff hiring to guest artists and live shows."

"So, you've got your hands in everything that goes on."

He gave me a thin smile. "You don't strike me as the type of person to have ever worked in the nightlife industry, detective. If you had, it wouldn't surprise you to learn that I don't know the half of what goes on downstairs. It's a night-club. I know exactly what it is I do. I don't know everything."

I squinted. "So, you mostly know what goes on, but only if it's convenient."

"That didn't sound like a question."

"Just an observation," I said. "How often do you see Alas-tair Gem?"

"I have bi-weekly meetings with him to brief him on our numbers, issues, reports," he said. "Eventually that'll slow down to bi-monthly updates once things even out."

"When's your next meeting?"

"This afternoon. Three p.m. at Gem Industries."

"I'd like to come with you."

Wes gave me a complicated smile that was hard to deci-pher. "May I ask why that's necessary?"

"Gem owns the place, doesn't he?"

"We both know the answer to that."

"I'd like to speak with him," I said. "I can go on my own, but I thought it might be smoother with an introduction from his friend."

To my surprise, Wes gave a laugh and spread his hands wide. "Fine."

"Did I miss something funny?"

"I have a feeling Gem might've met his match." Wes sat back in his seat and spun his mug around, the label of Gem Industries—a single diamond—glittered at me. "I'm eager to see how this plays out."

I pushed my chair back and stood, pulling a photo of Jane Doe out of my pocket. "Have you ever seen her before?"

The temperature in the air cooled considerably. "That's her?" Wes studied the picture, a shadow crossing his face. "She looks so young."

"Can you please answer the question?"

Wes brushed hair out of his eye. "No, I've never seen her before."

"You can't confirm whether she was here on the night she died?"

"Like I already told you, I was working upstairs—alone—until the bar closed. I couldn't have seen her."

"I thought she might be a regular."

"We opened a few weeks ago," he said. "We don't have regulars."

"Can I get a list of the staff working the evening of the nineteenth?"

Wes spun around to face his computer. He clicked a few buttons, printed out a list. Before he handed it over, he skimmed the names there, scratched at his chin. Then he reached for the highlighter and popped the top off before coloring out a few names.

"All but three people who worked on the nineteenth will be working tonight." He handed the sheet to me. "We're new, still hiring. We have a lot of the same people working every night. You want to chat with some of the employees, come by around seven tonight. You've got from the end of our staff meeting until doors open at nine."

I took the paper from him and ran my gaze over it. "I appreciate the cooperation."

"I've got nothing to hide, detective." Wes pushed his chair back and gave a stiff smile. "Oh, and detective?"

I spun around at the door. "Yes?"

"Word of advice," he said. "Gem had nothing to do with this. Not to mention, Alastair contributes generously to the police department every year."

"What's that supposed to mean?"

Wes cracked his knuckles, then winced and shook out his hand. "Alastair Gem is not a man you want to offend."

Chapter 9

"I expect you'll fill me in," Jimmy said as I climbed back into the car. "Dare I suggest it be over a bucket of chicken?"

I swerved into the left lane and put on my blinker for The Chicken Hut, a fried food joint near the station. We crawled through the drive thru line and put in our orders. A king-sized pail for Jimmy, a queen for me. A few minutes later, the tantalizing smell of fried chicken was working its way into the car's upholstery.

Jimmy had shiny fingers by the time we returned to the station parking lot. He mopped his chin with a napkin. "I'm ready to hear the details whenever you're done with that wing."

I sighed, tossing the wing back into the bucket. I wasn't all that hungry. It was hard to care much about food when a case consumed me.

"My sister brought Wes home last night," I said. "Like, on a date. Wes Remington—the manager of Rubies—was at my house. Rubies is Alastair Gem's latest venture."

"No kidding? That's neat."

"What's neat?"

"Gem is like the Tony Stark of the Twin Cities. His latest restaurant has the best food I've ever tasted—it set me back a year into retirement to eat there, though. Now I hear he's got an Emerald hotel coming soon that's gonna cost two grand a pop for a night. That man is rich, powerful, and handsome. The rest of us don't stand a chance."

"I beg to differ," I said. "Anyone who is that rich, handsome, and powerful has secrets to hide."

Jimmy shrugged. "Probably. Still doesn't mean I wouldn't date him, and I'm a happily married straight man."

"As it turns out, Wes doesn't have an alibi for the night of the murder. He says he was upstairs working, but we don't have anyone who can confirm it."

"Do you like him for Jane Doe's murder?"

I licked my fingers. "It's too early to tell. My head says yes. He's new to town and had easy access to the victim. But I don't have any clue as to a motive. Why would he grab her specifically?"

"We're looking for a serial killer. Is there any saying why they do what they do?"

"Maybe not," I agreed. "But my gut's telling me Wes isn't our guy. He seemed... surprised. A little sad. He doesn't strike me as the type."

"He could be faking. The good ones lie, and they lie good."

"You're right. It's just a gut feeling."

"Then there's the whole thing about him magically dating your sister," Jimmy pointed out. "Do you think he could be trying to get close to you to keep on top of the investigation?"

"It seems like a lot of effort to do that," I said. "But I can't pretend the timing doesn't strike me as strange. Jane is going to be pissed when she hears I interviewed him without telling her."

"You're just doing your job," Jimmy said, then pointed at the remainder of my bucket. "You gonna eat any of that?"

I handed the pail to Jimmy.

"What's next?"

"I've got lunch plans with Russo. He's going to be pissed too. I didn't exactly keep him up to date with my interview plans on the case."

"Is there anyone who's not pissed at you?"

"*You* better not be." I glanced over at Jimmy. "I just gave you my bucket of chicken."

He raised a hand and gave me a shiny-fingered salute.

"After Russo, I have to talk to my sister. Then, I'm tagging along with Wes to meet Alastair Gem. Tonight—"

"You're meeting Alastair Gem?"

"Want me to pass along your digits and a headshot?" I asked, laying on the sarcasm. "I'm a detective. He's a person of interest. Yes, I've got a meeting with him. I'd invite you along, but I'd prefer to go alone for this one."

Jimmy gestured to his bucket of chicken. "I'm too bloated to meet Alastair Gem today. Maybe next time. Give me a heads up so I can wear a fresh suit. You feeling okay to handle it?"

"I'll be fine with Gem, but I could use your help later tonight. We've got an invitation to Rubies to interview the staff who worked the night of the nineteenth. In fact, we could use a few uniforms on hand to help."

"I'll take care of it."

I pulled out a wet nap and wiped my fingers. Then I snapped a photo of the employee list Wes had printed for me before handing the hard copy over the center console to my partner.

Jimmy stared at me, then raised both hands. His fingers shined back at me. He gave me a look that said I was nuts.

I sighed, folded the paper, then reached over and tucked it into his suit pocket. Then I fished out an extra wet nap from my glove compartment, opened it, and handed it over to Jimmy.

"Have I told you how much I appreciate you as a partner?" he asked, scrubbing himself clean. "We make a good team."

"We sure do," I said. "I think you owe me a favor. The three names on the list that are highlighted—they're not working tonight. Have Asha run their names, get addresses, and track them down. I'd like to have everyone interviewed by tonight before anyone catches wind of what's happening."

"Aye-aye, boss."

"Do me a double-favor?"

Jimmy groaned until I gave his two buckets the side-eye. "Fine."

"Take Russo with you."

Another groan.

"I'll bring you a latte tomorrow," I wheedled. "Turtle mocha, extra whip."

"Fine." Jimmy opened the door and stretched. Then he ducked his head back in through the door. "I think you've got company, and he doesn't look happy."

I sighed as Jimmy moved out of the way. Russo appeared there a second later, then slid inside the car without waiting for an invitation.

"You're driving," he said. "Let's go."

"Russo—"

"You're lucky I'm not making you pay," he said through gritted teeth. "I'm not happy, detective."

"I can't help you with that."

"Oh, Kate." Russo's eyes darkened as they landed on me. "You are so very wrong about that."

"I THOUGHT YOU HAD PERSONAL business to take care of," Russo said the second we were seated at a table. He flagged down a passing server. "Two waters to start with, please."

I hissed across the restaurant chatter. "And I thought we were having a casual lunch date."

"I never said casual."

I glanced around the lakeside inn that had been converted from a vintage B&B into an elegant and exclusive restaurant approximately seven times above my pay grade. I fingered the cloth napkin and slid it over my lap, thinking how just a short time back I'd been licking chicken grease from my fingers.

"I hope you didn't spoil your appetite," Russo said as he glanced at me. "I can smell the fried chicken from a mile away."

"Thank you," I said. "It's the new Chanel blend."

A smirk tugged at the corner of his mouth. "So, personal business?"

I sighed, choosing to survey the nineteen different forks and spoons on the table before me, along with the neatly outfitted men and women scurrying about with little sticks meant to wipe crumbs off the tables. Dishes of fresh fruit sat piled high on the outskirts of the room, tucked between several discreet displays of tiny desserts.

The restaurant had been dressed to the nines in Christmas attire. A light scent of evergreen overpowered the lingering chicken odor clinging to my jacket. The gray skies outside were dimmed by thick curtains hanging over the windows. The dim ambiance was offset by a series of all-white Christmas lights, all-white Christmas trees, and all-white Christmas ornaments. Angels clung to rafters and fairy lights dipped and crossed above our heads. It was a winter wonderland.

"I'm sorry," I began, but stopped as a server swooped over and deposited a plate of olive oil swirled with delicately thin strips of basil leaves. Next to it, he placed a fresh loaf of piping hot focaccia. "This looks amazing."

Russo's eyes watched as I ripped off a hunk of bread and dunked it in the olive oil. With an amused twinkle in his eye, he glanced up at me. "You were saying?"

"Right. I am sorry I didn't keep you in the loop this morning, but I *did* leave on personal business. It just so happened my personal business intersected with work, and I decided to take advantage of it."

"Uh-huh."

Russo didn't believe me, but I didn't care. The bread tasted like clouds and the olive oil was smooth and spicy and just about the best thing I'd ever put in my mouth.

"I didn't promise I'd let you shadow me on the case," I said. "I *said* I'd keep you posted, and that's what I'm doing now. Posting you."

"I see," Russo said. "Then post away."

We paused to order. Russo recommended the salmon and salad, but I went for a hefty plate of lasagna with a side of French fries.

"Fries?" he asked.

I shrugged. "I like fries. This place probably has fancy fries. I've never tried fancy fries."

The amused half-smile on Russo's face was becoming a permanent fixture. "The case?"

I filled Russo in on my morning at Rubies while we nibbled on bread and an appetizer of calamari that he'd ordered on the sly. I left out only the bits about my sister.

"Which part of that was personal?" Russo asked when I finished.

I opened my mouth to respond, but my cell phone cut me off with a ring. A glance at the screen told me it was my sister. "This part is personal."

"Convenient."

I ignored Russo and stood. "Excuse me. I have to take this."

As I stepped away from the table, I saw a server carrying two plates of food that looked suspiciously like lasagna and salmon, along with a side of salad and fancy fries. I felt a bit guilty about answering the phone at a lunch outing, but I couldn't take the chance my sister was in trouble. Not with everything going on.

I answered, and my stomach plummeted when I heard labored breathing.

"What were you *thinking*?" Jane screeched into the phone. "What the hell did you do?"

"What are you talking about?" I asked, toying with a strand of hair that had fallen out of my ponytail.

"You know perfectly well what I'm talking about. You paid a visit to Wes, didn't you?"

"What did he say?" I asked.

"Not much," she fired back. "That's the problem. He did go ahead and cancel our lunch plans for today. Then, he cancelled my interview afternoon."

"Your interview?"

"My job. You know, the thing that was supposed to get me out of your house and into my own place? *That* thing."

"Don't tell me you wanted to work at Rubies. Come on, Jane. There are better jobs out there."

"I sure hope so because the chances of me getting this job after whatever you said to Wes are slim to none. I don't know if I'll ever even see him again, and I certainly won't be able to step foot back in the club."

"You know mom's got a job for you at the bakery. She'd love it if you went back."

"I can't believe you went behind my back on this."

"I was just doing my job."

"Sure, whatever," Jane said. "You're always just doing your job. That's the problem."

"Jane—"

"I don't want to talk about it anymore. I'll see you at home."

I dragged myself back to the table, suddenly not all that excited about fancy fries. I couldn't make eye contact with Russo, so I made do by sliding into my seat and fiddling with my napkin until he broke the silence.

"Is your new, bad mood something personal?" he asked dryly. "Or should I be expecting another update?"

I just stared at him. Something in my face must have told him I wasn't in a joking mood because his smile immediately dampened.

"I'm sorry," he said. "That was uncalled for. How about a fancy fry to cheer you up?"

"I don't feel like being cheered up," I said. "But thanks. I appreciate you taking me out to lunch. And I'm sorry about everything else."

Russo studied me for a long moment, watching as I reached for a fry, ate half, and set the rest on my plate.

"You know what?" he said suddenly. "I'm not hungry either. What do you say we order dessert and coffee and get out of here?"

"Don't be ridiculous. You're paying a fortune for these dishes. And fancy fries and salmon aren't as good cold."

"You're in luck; I know a secret trick to reheating fries that make them taste even better the second time around."

"That's impossible."

He gave me a smile. "Tiramisu?"

"Only if you get the gelato on the side."

"As if that was ever a question."

Russo flagged over the waiter and requested our dinners be boxed for the road, ignoring the curious look we earned in exchange. Then he ordered dessert along with two cappuccinos.

"They're not as good as your mother's," he explained. "But they'll do."

We finished our dessert in the closest thing to a friendly moment we'd ever had in our short time together. After Russo let me have the last bite of tiramisu, I sat back in my seat and rested a hand on my stomach.

"Delicious," I said. "Thanks again."

"Just wait until you try my re-heated fries."

The check came and Russo discreetly slipped his card inside. I watched, feeling a sudden flush in my cheeks as the server gave me a knowing wink.

"I hope you don't mind me saying," he said with a gigantic smile, "but the two of you make for a lovely couple. Have a wonderful afternoon."

"Oh, we're not—uh—" I stuttered.

"Thanks," Russo said and handed the book back. "We certainly will."

The server vanished behind a white curtain where I imagined he was running the card, leaving me to drown alone in a pool of awkwardness. Annoyingly, Russo didn't seem the least bit distressed.

Finally, I broke the silence. "Can I ask a favor of you?"

"Go ahead."

"There's a meeting I would like to take alone. It's not quite personal, but it's not quite business, either. It's a meeting with Alastair Gem. I don't know if you've heard of—"

"Of course I know who Gem is," Russo said. "I'd like to join you."

"Maybe you could meet up with Jimmy instead and help cross off the employees at the club who won't be working tonight. We can meet at Rubies around seven to take care of the rest of the interviews."

"Jimmy will be fine on his own. I want to go with you, but I'll wait in the car."

"Really?" I asked. "Why would you do that?"

He glanced down at his hands. "Sometimes it helps to have someone there. Just in case."

I considered his offer. "I can deal with that."

"It's a date," he said, then cleared his throat. "Should we take my car? It's got four-wheel drive."

"That'd be good," I said. "Gem's headquarters are over in Minneapolis, and if we want to be there by three, we should probably get going."

The check was returned, Russo signed it, and I grabbed our bag of leftovers. I handed them to Russo.

"You'll need these more than me at the hotel," I said. "I have food at home."

"But—"

"Sometime," I said with a smile, "I'll try your re-heated fries. I promise."

Russo quirked an eyebrow. "Deal."

"For what it's worth, I don't think you're a colossal pain in the ass."

"Thanks, detective. I like you too."

Chapter 10

By the time my car skidded into the precinct lot, any sort of friendliness had faded between me and Russo. He wasn't a fan of my driving technique, and I wasn't a fan of his commentary on said driving technique.

"You're still alive, aren't you?" I retorted as we climbed out of the car.

"Next time we go anywhere, we're taking my car," he muttered. "I need a pacemaker to slow my heartrate."

We stomped next to each other inside the office. I stopped in front of Jimmy's desk. "Are you coming with us to hear the autopsy results?"

Jimmy glanced up from the pack of Ho-Ho's on his desk and looked between Russo and myself. "I can see your friendly little lunch didn't ease the cold war."

"The food was great," I said. "It's my driving he has a problem with."

Jimmy looked over at Russo, his eyes widening. "You talked about her driving?"

"During my driving, through my driving, at my driving," I said. "At my braking, at my turning, at my skidding, at the distance between my car and the next. He couldn't seem to stop talking about my driving."

"Dude," Jimmy said.

Russo just shrugged. "I thought I was a dead man."

"I ain't saying you're wrong." Jimmy dropped his voice as if I couldn't hear. "But dude."

"I'm going down to talk to Dr. Brooks." I continued my storm trooper path to the elevator and punched the door-shut button before Russo could join me.

Melinda was in her office, hunched over a stack of papers when I found her.

She gave me one look and raised her hand in surrender. "I didn't do anything."

"It's Russo and Jones," I said. "They're complaining about my driving again."

"Well, have you considered the fact they might have a good—"

"Don't say it."

"I'm just thinking aloud. If everyone who rides with you has a near-aneurism, then maybe—"

"How about we focus on work here?"

Melinda gave me a patient smile. "I do have a few findings I wanted to share. I'll have the full report later this afternoon."

"Do you have a name for our victim?"

"We tried fingerprints and dental of course, as well as her DNA—no hits. Not a huge surprise, but there you have it. I did find a fiber that I'm running through the system."

"You think it might be from the killer's clothes?"

"Too early to tell. Even if it is, it will be a needle in a haystack to match with anyone."

"I figured." I bit my lower lip in thought. "Have you read through Russo's files for the other cases? Is it possible we're dealing with one killer?"

Melinda didn't meet my eye. "The MO is very similar between Russo's cases and this one. I would speculate there's a very good chance we're dealing with a serial killer or, at minimum, a copycat of some sort."

"What are the chances of a copycat?"

"I would say slim," she said. "I believe what we're dealing with is a progression, an accelerated need to kill. A copycat would... copy. Each case has some slight differences that can be attributed to the killer refining his process as he goes along."

"Wonderful."

"He's becoming more and more meticulous, and he'll only get better."

"Not if I can help it."

"I meant—"

"I know what you meant," I said, an urgent gaze passing between us. "We can't afford for him to get better. We don't even have a name for our victim yet, and he's probably already thinking about the next."

Melinda gave me a sad smile. "Go do what you need to do. I'll call you if anything else turns up."

I was lost in my thoughts as I headed upstairs. Russo and Jones were still waxing poetic over my driving skills, but after one look at my face, they both fell silent.

"What is it?" Russo asked. "What's wrong?"

I filled them in on Melinda's findings. "I think we need to go back to his first kill. There's got to be a personal connection there. Something that triggered him."

"We don't know who she is."

"We're missing something. What the hell are we missing?"

"Kate," Jimmy began. "Everyone's doing the best they can. Yourself included. Take a breath."

"It's not good enough," I snapped. "We need to be better, or there's going to be another young girl on our table before we can blink. It could be my sister. It could be your daughter, Jimmy."

"We all want to find this guy, Kate," Russo said. "Nobody more than me. But—"

"Great," I said shortly. "New plan for this afternoon. Russo, get Jimmy the files from your first cases. Jimmy, pore over them with a fine-tooth comb. Nothing is too big or too small. Something has been missed. Russo—"

He turned his gaze to me, challenging me to give him an order.

I hesitated, then averted my eyes as I spoke. "Russo, I think your time would be best spent knocking out a few interviews of the bar employees. See if they saw our girl leave with someone. Our killer is getting more savvy, and I'm thinking he wined and dined his last victim, got her to trust him—at least a little."

"With all due respect, detective," Russo said, "I think you can get someone else to do the interviews. I'd prefer to join you at Gem Industries."

"And sit in the car?" I shook my head. "No."

"I've got calls to make. My time won't be unproductive," he said firmly. "Get someone else to knock out the interviews."

"I'll do the interviews," Jimmy said, jumping in to stop the sparring. "It won't take me all afternoon to review the files. And whatever I don't get through I'll do tonight. My wife is away at a yoga retreat anyway."

I let my gaze land on Russo and burn holes into his skull. He shifted his weight but didn't outright flinch, and I had to give him credit for that.

"One word about my driving," I warned him, "and I'm throwing you out of the car."

"Oh, no, detective." Russo jangled his keys, glanced over his shoulder at Jones and threw him a wink. "I'm driving."

Chapter 11

"You don't have to babysit me, Russo," I said as we cruised down I-94 westbound toward Minneapolis. "You could've worked from the comfort of the office."

"My car's more comfortable than that thing you call an office. You haven't changed your mind about letting me come with you to meet Gem?"

"I have not."

"Well, then, you can deal with me sitting outside in my comfortable rental car on its heated seats with a fresh cup of coffee."

"This is me, dealing with it," I said. "Here we are, I guess."

"No kidding." Russo gave a low whistle as he surveyed Gem Industries. "What gave it away, the huge sign out front or the sparkling diamond on top?"

"Park out front." I ignored his sarcasm. "Is the FBI footing the bill for the meter?"

"I swear, that's the only reason you let me come," Russo said with a grin. "For my credit card."

"I won't deny it's a nice perk to having you around," I shot back.

Russo's grin grew brighter as he pulled into the valet station. A neatly outfitted man in a suit and excessively gelled hair was at my window before I could blink.

"FBI," Russo said as he rolled the window down and leaned over me. He brushed against my stomach, apparently oblivious to the tingles that erupted from our contact. He flashed the valet his badge. "My vehicle's staying right here for the next half hour."

The valet backed away slowly. I took out my own badge. "Police. I'm looking for Alastair Gem."

"Mr. Gem?" the valet looked shocked. "You, uh, you can't see him. It takes weeks to get an appointment."

"Not for me it doesn't," I said, sliding out of the car and crossing my arms. "Can you show me where to get a badge?"

"The front desk handles all that. I just drive the cars."

I glanced behind me at Russo. "I'll be back."

He acknowledged me with a nod before settling in and pulling out his phone. I entered the lobby ten minutes before my meeting was supposed to start and looked around for any sign of Wes. He was nowhere to be seen.

"I need to speak to Alastair Gem," I said to the receptionist at the front desk without preamble. I flipped out my badge. "Detective Rosetti. TC Task Force."

"I'm sorry," the receptionist deadpanned. "Mr. Gem is unavailable for appointments until April."

"Not for me, he isn't," I said. "I am here—"

"Kate?!"

The voice stopped me in my tracks. I spun around, my heels squeaking against the slick floor. I gaped at my sister, standing before me in a short black dress that flared out at her knees and left her legs bare. She was wearing glasses, which didn't quite make sense seeing as she had perfect vision.

"Jane!" I turned away from the receptionist and faced my sister. "What are you doing here?"

"I had an interview. I told you that," Jane said. "I'm just leaving. More importantly, what are *you* doing here? Are you following me?"

"No, I have a meeting."

"You actually don't have a meeting—" the receptionist inserted over my shoulder. "Mr. Gem is busy."

"And so am I," Jane said. "I'll see you at home, Kate."

My sister click-clacked out of the lobby before I could pester her further. I didn't have time to sit around and wonder. I turned back to the reception desk.

"I'm Gem's three p.m. Please call upstairs if you don't believe me."

"She's quite right, Ms. Karp." A gravelly voice rolled over my shoulder. "No need to call upstairs; I figured I'd come down to greet the famous Detective Rosetti."

The receptionist went sheet-cake white. She nodded, and her lips slid into a thin line.

With a sinking feeling, I spun to face the voice and came face to face with the man from the picture on Wes's desk. Alastair Gem's somewhat curly hair was lighter than I'd expected, offset by those same slate eyes I'd seen in the photo. Unlike the still image, the man before me was alive. Wildly, vibrantly alive.

There was a hint of curiosity in his eyes overshadowed by the broad smile still on his face that suggested he found me more than a little amusing. When he spoke, strong traces of a British accent pulled everything together.

He wore nice gray slacks offset by brown shoes and a stark white shirt rolled up to his elbows. A tattoo peeked out from underneath near his left elbow, though I couldn't make out the design. Under my gaze, Gem shoved both hands in his pockets and smiled. It was only after I'd completely taken in Alastair's presence that I realized Wes Remington was standing right beside him. Gem had a way of stealing the show.

"Alastair Gem," he said in that light, playful accent. "And you must be Kate."

"It's Detective Rosetti," I said. "I'm here on a—"

"I know, he filled me in." Gem cocked his head toward Wes. "Let's discuss this somewhere more comfortable."

"That would be good," I said. "I won't take up much of your time."

"Oh," Gem said, a twinkle in his eye. "I know."

Chapter 12

I followed Alastair Gem and Wes through the lobby. We strode underneath an all-glass ceiling that allowed brightness to stream in from all sides. Thin winter sunlight filtered through, giving a glittery wash to the premises.

The sprawling floor was made from a shiny black material, and the fountain in the middle was crafted from pure marble. Water shot upwards in all shapes and patterns as the fountain bounced along to a peppy Christmas tune. A coffee shop on one side boasted a sign saying The Diamond Bar and proclaimed to serve each latte with a shaving of 24 karat gold on top.

I raised my eyebrows as we wove our way through the opulent lobby flooded with businessmen and women skittering about in high heels and black suits and sparkling jewelry. It seemed that diamonds were a part of the uniform at Gem Industries.

I came to a stop at the far end of the lobby where a small atrium rose before me with exotic plants crawling up the walls and colorful blooms adding a sweet, pungent scent into the air. It felt like spring despite the fact we were in the dead of winter.

However, the star of the show was the Christmas tree in the center of the atrium. A few pine needles dusted the floor, and the familiar smell of evergreens danced in the air.

The tree itself looked as if it'd been frosted by gems—every branch touched by an angelic snowfall so real I had to reach out and touch it to feel that it wasn't cold.

Instead of the typical Christmas ornaments, the tree was decorated—fittingly—by gems of all shapes, sizes, and colors. Diamonds, rubies, emeralds, sapphires. Pearls, opals, amethyst. The star above the tree was made of a gorgeous moonstone that shimmered under spotlights.

"Do you like it?" Gem asked when he caught me staring.

I cleared my throat. "It's a bit over the top."

"Right." He winked. "I like over the top."

"I'd never have guessed," I said dryly. "Where would you like to discuss our business?"

"Let's go up."

We stepped inside an elevator as both Wes and Gem scanned cards on a panel, causing the doors to shut around us. Gem frowned, punched in a few numbers, and soon enough, we began to ascend.

The elevator was made of all glass but had been tinted for privacy. We could see out—they couldn't see in. From one side, we had a perfect view of Gem Industries headquarters. Tiny people rushed below us in a hurry. The floor glittered black against the daylight. The tree turned into a bright dot against the black.

The other side of the elevator boasted a view of the city skyline. It was this view I chose to study as we climbed floor after floor, bursting above the atrium and into the corporate floors above. My chest constricted with the suffocating weight of this man's wealth. He had a Christmas tree made of diamonds. A private elevator with a direct trajectory to the top of the city. His money made him untouchable.

"Coming?"

Gem's hand lightly touched my shoulder, startling me from my thoughts. When I turned, I noticed Wes had already vanished somewhere. The doors to the elevator stood open, and Gem gestured for me to step out first.

I did, noting the curious glint in his eye, a mixture of boyish-handsome twisted with an underlying concern. There was a severity to him that I hadn't first noticed. Behind the sheen of his snappy comments and glittering building was a startling intelligence, a cunning sharpness that had me on edge.

It shouldn't have surprised me, I thought as I followed him silently out of the elevator, my footsteps engulfed by thick carpeting on the floor of a magnificent lobby. It wasn't just *anyone* who could have amassed this much wealth. Even if Gem had come from a rich family, he would've had to be smart to keep it, grow it, change the city's landscape. Literally.

"Coffee?" Gem gestured to a golden machine that looked like it made a lot more than coffee. Maybe alchemy.

"No, thank you. I'd prefer if we just got started."

"Very well." Gem nodded toward a small table near the edge of the room. He pulled out a chair, gestured for me to sit. "I noticed you liked the view."

I sat down and studied him. "What businesses are you in, Mr. Gem?"

"Just Gem." He waved me off with a flick of his wrist. "I hate my first name, and mister is so formal."

"I prefer formal," I said. "I'm Detective Rosetti and you can call me that."

"Understood."

"As I'm sure Wes told you, I'm here on a homicide investigation." I waited for him to agree, but he simply continued to watch me. I took a breath. "Can I say something off the record?"

"I prefer *off the record.*" Gem finally looked interested. "I think we should call this whole meeting off the record. Otherwise, I'd have to get an army of lawyers involved, and neither of us want that."

I took a moment to cross my legs, stalling for time. "I was wondering if you know anything about my sister, Jane Rosetti, getting hired on at Gem Industries."

"Why do you ask?"

"I'm curious."

"Yes."

"Yes, what?" I asked, toying with the edge of a napkin on the table as I stared outside at the view. It was wintery bright—cloudy and overcast with hints of sunlight peeking through. The St. Paul skyline was visible in the distance while the Minneapolis sprawl spread around us like a Christmas tree skirt.

"Yes, my company has employed your sister."

"Legally?"

Gem laughed. "Do you think I'd tell a cop if it wasn't?"

I surveyed the penthouse office while I contemplated his answer. We were still in the lobby area, and a huge, reception-style desk sat in the center of the room facing the lobby doors. It was currently unmanned.

A granite wall stood behind it, water trickling down its face and guarded by shoots of live bamboo stretching upward from the ground and fed by the generous light from walls of windows. The sound of a trickling stream played as a soothing backdrop for the moment of silence. It almost felt like I was at a spa instead of corporate headquarters.

"Tell me about Wes," I said finally. "How long have you known him?"

"Wes Remington is a great guy," Gem said, eyeing me carefully. "He's very protective of the people he cares about. There aren't many, so when he does find someone he likes, they quickly become family. I've known him long enough to consider him family."

"Is he—"

"Is this about the case, detective," Gem asked, "or the fact that Wes is dating your sister?"

I felt my cheeks pinken. "Of course it's about the case."

"Just checking." Gem opened his arms wide and gave a dazzling smile. "Not that it matters since we're off the record."

"How'd you meet him?" I asked. "Wes doesn't have the same accent that you do."

"I'm from the UK," he said. "Wes is not. How is this relevant to the case?"

I ignored him. "Tell me more about Gem Industries."

"It's probably faster to list what we *don't* do." Gem leaned back in his chair and crossed his arms, looking entirely too relaxed seeing as he was sitting across from a homicide detective. "I own nightclubs as you know. Jewelry companies. We build apartments, condos, and resorts. We own office buildings. I have a few technology companies up my sleeve. We have one production company making our first movie. Our resume is quite extensive, so I'm sure I'm leaving a few off. My assistant can get you the comprehensive list if you'd like."

"I'd like that, thank you," I said. "Where were you the night of the nineteenth?"

Gem pulled up his phone and frowned in concentration as he glanced at the screen. "Checking my calendar," he narrated. "It looks like I was home."

"Alone?"

Another one of his nifty little winks. "Is this a personal or professional question, detective?"

"Still professional."

"I had a friend over that night for a little while," Gem answered vaguely. "We ate dinner, watched a movie."

"Ah. Does she have a name?"

"Topeka Rosales."

"From when to when was she at your place? And will she verify this alibi if we ask her?"

"I imagine so," he said. "I don't see why not. My assistant will get you her number and contact information. She was over from—oh, nine p.m. to just before midnight?"

I jotted down a note in the little booklet I'd pulled from my pocket. Topeka Rosales wouldn't quite cover Gem for the time of the murder, but if she did verify his story, it would help him some. Then again, a man with Gem's money and stature could buy an alibi quite easily. I'd have to find this Topeka and make sure her story didn't fall flat.

"Wes claims he was working all night on the nineteenth, yet nobody saw him in his office during the time of the murder," I said. "Are there any cameras that could confirm his story?"

"I have no doubt his story is true."

"Right, but I'm going to need to verify it."

"He wouldn't lie."

"I understand he's your friend, Mr. Gem, but—"

"I'm not lying to you, either, detective." Gem unfolded his arms and shifted one long leg over the other. "If I wanted to cover my tracks or Wes's, I would have done a better job—in advance—don't you think? I can't give you more than the truth, and it sounds like that's not enough. So, you'll just have to find another way to clear us of any wrongdoing. I'm sorry we didn't make your job easier."

Flustered, I glanced down at my notebook. I'd been a cop for years. The first female detective on the TC Task Force. Yet Gem had rattled my cage.

My phone buzzed. I looked down to see Jack Russo's name pop up on the screen. I silenced the phone.

"Husband?"

"I'm not married," I said.

"Boyfriend?"

I cleared my throat and gave him my best glare. "I think that's everything for today." I stood, well-aware I was ending the interview prematurely, but I felt like I was losing the battle on Alastair Gem's home turf. I needed to retreat and lick my wounds, then regroup and prepare for round two. He was smarter and more cunning than I'd given him credit for. "Thank you for your time. I'll be back with additional questions."

"Detective." Gem rose, unfolding his body to its full height, which was quite magnificent. He moved close to me, smelling of Christmas and spice and a touch of expensive aftershave. "Here's my direct line. Call if you need anything. I'd be happy to meet for dinner if there's more to discuss—personally or professionally."

"Thank you," I said stiffly. "Though dinner is quite unnecessary."

"Then maybe you'll consider swinging by my Christmas party," he said. "Christmas Eve in The Diamond."

"I don't think—"

"I'm sure you want to keep an eye on me."

Gem reached for his business card and snagged it out of my hand, his fingers brushing against mine and sparking something so warm I let go at once. He smiled as if he'd felt it too, then removed a silver pen from his pocket and rested the card on the table. On the back, he quickly scribbled the date, time, and location of the party.

"I'll have my assistant send a formal invitation," he said, handing it back with a pensive stare. "I'll include a plus-one for you. Just in case."

"No need," I said, tucking the card into my notebook. "I'm busy that night."

"Ah, I see. Well, let me walk you out, at least."

"I can handle that myself."

Gem followed me to the elevator and smiled as the doors began to close. "Merry Christmas, detective."

Chapter 13

I spent the elevator ride to the ground floor watching the city sprawl before me. Twilight hovered in the near distance, settling over sleepy buildings while the beginnings of nightlife pricked to life. The suburbs beyond had begun to sparkle, and a few errant lights from the nearby airport shelled out glittering winks like shooting stars.

Russo was waiting for me out front. I climbed into the warmth of his car, bringing a cool draft with me. He wore a curious expression while glancing me over from head to toe.

He cleared his throat and decided not to speak as he pulled away from the curb. I opted for the same decision. I wasn't sure where he was taking me, but I didn't care. I needed to think, to collect the information I'd gathered and sift through everything to make sense of it all.

"I made some calls while you were in there," Russo said eventually. "I wanted to check with the agency to see what information they have on local trafficking rings. I have a few addresses we can check out when you're ready."

"Let's start on that tomorrow," I said. "It's a long shot. For tonight, I think our best bet is focusing on Rubies. We know Jane Doe was there the night she died. Someone had to see her, talk to her, notice something. *Anything*." My voice rose in frustration. "Sorry. I didn't get anything out of Gem."

"He's a force of nature."

"You know him?"

"Gem might be a local hero, but his name's known around the country. He's got his fingers in a bit of everything."

"Anything in gray areas?"

"Define gray areas," Russo said. "He's never been arrested."

"Can you get access to his file?"

"It's in your inbox."

I sat back, impressed. "Thank you."

"See, Kate? Partnering with me doesn't have to be painful. It just has to be a two-way street."

"Neither Gem nor his buddy, Wes—manager at Rubies, and my sister's current squeeze—have solid alibis for the night of the murder."

"There's a lot to unpack in one statement," Russo said with a grin. "I'll leave your sister out of this because family is complicated. As for Wes and Gem—do you think they're good for the murders?"

"Honestly? I *want* to find something wrong with Wes and Gem. It would be so convenient."

"Why?" Russo asked. "Because your sister's dating Wes?"

"Of course not."

"It would solve your problem," Russo said. "Your sister can't date a man if he's in prison. I mean, she can, but it's a helluva lot more difficult to manage movie nights."

"I'm not trying to micromanage my sister's life."

"Okay then." Russo tapped his fingers against the wheel, glanced out the other window. "For what it's worth, I understand. Your worry about her, I mean."

"I only worry because historically, Jane has proven that she's not great at choosing men for herself."

"She's alive and relatively happy, isn't she?"

"I suppose."

"So, don't worry so much. Maybe she's doing better than you think."

"You don't have any place to—"

Russo raised a hand. "I'm not trying to get involved in your personal life. Let's just say, I get it."

"You have siblings?"

"Is this us, having a real conversation that doesn't involve arguing?"

"Mark it on the calendar."

"I have one brother," Russo admitted. "Younger."

"You're the protective big brother?"

"I tried to be." A tired look came over Russo's face.

I sensed I'd reached his no-press zone and backed off. "I see. Well, you're being very understanding about today."

"I just pretend to be a colossal prick."

I flashed him a smile. "Don't push it."

He smiled in return, flicking on a blinker and pulling us around to the precinct parking lot. The twenty-minute drive had flown by. Luckily, the roads had been somewhat cleared and salted, but if the clouds swarming above us were anything to go by, we'd be in for more snow overnight.

Russo threw the car into park. Before he could get out, I reached over the center console and rested a hand on his arm. He froze, then sat back in his seat.

"Why'd you really come with me today?" I asked. "And why'd you agree to wait in the car?"

"You're my partner," he said. "I trust you. You wanted to go alone, so I let you. That doesn't mean I don't want to be there as your backup."

I was suddenly aware of my hand on his arm, the warmth flowing between us. It wasn't the hot spark that'd sizzled when Gem had brushed against me. That had been an electrical fire. This was more of a cozy burn.

"Thanks," I said. "That means a lot."

"I'm just doing my job."

I withdrew my hand from Russo's arm. Together, we climbed from his car and made our way silently toward the precinct. Out of the corner of my eye, I thought I saw my mother's face pressed against the windows of her café. I purposely ignored her.

"Is that—" Russo pointed over his shoulder at café window.

"Yes, that's my mother."

"Does she have binoculars?"

"She does."

"Ah," Russo said. "She's one of a kind, isn't she?"

"That she is." I pushed open the door to the precinct. "Between her and my sister, sometimes I think I'm adopted."

"What about your dad?" Russo asked. "He was a cop."

My blood ran cold. "He was at one time. That didn't work out well. I sure hope I'm not like him."

"I didn't mean—"

"It's fine," I said. "Maybe we don't talk about personal business."

"I'm sorry, Kate."

"It's fine," I repeated, feeling the friendliness that had blossomed between Russo and I start to fade as my walls inched back up. "I've got a few things to take care of this afternoon, so I'll see you tonight at Rubies."

Russo looked like he wanted to say more, but one look at my face, and he clearly decided against it. "I'll see you tonight, partner."

"YIKES," ASHA SAID WHEN she saw me. "It's been a day, huh?"

"Quite a day," I agreed. "I need some help. Can you run a name for me? A few, actually."

Asha's fingers were poised above the keys. "Hit me."

"Wes Remington," I said. "Alastair Gem—"

"Gem?" she interrupted. "Like, the Gem who owns this city?"

"The one and only. Also, Topeka Rosales."

"Topeka," she said. "Huh."

"That's it for now."

"If I run Gem, he's going to know you're checking up on him," she said. "I guarantee that man knows everything that goes on in the city."

"Good," I said. "Let him know we're looking into him. The more aggressive the better."

Her eyebrows inched up. "This *is* something to do with your case, right?"

"Alastair Gem owns Rubies. Wes Remington is the manager there. Both had access to the club on the night our victim was there. Topeka is supposedly Gem's partial alibi. I'll want an address and phone number for her, too."

"I'll send them through to you tonight," she said. "Jimmy was looking for you, by the way."

I left Asha with her work and went to find Jimmy. He was seated behind his desk with a newly opened package of Red Vines. One of the licorice sticks sat between his lips like a cigarette.

Russo's eyes followed me across the room. I studiously ignored him as I reached for a strand of licorice and perched on Jimmy's desk.

"Find anything?"

He frowned. "I paid two bucks for those."

"Add a nickel to my tab."

Jimmy broke into a grin. "I just got back from checking on the three employees who won't be working at Rubies tonight. They all gave solid alibis during the time of the murder."

"Have you checked them out?"

"None of their stories set off red flags, but we're still doing our due diligence to follow up on the details," he said. "If you ask me, though, I think it's a wash. Hopefully something will turn up tonight. I think we've got thirty-two employees to interview, excluding Wes Remington. You talked to him?"

"A little," I said. "But I'm hoping something will turn up tonight. You ready to get going?"

"It's early, and I've got dinner plans."

"With your licorice? Get in the car. I'll drive."

Jimmy hauled himself to his feet. "Yes, ma'am. Russo?"

"He's got a problem with my driving," I said. "I'm sure he'll want to meet us there."

Jimmy raised his eyebrows at Russo.

"C'mon, partner," I called. "Before you retire."

Jimmy gave me a good-natured salute. Once we were in the elevator, he shifted his hefty mass from one foot to the next. "I don't suppose you want to tell me about your beef with Russo this time?"

"I don't have *beef* with him."

"Oh, then what do you call it?"

"He tried to have a personal conversation with me."

Jimmy put his hand over his heart in a faux-dramatic gesture. "*God forbid* someone ask you about your life."

"Tell me about it," I grumbled. "Why can't everyone mind their own business?"

"This is gonna be a fun night," Jimmy said. Frantically, he patted at his pockets. "Crap. I forgot my Red Vines."

Chapter 14

Our arrival at the club was greeted by a small crew of employees preparing for the night ahead. A bartender who introduced himself as Reggie let us in, a lemon in one hand and a sprig of mint in the other.

"Wes said you'd be swinging by," he said. "He told me to let you in. He also said for you to get started as soon as you can so that you can be out of here by the time we open. Sorry, his words, not mine."

"It shouldn't be a problem. Let's start with you. What's your name?"

"Reggie," he repeated. "Reggie Woo. Bartender."

I noted Reggie was taller than me, good looking, fit, one tattoo on his bicep. He wore a simple white T-shirt and jeans that looked worn and ripped but were probably at the top of the fashion pyramid.

"Is there some place we can chat, Reggie?"

"Sure thing. Let me set these down." He gestured to the fruit and herbs in his hand. "Take a seat in one of the booths. Wes is finishing up something in his office, and then he'll be down."

While Reggie ducked behind the bar and washed his hands, Jimmy and I took seats in a corner booth and surveyed the place. Dim lighting set off a ruby red theme around the club—unsurprising, considering the name. Each table had fake red gems embedded as a centerpiece. The dance floor sparkled with red chips. The lights glinted with a red-tinted hue. Soft Christmas music played in the background and a tree decorated with fake red rubies—no surprise there—stood to one side of the dance floor.

"I assume you change the music by the time evening rolls around?" I asked when Reggie returned. He passed two glasses of water across the table. "Thanks."

He grinned. "Yeah, but we've got a few hours until then, and we're feeling festive. Let me know if you're up for a drink—we've got a great holiday cocktail that tastes like eggnog."

"No, thank you—we're on the clock," I said. "More specifically, we are here to talk about the evening of the nineteenth. You were working?"

"I've worked every night since opening. It's a busy time. I was lucky enough to get my foot in the door early—I know once Rubies gets going, everyone will want a job here. I'm trying to get all the hours I can while they're available. I can sleep when I'm dead, right?"

He gave a bright grin, not seeming to realize that his choice of words was a bit off-color considering the circumstances.

"How long have you lived in town?"

"Forever," he said. "I grew up Downtown St. Paul."

"West 7th," I said, pointing to myself. Then I gestured to Jimmy. "Phalen Lake."

"Nice," Reggie said. "It's a great place to live... if you can survive the winter."

"Do you recognize this girl?" I slid a photo of Jane Doe across the table. "She was here on the night in question."

Reggie scratched at his chin as he examined the photo. "She looks dead."

"She is dead. I'm hoping for a name."

Reggie looked up. "She's dead, and her family doesn't know? That's awful."

"Did you see her?"

Reggie gave a shake of her head. "Can't say that I did. Granted, it doesn't mean she wasn't here—it doesn't even mean she didn't order from me. It's dark in here, and when the bar gets crowded, people are shouting orders at anyone who will listen. I just sling drinks as quick as I can."

"I understand."

"Plus, it seems like she was pretty—you know, when she was alive. Pretty girls aren't the ones buying the drinks usually."

"What do you mean?" Jimmy asked.

Reggie gave a thin smile. "The guys with the tables like to 'collect' girls. They buy bottles, the girls flock to them. They flash the money, girls get free booze, everybody wins."

"Until someone ends up dead."

Reggie's smile completely vanished. "You don't think—was she killed here? Or... why are you asking us about her?"

"We'll ask the questions," I said. "But no, we don't think she was killed here. This was one of the last places we believe she was seen."

"How do you know that without a name?"

"The stamp on her wrist," I said, and then in a sudden streak of inspiration, I pulled out my phone. Pulling up a photo of my sister, I pushed it across to Reggie. "Do you recognize her?"

Reggie studied the girl. "Don't tell me she's dead, too."

"Thankfully not," I said. "Did you see her? She was here that night, too."

"Actually, I think she does look familiar. She was hanging around at bar close. You know how I said pretty girls don't buy their own drinks?" Reggie extended a hand, tapped at the phone. "She did. I remember that clearly. It means she's one of the smart ones."

"Why do you say that?"

"I saw her toss a drink that someone offered her. She came to the bar to buy her own instead," he said. "It's smart. I'm not saying I've seen anyone drugged here, but it takes all kinds—know what I mean?"

"Do I ever." I pulled my phone back. "Was she with anyone?"

"I don't know what you mean. *With*—like on a date? I don't think so. Like I said, she was hanging around at bar close talking to a girlfriend. The girlfriend left at some point, and then this lady in the photo was left alone at the bar." He nodded, gaining steam. "That's how I remember her, actually. Some dude came up and started pestering her, asking for her number, trying to get her to go home with him."

"This is around 2 a.m.?"

"Yeah. We'd just flipped the lights on and were shooing out the customers. That's how I recognize her face."

"What happened then?"

"I was wiping things down, heard her raise her voice and tell him to back off." Reggie gave a thin smile. "The guy didn't get the picture. I was just about to step in when Wes came downstairs and took care of things. He's a good guy; I like working for him."

I glanced at Jimmy. Reggie's story matched Jane's which meant that while Wes didn't have an alibi for the exact time of the murder, he was most certainly at Rubies during bar close.

"Thanks," I said. "That's helpful. And if you think of anything else—"

"I'll call you," he said. "You want me to send over the next guy? Maybe Bobby saw her—he was working the front door that night giving stamps."

"Send Bobby over," I agreed. Once Reggie had disappeared, I turned to Jimmy. "What do you think?"

"Nothing much, yet," Jimmy said. "Except that Reggie's story matches Wes's, which leads me to think he might be telling the truth."

"Maybe," I admitted. "We'll see."

Our next guest was a beefy security guard who topped out around six feet and looked like he could tow a train with his pinky finger. He had one tattoo on his face, a pierced ear with a huge diamond in the lobe, and a shiny bald head. Bobby had stuffed himself into a suit and managed to look like an uncomfortable sausage.

"Bobby Legatt," he said in introduction. "I've been working every night this week."

"We're most interested in the nineteenth," I said, nodding to Jimmy who pushed the picture of Jane Doe across the table again. "Recognize her?"

Bobby studied the photo for so long his eyes appeared to cross. "She looks dead."

"She is."

"I didn't see no dead people."

I let out my breath slowly and tried for patience. "She would've been alive when she came here. We're looking for her murderer."

"She was killed?"

"That is what murder means," I said. "We found her body dumped not far from here. She had a stamp on her hand, and I hear you were the one giving out stamps that night."

"I'm the stamp man," Bobby said proudly. "But I've stamped hundreds of wrists just this week. I don't remember her."

At first, I was tempted to believe Bobby, but then he glanced over his shoulder. Unfortunately, I didn't think Bobby was very smart. When he looked back, his face was red as the gems on the Christmas tree.

"Sorry," he said. "Can I go?"

"Hiding information from the cops is a criminal offense." Jimmy jumped in with a glance in my direction. "If we find out you're lying, Bobby, you'll get in trouble. Obstruction of justice in a homicide investigation—that ain't good, my friend."

"I told you, I don't know her."

"Maybe you didn't know her," I said, "but did you see her?"

"Maybe," he hedged. "You say I stamped her hand, so I believe you. Doesn't mean I talked to her. I wouldn't know her name."

"Do you check IDs?"

"Yeah," he said. "So?"

"Did anyone use a passport to get into the club the night of the nineteenth?"

"There's always a handful," he said. "I still don't remember their names."

"Thanks, Bobby." Jimmy looked down at his hands. "We've got the FBI coming later—mind if we send them your way with a few more questions?"

"The FBI?" Bobby's eyes just about popped out of his head. "Why're they here? I thought you were the police."

"It's a big case," I said, silently thanking Jimmy for his foresight and seeing where he was going with this. "Real big. We've got Mr. Gem himself involved, the FBI, and the mayor will be hearing the details, too. Trust us, we won't stop until we've uncovered every lie. The killer's going down."

Bobby raised his hands. His fingers trembled. "I'm no killer."

"We're not saying you are," I said. "We just want this girl's name."

"I don't have to talk to you." Bobby sounded unsure, but when we didn't argue, he stood up and took a huge breath. "I don't have to talk to you. I want a lawyer. I don't know nothin.'"

"That's fine, Bobby," I said. "I'll tell you what—you think of anything, give me a call. You don't need a lawyer. We don't think you've done anything wrong."

Bobby accepted my card with a dubious expression. "You mean it?"

"Swear on it."

He shoved the card in his pocket and stomped off with footsteps loud enough to pierce through The Little Drummer Boy humming through the background speakers.

"He's hiding something," Jimmy said. "He recognized her."

"He didn't kill her."

"Of course not," Jimmy said. "A muscle head like him? No, he's not smart enough to know the right end of a gun. But he's scared of someone. Or he was paid off. Or he just hates cops. And that's what we need to figure out."

"We'll sic Russo on him when he gets here," I said to Jimmy. "That was a brilliant idea."

"I'll let you handle that part, seeing as you and Russo are best friends," he said. "Plus, I want to try one of them holiday cocktails."

"Jimmy."

"Virgin," he corrected, heaving himself out of the booth as Russo entered the club and scanned the room, beelining toward us. "Also, I just don't want to be here when Russo gets here. Sitting between the two of you... I never know if you are going to fight or make out."

"Jimmy!"

"See you."

"Chicken."

Jimmy lumbered away, waving a hand dismissively behind him.

"What've you got so far?" Russo asked as he arrived at the table. He watched Jimmy saunter up to Reggie and order a drink at the bar. "Anything?"

"We need you to interview Bobby Legatt," I said. "He's got a box of rocks for brains, but we think he saw the girl. He's scared of cops, terrified of the feds."

"What else have you found?"

"Not a whole lot," I said. "I'll divvy up the list. After Bobby, we can split things three ways. With any luck, we'll be out of here by nine and home before the snow starts falling."

"Kate—"

"That'll be all," I said. "Bobby's in the restroom. Catch him when he comes out, will you? We can't afford to have him spooked."

Chapter 15

By the time nine p.m. rolled around at Rubies, the overhead lights had flickered completely off. The still-vacant dance floor was lit only by the glow from green and red spotlights spinning around the room, and a hint of the reflection from the stones embedded in the floor.

A Christmas song remix was playing as the first partygoers found their way inside and feebly wandered toward the bar. Bobby was at the door stamping his way through the night. Reggie was behind the bar pouring the first of the cocktails. The rest of the servers, shot girls, bus boys, and bar backs were buzzing with energy that was sure to fade by the time two a.m. rolled around.

I stood with Jimmy and Russo at the entrance swapping notes. We'd let the other officers go home already. I sighed as Russo shook his head and handed me a few sheets of looseleaf.

"So, we've got a goose egg," I said. "Nothing."

"Someone saw something," Russo said. "We know Bobby—or someone—stamped Jane Doe. Whether he's lying about remembering it, I can't tell."

"Did you whip out the FBI badge?" Jimmy asked. "He seemed terrified of your little acronym."

"Little acronym." Russo stared at Jimmy, but my partner was unfazed. He was too close to retirement to care about much of anything. "Yes, I showed him the badge. He'll call."

"How can you be so sure?" Jimmy asked. "He doesn't seem like he knows how to work a phone."

"Just watch." Russo looked at me. "Anything else?"

"One of the waitresses—Cindy Rowe—said she thought she saw Jane Doe sitting at a table," I said, glancing at my notes. "But she couldn't remember which table or who she was with."

"We could shake down some of the patrons," Russo suggested. "Management wouldn't like that much—maybe it'll force someone to talk."

"I think we need to get a list of credit cards used that night," I said. "Buying a bottle is expensive."

"If our guy was out trolling for a victim, I don't see him laying down a credit card," Russo said. "I don't think this guy is looking for attention, and around here bottles draw attention. I think he wanted to be low profile. Scour the place for his next victim."

"Maybe if I camp out here for the night and tuck myself into a corner, he'll come back, and I'll be able to pick him out of a crowd."

Russo shook his head. "Needle in a haystack. Historically, he's not hitting the same place twice."

"Fine. You got any better ideas?" I snapped. I felt Jimmy's eyes on me. "Sorry. Long day."

"Let's call it a night," Russo said. "Resume in the morning. And if it comes to it, I'll sit in a corner with you, detective."

"That sounds like a deal to me," Jimmy said. "I've got a Chipotle burrito at home with my name on it, and it ain't getting any warmer."

We left Russo standing at the entrance to the club while Bobby stamp, stamp, stamped his way through a line of patrons waiting at the entrance. He moved slowly, keeping the line long despite the empty dance floor inside.

"Making it look busy," Jimmy said. "What a load. Did you ever go dancing when you were younger?"

"I'm still young."

"You ever go dancing?"

"What do you think?"

"Right." He raised his eyebrows. "So, are you getting along with Russo?"

"No comment."

"What I don't get is why you care so much about what the suit thinks. He'll be gone in a few days."

"He brought up my dad."

"Idiot."

I snorted a laugh. "Finally, we agree."

"Come on, Kate," Jimmy said. "Don't let that get your goat. Your dad's shadow has been hanging over your shoulder for too long. You're above it."

"It's not something I can just forget about, Jimmy."

"No, but you're a good cop, and we all know it. Your dad was a good cop too," Jimmy said. "Don't forget—I'm old. I was around when he went down. A lot of us, you know, we thought he caught the brunt of something that wasn't his fault. He was the fall guy. The face for the media. The mayor needed someone to blame the mess on—election year."

"If he was innocent, none of it would've stuck."

"Maybe, but are any of us truly innocent... of everything?" Jimmy shrugged. "Maybe you are. But I'm not. Most of the guys I know—especially back in the day—were not. Your dad caught an unlucky break."

"He shouldn't have been in bed with the mob."

"Your dad's a Rosetti. You go to Christmas, and you're in bed with the mob."

I rolled my eyes. "Thanks, Jones. Your advice is oh-so-helpful. Maybe you should look into retirement."

We pulled into the precinct parking lot and Jimmy gave me a look. "Russo's just doing his job. I don't like that he's here either, but you're going to have to deal with him."

"Yeah, I know. Thanks, Jimmy. Enjoy your date."

"I always have a good time with Chipotle."

"I believe it after seeing you with the chicken bucket earlier."

He grinned. "Get some sleep, detective. Sweet dreams."

I set my sights toward home. The light flurries that'd started while we were tucked under the ruby lights at the club had continued, tickling at my face as I raised and lowered my window because I'd been too lazy to scrape the snow off the side. I only had four minutes to go. It'd take that long to warm the car up.

The four-minute drive home turned into twelve thanks to the rapidly deteriorating road conditions. I managed to shove my car into the slim driveway that really wasn't meant for cars just in case the plows came by overnight. The last thing I needed was a ticket from some new boot who hadn't learned the ropes yet.

I made my way inside, halfway expecting to hear the clatter of two people untangling from a naked cuddle session upstairs. My rules about no boys and no booze had been broken on Jane's first night here, and I hadn't really felt the desire to enforce any of it.

"Hello?" I called out. "Jane, I'm home! Can we talk for a second?"

I stilled in the foyer, listening. Something was different.

My hand found its way to the gun in my holster instinctively.

"Hello?" I stepped forward and rounded the corner into the living room.

Nothing. Pitch blackness.

That's when it hit me—the very absence of sound and light had thrown me off. One day with Jane at home, and already, I'd gotten used to her. I stared at the Christmas tree. It looked like a ghost, unlit, with some of the ornaments twinkling under the thin strips of moonlight streaming through the window.

I eased over to the Christmas tree, flicking on the colorful lights. As I did, I slid out my phone and dialed Jane. While I waited for her to answer, I headed to the kitchen and found the counter and sink to be surprisingly spotless. The only thing out of place was a brand-new purple toaster.

I stifled a thin smile at the shiny monstrosity. The smile shrunk, however, with each passing ring that Jane didn't answer her phone. I glanced at the tree, the capped bottle of wine, and found myself wishing she'd just come home. In part, so I didn't have to worry about her. Another part, however, had nothing to do with Jane and everything to do with me. I wanted the company.

"Jane," I said when her voicemail clicked on. "I assume you're still staying with me... Is everything okay? Give me a call when you get this. Please."

I hung up, poured that glass of wine, and made my way to the couch. I kicked off my heels and pulled on a fuzzy pair of socks that were about an inch thick, completely unattractive, and felt like pillows of heavenly clouds against my feet. Sliding my toes under a blanket, I sipped my wine, watched the tree, and waited.

As the minutes clicked by, the unease grew. I put down my wine glass, too queasy to finish it. Where was Jane? And why hadn't she called?

My brain clicked through a series of awful scenarios: The killer had struck again. The killer was Wes, and he had her captive somewhere. Alastair Gem was out for revenge after my visit today. He'd picked on Jane because he'd known it would hurt me the most.

I picked up my phone, re-dialed Jane's number. It went to voicemail. The second time, I didn't leave a message. I'd try her back later. After all, it was still relatively early, and Jane was a known night owl. There was a chance she'd gone out on a date, met a few girlfriends—she could've been at Bellini's chatting with Angela. I supposed she could've been at whatever new job she'd gotten, but work had never been a priority for my sister.

I called Bellini's.

"What's up, cuz?" Angela answered. "Your girlfriends aren't here tonight. Neither is that cutie you were with the other day. Anything happen with him?"

"Not exactly," I said. "Say, has my sister stopped by tonight?"

"No, I haven't seen her in a while. Was she supposed to?"

"I was just curious. She's out and about, and I was thinking of meeting up with her."

"Come on over. You can wait for her here. The weather's nasty out there, so it's empty. I'll be able to have a drink with you."

"Thanks, Ang. Maybe another time."

While talking to Angela, I'd shuffled back into the entryway of my house. I reached for the bundle of supplies I'd set on the table when I'd first come home and grabbed the files from Asha. I pulled up the emails from Russo on my phone before climbing back under the blanket.

I tried to focus on the files, but even the tempting thought of digging into Alastair's past wasn't enough to keep me from fidgeting and staring at my phone screen. Where had Jane gone?

The hour was creeping toward eleven p.m. I scrolled down Gem's file on my phone and found contact information for Wes Remington. I punched the number in my phone. Stared at it. Hovered my finger over dial. Removed hovering thumb.

I shouldn't be using work resources to contact Wes Remington for information about my sister. That would be crisscrossing lines that had no need to be crossed.

But what if? A small voice popped up in my head. What if Jane was in trouble?

I depressed the button. Wes's phone rang through to voicemail. I was too shaky to leave a message.

The prick of something in my back pocket gave me one more genius idea. Pulling Gem's business card out, I recalled his invitation to use his personal number at any time—for any reason. Business or pleasure.

This wasn't pleasure, but it was personal.

I punched in the numbers and waited. Unlike my last few phone calls, I didn't have long to wait. The deep voice answered in a few seconds with an English accent.

"Good evening, Kate," Gem said nonchalantly. "What can I do for you?"

"It's personal."

"Even better."

"Do you know where Wes is tonight?"

"I'd hoped you meant personal with me."

"It will be personal if anything happens to my sister."

"Ah." Gem hesitated. "You live in the West Seventh neighborhood?"

"How do you know that?"

"Tit for tat. You pull info on me, and I pull info on you. Don't worry, I won't use it against you."

"Aha."

"I'm headed to see Wes. I'll pick you up on the way."

"But—"

"You're looking for your sister?"

"Yeah—er, yes," I said. "You know where she is?"

"I do. She's employed by Gem Industries, and I happen to know she has a shift tonight."

"A shift where?"

"Rubies. I'll see you in five minutes."

"I can drive myself."

"We've accumulated four inches of snow in the last hour, and it'll only get worse. Let me—the car is warm."

I peeked out front and saw that some neighborhood bozo had attached a plow to his huge truck and kindly plopped a gigantic pile of snow in front of my driveway. I'd be digging halfway to China to get my car out, and then I'd be turning around and doing it all over again the next morning.

"How will I get home?"

"I can drop you anywhere after. At any time."

I pursed my lips and considered my options. I could stay home worrying about my sister, or I could go to the location our victim had been seen last, blend in, ask a few questions, poke my nose around. "Why are you doing this?"

"I have my reasons."

"Fine," I said. "I'm bringing my gun. So, forget about any funny business."

Chapter 16

I couldn't quite say why I'd chosen the outfit I had. Maybe it was the name of the club. Maybe it was because Jane had left an extra dress in her closet that happened to fit me just right. Or maybe it was because I knew Alastair Gem was on his way to pick me up, and I didn't want to be caught looking like a drowned rat again.

When he pulled up in front of my house, I was ready thanks to the quickest transformation humanly possible. I'd pulled my hair into a tight bun that I hoped looked sophisticated and added a swipe of mascara to my lashes in hopes that counted as a makeover.

A few squirts of my best perfume and a tube of red lipstick that hadn't seen the light of day since 1999 topped off my outfit, combined with a pair of tall black stilettos that had grip on the bottom to help with the slippery sidewalk.

Lastly, I'd dug out a pushup bra that I'd bought sometime during my last relationship—back in the ice age—and popped Jane's dress over the top. It was Christmas red and fell halfway down my thighs, a slim fit with simple, spaghetti-strap sleeves holding it in place.

By the time headlights flashed out front, I was adding a faux fur black coat I'd gotten for thirteen dollars at TJ Maxx but made me feel like at least a hundred bucks. I situated my gun in a somewhat comfortable position, grabbed my phone and a clutch, and stepped into the flurries of snow.

By the time I locked the door, a shadow had appeared behind me. I reached for my gun and slipped all at once—a dangerous combination. Fortunately—or unfortunately—an arm reached out to steady me before I could take a dive off my front steps with a loaded weapon.

"Cripes," I snapped at Gem, taking a step back and straightening my jacket. "You just about killed me."

"I saved your life." Gem's eyes glittered down at me, his lips quirked into a lopsided grin. "You're welcome."

"If you hadn't scared the crap out of me, maybe I wouldn't have fallen."

"Almost fallen," Gem reminded me. "Because I saved your life."

"Right. By the way, I don't need help to the car."

"I beg to differ."

Gem stuck his arm resolutely out as I took a glance at the accumulating snow, the waiting car—scratch that, limousine—and the gorgeous man offering me his arm. Reluctantly, I hooked mine into his, grumbling as we slipped and slid our way down the steps and across the walkway.

"You need someone to salt your sidewalk," Gem said.

"I need someone to clean my house and cook for me," I scoffed. "Doesn't mean I can afford it. I'll toss some on when I get home."

"If you'd like, I could have someone—"

"No, thanks."

"I appreciate you hearing me out."

I hid a smile as I slid into the limo first, followed closely by Gem. Once we were situated, the driver glanced in the rearview mirror. One cursory look at me before his focus returned to Gem. I idly wondered how many women Gem charmed into limousines on a regular basis.

"To Rubies," Gem said.

The driver took off while I was still trying to figure out how I'd ended up in a limousine on a weekday night dressed in a little red dress. Of course, Gem had a driver, and a limo, and people who did everything for him. He was a billionaire. If I had that kind of money, I would probably hire a chef at least. Maybe a housekeeper. Definitely someone to shovel my sidewalk.

"So..." I cleared my throat when Gem didn't show any sign of speaking. "Are you positive my sister is at Rubies?"

"She was supposed to start work there tonight," Gem said. "I'll let her fill you in on the rest."

"She wasn't answering her phone, and neither was Wes. I thought they might be together." I glanced out the window. "I panicked when I couldn't get ahold of her."

"Understandable, considering all that's been going on in town."

We drove the rest of the way to the club in silence. When it was time to disembark, I hustled out before either the driver or Gem could open my door. When Gem appeared by my side, I declined his extended arm.

"How would it look if I walked in on the arm of the boss?" I raised an eyebrow. "We can't have that."

"I beg to differ."

"Well, I'm a detective. I prefer to keep a low profile."

"I thought this was a personal visit."

"That doesn't mean it's a date."

"If you're interested in making that happen, it can be arranged." Gem grinned. "Just say the word, detective."

"The word is no. But thanks," I added. "For the ride."

"Anytime." Gem dropped his arm, but he kept his hand lightly on the small of my back until we reached the front door.

We bypassed a line of women shivering in tiny skirts and tinier dresses. The bravest of them wobbled on high heels. The snow was still coming down, and though I was wearing my own little dress, I didn't have to stand outside and wait. I'd been outside for two seconds and could've sworn my leg hair had grown as many inches.

"They must be freezing just standing out here," I said. "Poor things. You need some heaters."

"Heaters?" Gem stopped mid-stride. He turned, focused on me. "That's a brilliant idea."

"If you're going to torture them by making them wait outside, at least make it comfortable. Throw in a few s'mores sticks and you've got yourself a party."

"Will you wait for one second?"

"Um, okay." I moved to head toward the back of the line, but Gem grabbed my arm and tugged me around to the front.

"You're with me," he said. "Let's go."

Gem hopped on his phone, quietly murmuring into the receiver while I sidled near the front entrance and tried to pretend the wind wasn't whistling through my clothes. To distract myself from the chill, I watched the front of the line where Bobby was standing next to a bar stool used to prop the door open. He had a stamp in one hand and a frown pasted on his face.

He flicked through IDs one at a time, presumably scanning names and birth date, then squinting up at the person in question to match their photo with their image. The only time his frown softened was when a girl gave him a pretty smile to match her picture. Then it turned into a sort of ugly leer that made him somehow look like a man in a hot dog costume.

He glanced up as he ushered in a large group of women. One of them wore a Happy Birthday sash while the rest of her cronies had on sparkling crowns and pink dresses.

Bobby's eyes met mine. He squinted, and it had a way of making him look meaner than before. It had me wondering if his dumbness was all just an act—if maybe, there was more to Bobby than a pair of meaty hands and a blank look.

But when Gem laid a hand on my shoulder, Bobby's expression went from mean to surprised. I didn't blame Bobby for that part. I was just as surprised as anyone to be showing up to a club with Alastair Gem.

Gem reached for my hand and pulled me toward the entrance. By the time we were there, Bobby had managed to pull his expression into some semblance of a straight-face and bowed his head to his boss.

"Aren't you going to ask for my ID?" I asked as Bobby waved us through. "What if I'm not twenty-one?"

"Uh," Bobby said. "But you're a cop."

Gem winked. "I think it was a joke."

Bobby looked deflated. "Yeah, sure."

As we passed into the club, Gem spoke in low tones to Bobby. "There'll be a delivery truck coming soon, and they're going to set up outside. Let them."

"Yes, sir."

We moved further inside and were immediately engulfed by a thumping *All I Want for Christmas* while a beat screeched beneath it sending dancers diving for a spot in front of the tree on the dance floor.

"I'd say your newest business venture is a smashing success," I said, surveying the crowd. "It's packed."

"The first week is always a success," Gem said. "It's what happens after that that matters. In the meantime..."

Gem grabbed my hand and led me toward the dance floor as I dug in my heels and shook my head. "I don't dance."

"A drink?"

"No, I'm okay."

"You're not on duty, are you?"

"No, but—"

"Then you should really try the eggnog cocktail. I perfected it myself."

"I thought you had people to do that for you."

"What's the fun in that?" He winked and nudged me deeper onto the dance floor. "I normally don't dance at my own clubs, but with the right woman..."

"Not happening."

"Just one song."

"I'd rather not. How about that drink?"

Despite my declined offers to dance, it was impossible not to be jostled and bumped against Gem as we wound our way through the throng of people pulsing under the lights. In a way, we were intertwined in our own dance.

Gem's arms came around my waist as he blocked a man the size of a linebacker from taking me down in a tackle as he drunkenly tried to chicken dance. Another woman nearly stepped on my toe, and my pinky digit was saved only by Gem's quick twirl, which landed me once again against his chest.

The feel of him was becoming all too familiar. The way he smelled, the lean muscles beneath his perfectly cut suit, the way his hand felt as it brushed against my body. A girl could get used to it. *Another* girl could get used to it. Not this girl.

To free myself from dangerous thoughts of Gem, I beelined for the bar. Reggie was working along with four others, two of them women. Before I could shout out my order to the sea of bartenders, I caught sight of a familiar figure. I made it to Jane's side before she knew what hit her.

"I'll take one of your Eggnog things," I said in her ear. "Make that two."

Jane started to respond automatically, stopping only when she glanced up and recognized me. "Kate?"

"Surprise!"

"T-that's my dress," she said. "What are you doing here?"

"I called you a few times. You didn't answer. I got worried. And thanks for letting me borrow your dress."

"And you knew I'd be here because..."

"I'm a detective."

She rolled her eyes. "Right. You called Wes."

"I did, but he didn't answer either. Hence my panic."

"Kate—I'm fine!" Jane's cheeks blushed pink. "Don't let anyone see me with you. I'm working. It's not good for us to associate with cops."

"You're a waitress."

"That's what you think!"

I glanced at her tiny black skirt and bright, ruby-red tube top, along with the tray in her hand. "Am I wrong?"

She opened her mouth with a retort but stopped herself, eyes glittering. "I don't have to explain myself to you. But I don't bother you when you work—please don't bother me."

"I'm worried about you, Jane! We're investigating a murder. This is the last place a pretty young woman like yourself was seen. We believe she knew her killer. It could be an employee, a guest, who knows? My point is, there might still be a murderer on the loose in the nearby vicinity."

"Or there might not be," she snapped. "You don't know yet, and that's the point. Also, you don't own the rights to worrying."

"What are you talking about?"

"You're worried because I'm slinging a few drinks at a nightclub?" Jane rested one hand on her slim waist. "At least nobody's shooting at me, Kate. The worst I see is a bar brawl or some idiot puking on the dance floor. You wear a gun to your job every day. You catch killers on a regular basis."

"Come on, that's different. It's my job."

"This is my job! You think I don't worry just because you have training? You think that mom doesn't dread the fact that you're on the streets every night as she goes to sleep? Of course we do. We worry and stress and hate the fact that you put your life in danger. But we don't chase you down, call your phone, and freak out when you don't answer. I just want the same respect."

"I didn't know..." I hesitated. "I didn't know you felt that way. I'm sorry."

"Sometimes, I think you believe that you're the only one who cares, but that's not true."

"I know that. I don't doubt that you care."

"Then have a little faith in me. I know you're working a scary murder investigation, but then again, when aren't you? I'm thirty-two years old. This is my job. Nothing sinister about it."

"I'm sorry."

My sister's chest heaved as she digested my apology. "It's fine. I guess I just get sensitive when you and mom feel like you have to watch over me. I know I might not have my life exactly put together, but you have to let me figure my own stuff out."

"I'll stop interfering with your work and your relationships," I said. "But when it comes to the case, I'm going to follow the evidence—wherever it leads. If I have to interview Wes again for the case, I'm not going to hold back because you're interested in him."

Jane watched my face for a long moment. "I know. That's why you're so good at your job."

I gave her a dry smile, wondering if the reason I was good at my job was the same reason I was awful at relationships. With my sister, my mother, my father, and any male on the planet. The only women who I spent any time with outside of the office were people I worked with. People who were surrounded by just as much death as me.

Before I could start feeling sorry for myself, Jane's eyes widened as she looked over my shoulder. It was becoming a trend this evening. And even before Gem's hand touched my back, I knew he was there.

"You're here with..." Jane whispered, then cleared her throat. "I mean, good evening, Mr. Gem. Can I get you something to drink?"

Gem raised his hands in response. He carried two spiced eggnog cocktails, handed one to me and kept one for himself. "How are you finding the job, Ms. Rosetti?"

"It's great," she gushed. "I love it. I-I'm sorry if I worried you guys tonight or anything, but I've been here the whole time. Just really busy—swamped, actually. In a good way."

Gem winked. "I told your sister she was overreacting. But she wanted to see you for herself."

"Of course." Jane nodded vigorously. "I understand."

"We'll leave you to it then." Gem glanced toward me and extended his arm. "Kate?"

I had no choice but to hook my arm through Gem's again as he led me around behind the bar. Glancing over my shoulder, I caught sight of Jane spinning around with her lips parted in shock as we walked. I ditched my eggnog cocktail on the bar and gave her a shrug as I disappeared from her line of sight.

"I wanted to show you something," Gem said as he wound his way through the blinking Christmas lights to the dimmer back hallway. "We got this all sorted. I thought you'd appreciate it."

Gem raised an arm and pointed toward the corner where wall met ceiling. It took me a second of squinting to let my eyes adjust before I saw the slight red glow. "A camera?"

"After what happened the other night, I'm not taking any risks," Gem said. "We've got three angles at the front entrance. Cameras along the back hallway so anyone coming or going from the offices will be seen. The dance floor, behind the bar, and storeroom are also covered. The only places left off are the bathrooms, but of course you can see people entering and exiting, and there are no opening windows inside. We have the back alley covered as well, just in case."

"Wow." I blinked and snapped my fingers. "You make things happen, just like that."

Gem just shrugged. "Wes is upstairs. Do you want to talk to him?"

"Not particularly."

"Well, I could use a coffee. You tossed your cocktail. He's got a machine that can fuel us both. Shall we?"

Gem and I made our way upstairs. He gave a quick knock on the halfway closed door to Wes's office, then pushed it open without waiting for a response.

Wes was faced away from us, poring over a spreadsheet on the computer. When he spun around, his face cracked into a wide grin at the sight of his friend. Then he saw me, and the smile faded just as quickly.

"Nice to see you," I said briskly as I came to a stop before him. "Always good to see you wearing clothes."

Gem's eyebrows went up as he looked to his friend. "Oh?"

"Ah, he didn't tell you about that?" I smirked at Wes. "We had an interesting first encounter."

Wes winced. "I didn't share for a reason."

"Do tell," Gem said.

Wes cringed again, but my phone buzzed and saved him from an embarrassing explanation.

Pulling my cell from my clutch, I peeked at the screen and saw Russo's name across the top. As I hit answer, I backed out of the room. "I'm sorry. I should take this."

"Rosetti, good evening," Russo said across the line. "I hope I didn't wake you."

"I'm up."

"Good. Any chance you can swing by the Brownley?" Russo spoke of a decent hotel in the heart of the city. "I've got an interesting bit of information to share with you."

"Can't it wait? It's late."

"Are you at home?" The way Russo asked the question told me he knew I wasn't.

I ignored him. "Can't you tell me over the phone?"

"Only if you tell me why you're at Rubies after we specifically agreed to call it a night. I would've gone with you if I'd known."

"This wasn't a planned trip."

"I haven't decided if I believe you." Russo hesitated. "Are you there with Gem?"

"He's here," I hedged. "As are lots of other people. The man knows how to run a club, I'll give him that."

"Which leads me to my next point," Russo said. "One of Gem's employees—a bouncer by the name of Bobby—called me just now. He mentioned that he lied during his interview. I'd prefer to discuss the rest of what he told me in person."

"C'mon, Russo! You know I'm dying to hear what Bobby had to say, but I didn't drive here. I can't get to you just yet."

"If you change your mind, I'll be waiting in the lobby in thirty minutes. I'd invite you up to my room where it's more comfortable, but I'm afraid you'd get the wrong impression."

"Right."

"If you're not interested, tell me now, and I'll see you in the morning."

My curiosity got the better of me. Plus, Gem had offered to drop me off anywhere I needed to go—and the Brownley wasn't far.

"I'll be there in half an hour."

"Good," he said. "And Rosetti..."

"Yeah?"

"Come alone."

Chapter 17

I returned to the office, phone in my pocket. "I'm sorry, but that was work. I have to get going."

Gem visibly tensed. "Is everything okay?"

"Fingers crossed we've got a break in the case." I watched Wes's face as I said my news, but he didn't seem to register much of anything. Gem, however, raised his eyebrows.

"That's great news." He stood and gestured toward the door. "I imagine you need a ride somewhere?"

"If that's okay."

"I wouldn't have offered if not. Is there anything else I can do to help?"

"You've done plenty," I said. "I just need to get to the Brownley."

"The hotel?"

"No, the circus. Yes, the hotel."

The eyebrow that had inched up earlier went higher. "For business?"

"I'm meeting a partner there." I held my gaze on Gem and dared him to press further. "Even though it's none of your business."

"Yes, ma'am."

Gem led the way outside. Bobby wasn't at the entrance this time, which made me do a double take. I was just about to ask Gem if Bobby was on break when I caught sight of the massive truck out front. Already, several heaters had been unloaded and placed along the edge of the ruby red rope that kept the customers in line.

"Wow," I said. "You work fast."

"Not always." He winked, then hooked my arm in his and pulled me through the curious crowd that leaned as an entity toward the heaters.

As we climbed into the car, Gem gave instructions to his driver to head to the Brownley, a hotel along the Mississippi River on the St. Paul side just off Highland Village.

"So, this partner—"

"He's a fed," I said. "End of story."

"You're not happy to be working with him? Tell me the movie clichés are real."

I rolled my eyes. "It doesn't matter if I'm happy or not. All that matters is catching a murderer."

"I see."

We pulled up outside of the hotel after a mostly quiet ride. Gem left me alone with my thoughts, which I desperately needed after this evening. The thought of coming face to face with Russo didn't lighten the load any, either.

The driver finally eased to a stop after an extended twenty-minute commute. I hadn't realized how long it'd taken us until I glanced at the time and saw it was just after midnight.

"The roads are awful," Gem announced. "This snow isn't going to let up until afternoon tomorrow. Let me wait and give you a ride home."

"I can catch a cab just as easy as you can sit here."

"I like to finish what I start."

"Which means?"

"That I'd prefer to see you home safely."

"I don't know how long this will take." I met Gem's gaze and was surprised to find concern there. "Look, I appreciate all you've done, but I can handle it from here. I'm a big girl."

He gave a thin smile. "It's not a matter of handling it yourself; it's about accepting help when it's offered."

"Well, you can afford to just buy your help when you need it. The rest of us have to fend for ourselves. I'm tough, Gem. I'll survive."

"I've no doubt." He opened the door and came around the limo as I was still scrambling to open my door. "I'll leave you here, then. But for the record, I'm not happy about it."

I stepped out of the car, the evening rushing back to me in a whirl as I caught Gem's scent. It must have clung to me from earlier. It gave me pause as I stood before him, digesting the concern that radiated from his expression.

"Thanks for everything tonight," I managed. "I really appreciate it. All of it."

"You're welcome." Gem reached a hand upward, pushed a strand of hair away from my forehead. It stuck, thanks to the snow, and as he tried again, his lips turned into a handsome frown.

"Goodnight, Kate." He leaned in, kissed me gently on the cheek. "I hope we can do this again sometime. Preferably without the threat of jailtime hanging over us."

"We'll have to see about that."

I left Gem standing outside while I hurried into the hotel, my heels spiking their way through the fluffy snowfall coating the sidewalk. A doorman was rapidly shoveling the walk, trying to keep ahead of the buildup. It was a losing game this evening.

"Welcome, ma'am," he said. "May I help you with your bags?"

I glanced down at my bare legs, skimpy red dress, and jacket. "My bags?"

"Er—right." His face colored and he ducked his head to keep shoveling, but not before he took one last long look at my legs.

It was with annoyance that I pushed the door open and let myself inside. Once I was free from the snowfall, I shook the flurries off my coat and stomped my feet a few times before making my way to the front lobby.

I stopped for a peek at the wall-length windows. Gem and his limo were still there. He leaned against the car, arms folded across his chest, and watched the building. Our eyes connected through the glass when he saw me stop to stare. I wondered if he'd wait for me, or if he'd drive off as promised.

A throat cleared behind me. "Did you forget something outside, detective?"

I jumped, turning to find Russo standing beside me. "You crept up on me."

"I don't think that's the case. If you ask me, you've been a little..." Russo's gaze slid outside as he took in Gem's posture against the car, "distracted."

"I'm fine," I snapped, circling around. "Where do you want to talk?"

"Are you sure this is a good time?"

"As good a time as any. Do they have coffee around here? I'm freezing."

"I'll say so." Russo's eyes flicked politely over my body. "I think I have an extra bathrobe in my room if you'd like."

"Ha-ha. Let's just get this over with. You said Bobby called?"

"Let's get that cup of coffee." Russo reached out, steered me toward the lobby with a hand on my shoulder. He cast a glance backward as we strode away, and I had no doubt he was checking to see if Gem was watching us. "There's no rush."

"WHAT DO YOU THINK YOU'RE doing?" I asked once we'd been seated at the deserted hotel restaurant.

Russo met my gaze. "Ordering?"

He spread the menu before his face. The restaurant wasn't technically open, but the front desk attendant had seen Russo's badge and said they could make an exception for him.

"Are you hungry?" he asked. "I've had their pancakes, and—"

"Their lox is the best," I said. "If you're getting something, go for the bagel."

He grinned over the menu, then went back and pretended to examine it further. This evening was the first time I'd seen Russo in anything but his uniform suit. And while he looked good in formal attire, I couldn't help but appreciate the way he seemed more relaxed, more human, wearing a soft gray sweater and a pair of faded jeans. His hair was just slightly damp as if he'd showered recently, and even from across the table, I could smell a nicely scented aftershave.

"Like what you see?" Russo didn't look up from the menu. "I can feel your eyes on me."

"Sorry. It's just—I'm not used to seeing you out of a suit."

"I'm a person, too," Russo said with an amused smile. "I'm not always in a suit."

"It's easier to think of you as a suit."

"Why? So you can automatically dislike me?"

"Something like that."

The truth was, I didn't want to see Russo as a human. It made me too self-conscious to be around him—alone—in a hotel this late at night dressed like... well, my sister. People could get the wrong idea.

"Kate, I just wanted to say—"

"Detective."

"Kate," he continued. "Look, I do have an update on the case. But I also wanted to take the time to apologize. I should have never brought up your dad."

"No, you shouldn't have." I grudgingly fell silent until a woman came by and asked for our orders. I asked for coffee.

"The same," Russo said. "And two lox bagels."

"I'm not hungry."

"A night on the town always makes one hungry."

"It wasn't a night on the town."

"So those are your pajamas?" Russo folded his menu and set it on the table. "Excuse me."

I shook my head, glanced away.

"Come on, Kate. We've already proven we can get along. Can we not fight it for once? I'm not asking you to be my best friend. Just drop your guard for half a second so we can have a conversation. We're going to be working together until we catch this guy."

"Which will hopefully be tomorrow if we're lucky. If your break is as good as you say it is."

"I didn't say it was a break in the case. I told you Bobby called me."

"And that's why you dragged me across the city in a snowstorm? To go over a phone call?"

Russo shifted in his seat. "I prefer face to face when discussing business. Especially since Bobby so kindly let me know that you were out and about with one of our suspects."

"Gem's not a suspect!"

"He's sure as hell a person of interest. If he wasn't, then why'd you go talk to him this afternoon?"

I gritted my teeth.

"I'm not trying to tell you what you can or can't do," Russo continued. "I'm just trying to look out for a friend. I don't believe that Gem can be trusted. He's slick, he's got money—and he's got ties to the case."

A rush of cold slithered down my spine. "Don't tell me you called me to the Brownley just to break up my night with Gem?"

"I'm trying to help," he insisted. "I don't care what you do with Gem—once he's cleared from the case. But he and Wes don't have solid alibis. There are conveniently no cameras where they should be in that club."

"There are now. They put them in last night."

"Again, convenient."

I wanted to argue further, but I realized Russo had a point. And if we were going to solve this thing, I couldn't argue with everything he said for the sake of arguing. So, I cleared my throat and nodded. "I agree."

He quirked an eyebrow. "You do?"

"I went tonight because I was worried about my sister. Turns out she got a job at Rubies despite my meddling in her life and attempts to convince her otherwise."

"Ah."

"She wasn't answering my phone calls and neither was Wes. I got worried."

"And Gem works into the picture, how?"

"I called him to ask about my sister. He gave me his business card and permission to use it. So, I did. One thing led to another, and he offered to pick me up and take me to Rubies to check on her. Seeing as my car was snowed in, I didn't have much of a choice but to take him up on the offer."

"Did you learn anything at Rubies?"

"Nothing concrete. Though I will admit it's uncanny how quickly those security cameras went up after the murder. While Gem strikes me as the sort of guy who gets business done quickly, that doesn't explain why they weren't there in the first place."

"Touché." Russo pulled his coffee toward him and took a sip.

While he held lightly onto the handle, I wrapped both palms as far around the mug as I could get them. I was still chilled from my jaunt outside through the snow and took a sip of the coffee, the warm liquid helping heat me from the inside. The added jolt of caffeine would be welcomed, too.

"The offer of the bathrobe still stands if you're cold," Russo said, obviously watching me hoard the coffee to my chest. "Alternatively, I could find you a comforter and wrap that around you."

"Let's talk about Bobby."

Russo smiled, set his cup down. He pulled the bagel closer and began doctoring up the toasted bread with cream cheese. "He called tonight, and I answered. It was immediately clear that he was at work. I could hear the music in the background."

"Was he upset? Scared? Nervous?"

"He sounded a little surprised." Russo squinted at his plate. "And maybe a little nervous, but it's hard to tell with a guy like Bobby."

I nodded. "He looked shocked to see me next to Gem. I'm not sure if he was just surprised to see Gem with a woman like me... or if it was something more."

"Oh, I don't think it was the former." Russo bit into his bagel. "I think Gem's a smart man."

"What's that supposed to mean?"

"He sees what he likes. Goes after it."

"Don't tell me you're talking about me. If that's the case, you've got it all wrong."

"Do I?"

More flashbacks from my evening next to Gem. "If he's trying to get close to me, it's because of the case. He wants to know what's going on with his business. Understandably, he doesn't want any problems for Gem Industries—and a murder is one very huge problem."

"Maybe."

"Bobby," I said, circling back to safer territory. "He sounded nervous?"

"He told me that he lied earlier during the interview. He did remember seeing our victim alive, but he doesn't remember her name."

"You believe him?"

Russo shrugged. "Who knows? It's hard to say over the phone. I'm not sure what this guy's end game is yet."

"Is that it?" I asked. "You called me across town to tell me something we already knew?"

"We hadn't had anyone confirm she was there—for sure. Now, we have that."

"If we believe him."

"True, though he said—unprompted—that he saw our vic leave with a guy *and* a girl."

I lowered my coffee cup to the table. "A guy and a girl? There were two people?"

"That's what he said. Now we just have to determine if we believe him."

"What incentive does he have to lie?"

"I haven't figured that out yet, but he lied once already. I get the sense he's not being fully honest, but I haven't figured out which part doesn't fit."

"Why wouldn't he tell us that right away?"

"Maybe he recognized one or both of the people leaving with Jane Doe."

I shook my head. "I'm not getting how this guy's brain works. He calls you to tell you that he lied initially, and then when he promises to tell the truth, he gives us half of it all over again."

"He might've known we suspected something and wanted to beat us to the punch. Or, I dunno, seeing Gem with you might've shaken him. What if it was Gem he saw leave with Jane Doe and one other girl? He could've seen Gem's visit as a sort of intimidation."

"Then why not name him?"

"Chickened out on the phone?" Russo shrugged. "Gem's a formidable opponent. He can silence people with the sort of money he has."

"That doesn't mean he would."

"Do you know Alastair Gem well enough to say that for a fact?"

I zipped my lips.

"If Bobby is telling the truth, who was the girl? And what happened to her? Was she in on it, or was she another victim, and we just haven't found her yet?" Russo asked. "Or, was he lying about the whole thing... and there *was* no other girl, and he was just saying that to throw us off?"

"Maybe Jane Doe was working at the bar," I said with a raised eyebrow. "Maybe she was working...but not employed by Gem Industries. Off the books sort of work."

"A prostitute? Could be. I wondered that myself."

I wrinkled my nose. "We're missing something. It doesn't feel right."

"I agree. But what?"

"I think we need to look into Bobby, really figure out if he's telling any semblance of the truth. And if not, what is he hiding?"

"I'd agree," Russo said. "In the meantime, let's flash Jane Doe's picture around at some popular places. See if we can't get anyone who's seen her around before."

"I don't have any better ideas."

"I'll take that as a yes," Russo said. "It's a date. I'll meet you at the precinct at ten. It's late."

"It is." I finished my coffee, pushed my bagel toward Russo. "Thanks for the information and the caffeine."

"Is Gem going to be waiting out front for you?"

"I honestly have no clue. Either way, I'm planning to call a cab. I told him not to wait."

Russo nodded, a hint of relief behind his gaze. "I'll walk you out."

We strode through the lobby. Russo stopped at the front desk to pay our bill. Meanwhile, I sidled to the front entrance and tried to decipher the sinking sensation in my gut when I saw the space where the limo had been... and where it was no longer.

I was on the phone with a taxi company by the time Russo joined my side. He shoved his hands in his pockets, glanced outside. A small smile perked up his lips as he saw the front walk empty save for the doorman.

"I need a cab," I said. "I already tried Uber. It's a three hour wait. I might as well sleep on the lobby couch and go straight to work in that case."

"The woman at the front desk said the cab companies are swamped," Russo added apologetically as I looked forlornly at my phone. "They're declaring a snow emergency. As you discovered, Uber is backed up for hours."

"Yeah, I figured that out."

Russo raised onto his toes then lowered. "You want to finish that bagel while you wait? I'd offer to drive you home, but it's nasty out there. My car wouldn't make it two feet before we got stuck."

"I want to be home." I stared sadly outside at the piles of snow building up. "I'm going to see if they have another room here. I need some sleep and a shower. Work isn't going to stop tomorrow."

"If you're going to stay here, I have an extra room."

"What?"

"I have a suite. You know, a two bedroom. Two locking doors. Two showers."

"How'd you manage that?"

"I travel a lot."

"Nice upgrade. Still, it's better if I just get my own space."

"It's a few hours, and I promise not to bother you."

I hesitated. I really didn't want to spend the two-hundred-dollar-plus nightly rate on the room. I didn't exactly have money to burn, but the idea of staying in such close proximity to Russo had me equally on edge.

"I don't know," I said. "I don't want to impose."

"I insist. You can have that bathrobe I've been talking about. Don't worry, I haven't touched it."

"I'll tell you what," I said. "I'll request an Uber. While I wait, maybe I can use your spare shower."

"Hell, go wild. Watch some TV while you're at it." Russo reached into his wallet, handed me one of two room keys. "Just don't order the good stuff. The FBI won't approve those charges. I'll give you half an hour to get settled—I've got a few phone calls to make."

My face colored as Russo winked.

"Nobody hears about this." I pointed my finger at him as we stepped into the elevator. "You breathe a word about this to a soul, and you're dead."

Chapter 18

He stood outside waiting patiently.
Patience, patience, patience.

It's how he'd managed to stay ahead of them.

All of them.

It's how he'd stay ahead of the rest of them.

All of them.

Even the freak detective who was ruining everything.

"Where are you taking me?" The giggly voice broke through his thoughts. "I thought you'd never ask me out."

He smiled. "I've had my eye on you since the moment we met."

It wasn't a lie. He'd known she'd been the one the second he'd seen her. She was just what he needed. Just what he wanted. Just what he *craved*.

And better yet, she'd throw off the cops. She was different.

"Isn't this romantic?" The young blonde spun around, her arms spread wide. "All this fresh snow—so pretty. A handsome guy... a sneaky little romance. Come on, tell me already. Where are we going? You said your apartment is nearby?"

"Oh, yes," he said with a smile. "And I have plans for us. But why wait until we get to the apartment? My car's right here."

"But won't we be more comfortable—"

"I think we'll be plenty comfortable just like this." He stepped closer, slid his hand under her dress. Drawing the woman near, he let his breath trace in tantalizing swirls over her shoulder. Then he whispered in her ear. "I want you, darling. I need you. Why wait?"

"Okay," she said breathlessly. "Why wait?"

He smiled, his heart pumping with adrenaline as he tasted her desire. He could feel her need for him. Small puffs of air landed on his face. She gasped when he squeezed her thigh, hiking her dress over her waist, baring her skin against the frigid cold. Her fingernails dug into his back, tore at his jacket.

And soon enough, it was all over.

I LET MYSELF INTO ROOM 703 and hesitated for a split second in the entryway, surveying Russo's private space. It might not be his home turf, per se, but he hadn't expected me to be invading it.

The suite opened into a small living area with a door on either side, presumably leading to each bedroom. I scooted along, through the living area, trying not to peek into Russo's room.

My attempt at self-restraint didn't work. I was a detective for Pete's sake. Plus, his door was open, so it wasn't exactly snooping if I could see inside without stepping foot over the threshold.

The left half of Russo's bed was ruffled, as if he'd been resting there before leaping from the sheets to derail my evening. Aside from that, the room was in order. One travel suitcase sat on a chaise lounge pushed before a window with a view of the glittering St. Paul skyline.

A pair of workout shorts hung over the arm of the chair, nicely folded but obviously used. I raised my eyebrows, wishing away the image of Russo's neatly sculpted body. The man obviously was accustomed to traveling and living out of a suitcase. I doubted even CSU would be able to find a hair in Russo's room once he checked out.

I backed away from the bedroom doorway and surveyed the living area. It was neat, efficient, and somewhat bland—obviously meant for business travelers. The second room was across from a small kitchenette. I grabbed a cup of water then let myself into the bedroom, closing and locking the door behind me.

The room was, as Russo had promised, unused and neat as a pin. A plush robe hung on the back of the bathroom door. I stared greedily at it, willing it onto my body. When my mind voodoo didn't work, I dropped my purse on the bed and wandered toward the bathroom, running the soft fabric of the robe between my fingers.

A five-minute shower couldn't hurt. After all, my poor body had been squished into a tight dress all night. My feet had been accosted by mounds of snow. Who knew what sort of virus I'd picked up winding my way through the sweating dancers at the club. I'd earned a long, hot shower.

Plus, that might be the ticket to perk me up. It wasn't lost on me that I was alone in a hotel with Jack Russo—gorgeous FBI agent and major pain in my ass. Not only that, but I was in his room. Possibly-almost in one of his showers. There was no time for a mental lapse in judgement from tiredness.

Before I knew it, I'd eased into the bathroom and stripped off my heels and dress. The water cascaded from the faucet sending lazy spirals of steam seeping from behind the curtain and fogging the mirror.

I hit the fan that, to my dismay, sounded more like a garbage disposal than a bathroom vent. I let it run and slipped into the shower, planning to be done well before Russo returned to the room. I figured I had at least twenty minutes on the clock. I didn't need more than five to warm up my extremities.

Unfortunately, three minutes into my allotted five, I was in for a surprise.

A very, very unwelcome surprise.

My fist reacted first. Straight into the face of said gorgeous FBI agent.

"Russo!" I screeched, yanking at the shower curtain and clapping it around my body as he bent forward and groaned in pain. "What the hell are you doing in here?"

Russo's face had appeared on the other side of the shower curtain just as I'd opened my eyes after a luxurious lather, rinse, and repeat using the complimentary hotel supplies. Then it had disappeared quite quickly as he'd lurched forward.

He straightened, pinching the bridge of his nose as blood dripped down his chin. "Damn. You've got some right hook."

"Give me the robe!" I waved at it. "Actually—don't. Don't touch it, you'll get blood all over it. Shut your eyes already! Don't peek."

Russo turned away from me and closed his eyes, but not before our gazes met in the mirror's reflection. And his eyes flicked down for the briefest of seconds before clamping shut.

"Nice," I grumbled.

"You're covered."

"By a clear garbage bag." I let the shower curtain drop to my feet and exchanged it for the robe. "You never answered my question. What the hell are you doing in my bathroom?"

"Your bathroom?" Russo retorted.

"Yes."

"Are we just going to ignore the fact that you punched me in the nose?"

"I thought it was pretty obvious why I did that."

Russo reached for the toilet paper and wrapped a huge wad around his hand before raising it to stem the quite impressive flow of blood. I hoped it wasn't broken. That could lead to some hefty red-tape.

He eyed me skeptically. "Who'd you think I was?"

"You know, I'm not sure. See, I wasn't expecting *anyone* to come into my bathroom while I showered. That's rude and creepy, and not to mention, very unprofessional."

"Sorry."

Russo didn't sound sorry. He sounded amused.

I rolled my eyes and kicked the mutilated shower curtain back into the tub, then leaned over and flicked the water off.

"I hope the FBI covers destroyed curtains," I said dryly. "Not sure how you'll explain that on the expense report."

He barked a dry laugh that sounded nasally thanks to the tissues shoved against his nose. "I think I'll put that on my personal card. Or better yet, I'll add it to the furthering my education bucket. Lesson Number One: Don't sneak up on Kate Rosetti in the shower."

"Again, I thought that would have been obvious." I tightened the robe around my body, noting it was just as soft as it'd looked. "You still didn't explain why you're here."

"It's my room."

"You said thirty minutes. That was fourteen, max."

Russo's face—or what I could see of it—sobered. "I really am sorry to have startled you. But you weren't answering when I called through the door, and I got... well, I thought I should check on you."

"Probably this stupid thing." I pointed upward. The fan confirmed my theory with a crunch that sounded like a fork caught in a sink disposal. "Plus, I was washing my hair. But the door was locked. How'd you..."

"FBI." Russo gave a cheeky grin that was made somewhat terrifying by a streak of blood on his teeth.

I raised a hand, gestured at my own mouth. He turned to the mirror and blanched at his reflection.

"Yikes," he said. "I don't know how you got this much blood to come out without breaking my nose."

"Maybe I did?" I tried not to sound hopeful. "You sort of deserved it."

"I've had my nose broken before." He winked in my direction. "Nice try. But no cigar. Give me a minute to clean up, and then we need to talk."

I slipped out of the bathroom. Russo shut the door behind him. There were a few curse words punctuated by the faucet turning on and off. I didn't want to see the towels when he was through with them.

I didn't take pride in having to hit Russo, though even I had to admit it was a solid strike. My instructor at the academy would have been proud. Jimmy would have been impressed. My mother would have been horrified.

By the time Russo had emerged from the bathroom, I'd managed to morph my expression into one of sympathy. "I'm sorry I smoked you in the face."

"I asked for it." Russo ran a hand through his hair. His face was slightly red around his nose, and it was possible the darkening on his cheeks might possibly turn into a black eye. "Though I had a reason. I got a call downstairs."

My gut clenched. "Is it Jane?"

Russo's eyes flicked toward the mirror, then toward the carpet. "They found another body."

My breath came out in a gasp. "It's not—is she from Rubies?"

"I don't know if it's your sister." Russo met my gaze. "But listen, detective, I have no reason to think it is. There are hundreds of thousands of women in this state."

"Yeah, but they're not all...Wait a minute. Who called you? Why didn't I get called?"

"You probably did get called." Russo thumbed toward where my purse lay on the bed.

In all the excitement, I hadn't checked my phone for messages. I also hadn't brought it into the bathroom. I scrambled for it, flicked on the backlight to the screen. Sure enough, two missed calls from HQ and one call from Jimmy a few minutes later—probably wondering why I wasn't answering.

"This isn't good." I stood. "Can you, uh, give me some privacy? I need to get dressed. Then, I'll need you take me to the crime scene. I know it's snowing out there, but—"

The panic rose in my chest as I grasped at the flimsy fabric of my dress, already realizing there was no way I could show my face looking like this—at this hour—in a snowstorm. I'd have to stop home. But there was no time...

"Kate."

The sound of my name had a soothing effect. I turned to find Russo holding out an FBI tracksuit, along with a windbreaker.

"It'll be a little big on you," he said, "but it'll do."

I swallowed with relief, my mind still thinking about Jane, as I accepted the clothes. "Thank you. But what will we say about the driving situation when Jimmy—"

"Tell him I picked you up from the club where you were doing recon and made you change in the car." Russo easily fed me the lie. "It's almost true."

"And your nose?"

"Shower is slippery." He winked. "I'll leave you to get changed. I swear I won't peek."

Russo let himself out of the second bedroom, closing the door behind him.

I didn't bother to lock the door before opening my robe and slipping into the borrowed clothes. After everything we'd been through, I realized I trusted Russo. And I genuinely felt bad about blackening his eyes.

I quickly dressed. The sweatpants material was soft against my skin and smelled clean, suspiciously like Jack Russo himself. I wouldn't mind adopting these clothes permanently. Except for the connotations that would be attached to such a thing, along with the fact it was a little creepy to steal someone's clothes.

Opening the door, I found Russo waiting for me in the living room. He was staring at the blank TV, his eyes glazed over. The agent looked tired and worn. A little saddened. The slouch of his shoulders was new.

"You okay?" I asked quietly.

"Yeah—yeah." He shoved himself to his feet, a smile flickering sadly over his face. "Let's get going. You look good in that outfit. If you ever want to wear the FBI letters permanently, I'm sure we'd have space for you."

"I'm sorry," I said. "Again, about your face. I just... reacted back there."

He waved his hand. "I've had worse. Or better? Anyway, shall we...?"

We both stood still, holding onto each other's gaze. There was a heaviness between us that felt fragile. An egg, balanced on the edge of a spoon, ready to crack and splatter at a momentary flinch.

Russo started to say something as I opened my mouth to speak. Neither of us took the initiative. Another awkward gaze followed. Russo scratched at his jaw, then gestured toward the door.

"I called Jimmy and let him know I'd be picking you up," Russo said finally. "We'll meet him there. Are you ready for this?"

"Of course. It's my job."

"It's not her, Kate," Russo said again. "It's not your sister."

"Do you know that for a fact?"

Russo's stare was blank.

"That's what I thought." I draped my dress higher over my arm and ignored the white-knuckle clutch I had going on my purse. "Let's move."

Chapter 19

The drive to the crime scene was a bear. It would've been rough even for a local driver, and while I hated to admit it, Russo did pretty good for an out-of-towner. Aside from one fish tail on a slippery exit ramp that almost killed us, the drive was quite enjoyable.

"You'd think crime would quiet down on a night like this one." Russo threw the car into park. "What sort of criminal wants to do their getaway driving in a foot of snow?"

"The kind who thought their mess wouldn't be discovered until morning," I pointed out. "Who found the body?"

Russo just shook his head. I'd been peppering him with questions the entire drive over, but it'd quickly become an exercise in futility. He'd already told me everything he'd heard on the call.

We climbed out of the car. I'd borrowed a pair of sneakers from Russo and a few extra pairs of socks to pad his much-larger size against my foot. It was naturally awkward to walk through a foot of snow even with the right footwear. Walking with shoes three sizes larger than mine would be an absolute joy.

The crime scene was again on the St. Paul side, but instead of the river road, the body had been dumped lakeside in a small park near a college campus. I wondered again if he was targeting the college area for its selection of young women, or if it was a coincidence.

The scene was already flooded with light and techs by the time we arrived. Melinda was leaning over the body. She'd traded out her usual high heels for fluffy boots with pom-poms on the sides that matched both her scarf and her hat. Her hands were bare, save for a thin set of gloves, and she held what looked like a flashlight.

Russo hung back while I lurched forward, losing one shoe in the process. I returned, yanked impatiently at the laces, and pressed forward until I reached the ME's side.

"Detective..."

Melinda's voice faded into the background. My gaze was already on the face of a young, dead girl. Unfortunately, I recognized her.

I just couldn't place her.

I exhaled a huge breath of relief at the realization that it wasn't Jane lying mutilated and unbreathing on the ground. At the same time, my body filled with hate for the fact that my relief would be someone else's horror—this girl was undoubtedly someone's daughter, sister, friend.

"I've seen her before," I murmured. "Where do I know her from?"

"You didn't listen to a word I said, did you?" Melinda straightened, gave me a curious look. "You know, if it had been Jane, I would have called you straightaway. It's not your sister, Kate. You can breathe."

I did as she instructed. "I wish that fact made this moment better. But this poor girl is still dead."

"Yes, well..." Melinda shook her head, but she didn't let the emotions give her pause. She couldn't—none of us could. If we did, we wouldn't be able to do this job. "Are you okay, Kate? Jimmy's on his way—he can take the lead if you need the night off."

"No, I'm fine." I flicked a glance over my shoulder. "Russo, come over here. You should hear this, too."

Melinda gave me a curious look. "You're friends now?"

"Don't push it."

"Must have been some lunch date." Melinda gave my clothing choices a smirk. Then she glanced at my feet. "You're nuts."

"Keep your head in the game." I gestured toward the body. "Who found her?"

Melinda waited until Russo had picked his way through the snow. She sized him up once he came to a stop, and if I wasn't mistaken, amusement danced in her eyes as she glanced between us.

"The body was dumped," she said. "Our victim wasn't killed here; the crime scene is far too clean for that. I've got her estimated time of death at just over two hours ago. We're lucky—at the rate this snow is falling, if our runner hadn't been out and about, we might not have found her for days, until some of this mess melted."

"Who's running in this weather?"

"Some guy training for the Boston marathon. He was fitting in a quick jog around the park after a late night at work and stumbled across the body—literally."

"Runners are crazy."

Melinda looked over at me. "Hey, now. You run with me sometimes."

"I only go with you when you agree to run to the doughnut shop. What happened here?" I pointed to a few markings in the snow that almost looked like a scuffle. "Is this from the runner?"

Melinda nodded. "He tripped over the body, nearly had a heart attack—or so he said. He called 911 just as soon as he could get his mittens off and stayed here until the first cruiser arrived. We let him go after taking down his info. Poor guy was terrified. And frozen."

"Do we know if she's connected to our other vics?" Russo asked. "She wasn't dumped at the riverbank this time."

"No, but there is a lake just down the slope from the path." Melinda scanned the horizon. "And there's a parking lot not far from here. Drag marks indicate our killer parked there and left her here."

"Any footprints?" I asked.

Melinda shook her head. "He was careful. And if he slipped up, we missed it. The snow covered everything."

"Maybe the killer's smarter than we thought," I said to Russo. "It's actually the perfect night for getaway driving."

Russo just raised an eyebrow. "Any chance you feel like guessing at a cause of death?"

Melinda leveled her gaze at Russo. "You're lucky it's cold, and I don't feel like arguing. The cause of death looks to be consistent with our Jane Doe."

I shook my head at the news. I'd been too late to help this woman. A fact that would grate on me, even if I knew it wasn't my fault.

Russo and Melinda must have been thinking along the same lines because a silence settled over us as we studied the figure on the ground. Like our last victim, this woman wasn't dressed for the cold. She wore a slinky, velvety dress that had been hiked inappropriately high over her waist, exposing an even slinkier thong.

I itched to pull her dress down, but I couldn't risk tampering with evidence, so instead, I averted my eyes to her face. She was pretty, even beneath the thick layer of makeup that acted as a mask against her deathly pale skin. Her lips had purpled, mixing with tattered blood-red lipstick. Her jewelry remained intact—a gold necklace, huge diamond studs, rings on several of her fingers.

Russo cleared his throat. "Any word on ID?"

"Right." Melinda shook off the somber quiet and brushed at her eyelashes where several fat snowflakes had landed while she'd been still. "Technically, no. She didn't have her wallet on her."

"But?"

"But a look at her face is ID enough for most people," Melinda said. "Her name's Leslie Rosehip, and she's something of a local celebrity. She's famous on Instagram and just recently won the Miss Minneapolis contest. She does a ton of events around the cities."

"I knew she looked familiar," I said. "But I couldn't tell you where I saw her. It must have been on TV somewhere."

"Lassie," Melinda said. "Lassie told us about her just last week. She was going to try and get Leslie to do an interview for her blog."

"That's right!" I snapped my fingers. "Lassie had us read over her e-mail. I forgot about that. I wonder if she ever got a response?"

Russo shrugged. "It doesn't look like she's getting one now."

"Thanks for that," I said. "As if that wasn't obvious already."

"One more thing." Melinda interrupted the start to a quarrel as she knelt in the snow and reached for the victim's arm. She pulled it toward her, flipped it over so the palm faced upward. Then she flicked on the flashlight-thing in her hand and shined it at Leslie's wrist.

But this wasn't any normal flashlight. It was a blacklight. And there was no stamp.

"Did you try the other wrist?" Russo asked.

"Of course she did," I snapped at him. "So, he didn't go back to the same locale. What does that mean?"

Melinda shut the light off and stood. "I can't deny the similarities between the cases, but Kate—we could have a copycat. There are differences with this victim, and until I get her—"

"—on your table, you can't say anything conclusively," I finished. "Yeah, yeah. You're doing the autopsy first thing in the morning?"

Melinda nodded. "You're welcome to join. I'll be starting at eight a.m."

"Has her family been notified?"

"I don't think so." Melinda glanced over her shoulder, thumbed at two officers standing a short distance away pretending not to eavesdrop. "They were the first officers on the scene. Go ahead and ask them to confirm."

"You want to do notifications?" Russo asked. "We can—"

"No," I said quickly. "But I do want to get to the Rosehip family residence first thing in the morning. We'll join you after we're done there, Melinda."

She crooked one eyebrow at the word 'we', but simply gave a nod in agreement. "I'll take a flat white, since you're asking."

"You drive a hard bargain." I grinned. "Russo's on coffee duty tomorrow. You get that, suit?"

We stuck around for a bit longer, poking around the perimeter just in case the snow hadn't obscured some traces of evidence, but we were out of luck. The tire tracks from the car quickly became blurred in a muddy mess—and even where the indents were clear, there was too much snow piled on top to be of use to CSU.

We scoured the walking path, but it didn't appear the victim or her killer had done much meandering once they'd reached the park. As Melinda said, our girl had been dead on arrival, and our killer hadn't stuck around.

Leslie's body didn't tell us much on sight, except that she had been ready for a night out on the town. Not surprising, seeing as she was essentially a professional socialite. I'd have to ask Lassie to confirm, but I'd bet Leslie had been a regular on the nightlife circuit.

An idea popped into my head. I texted Lassie and asked her to meet at my mother's café at eleven a.m. My treat, her gossip.

Lassie's agreeable response was swift. It wasn't a surprise that she was still awake—snowstorm or not. She'd be out hounding her next story, or at home, plucking away at the keyboard.

Closing my phone, I turned to Russo. "Are you okay here?"

"I'm good if you are," he said.

"You need a ride back?" Jimmy huffed over to where I stood next to Melinda. "I can drop you off if you want, unless..." His eyes scanned over the agent.

"Russo picked me up. He can drop me off," I said, not quite meeting Jimmy's eyes. "Thanks, though. I'll see you in the morning. You want to come to the interview with the family tomorrow? We're going to see the Rosehips first thing."

Jimmy glanced between us. "I think three's a crowd. I'll sit in on the autopsy and get Asha running on her investigation. I'll see you once you're back. Have fun, you two."

"He's a peach," Russo said when Jimmy headed toward his car.

"At least he's never seen me naked," I hissed under my breath.

"But have you punched him in the face?" Russo grinned. "That's how real friendships start."

"Then come on, my friend. You're driving me home."

Chapter 20

By the time I made it home, the hour had transitioned from late night to early morning. In my book, at least. After a quick check in my spare bedroom, I confirmed that for Jane, it was probably still considered a late night seeing as she hadn't made it home yet.

Since there was no chance for sleep, I tooled around downstairs, popping a mug of water into the microwave and tearing open a packet of hot cocoa. Once mixed, I added a dollop of whipped cream on top and hoofed it over to the sofa, flicking the TV on to an old re-run of Matlock.

While I slurped my drink, I folded my legs underneath me, all too aware that I purposely hadn't changed out of Russo's clothes. I'd kicked off his damp shoes at the door, but the sweats had stayed. I told myself it was because they were too comfortable to give up just yet.

As my hot chocolate vanished, I thought about the crime scene, weighing the likelihood that we were dealing with a second killer. My gut told me we weren't. Every one of my instincts screamed that this was one killer. One murderer, morphing as he learned. Getting smarter. Faster. More dangerous.

The case morphed into thoughts of Russo and Gem—two vastly different men, both of them inexplicably intertwined in my life at the moment.

At the moment.

The phrase hit me with surprise. In just a few days, hopefully, we'd have our killer. That would mean Russo would jet back to DC and Gem would be left alone in his diamond tower. Both men had blown into my life like a twister, and they'd leave it behind just as quickly.

To avoid dealing with my thoughts on that particular subject, I drained the rest of my hot chocolate and rose from the couch. I dumped the mug in the sink then headed to the hallway to grab Russo's shoes. I'd just tossed them in the dryer for a quick spin when the sound of a lock turning in the door stole my attention.

I reached for my waist on instinct, realizing a beat too late that I'd left my gun upstairs in my bedside drawer after I'd checked on Jane's room. Russo's sweats didn't have a great spot to hook a gun, and also, I hadn't suspected I'd need one in my own home.

"Oh, you're up?" Jane paused in the doorway, her lips turning up in a sheepish smile. "So, then, it's a really good thing I told Wes he couldn't sneak back tonight with me, I guess."

I glanced at my watch. "It's after four a.m."

"Um, right." Jane closed the door, flicked the lock. "I know how to tell time."

"No call, no text?"

"You knew I was working!" Jane kicked off her high heels and peeled a purse from her shoulder, dropping it on the entryway table. "You literally came to my club to spy on me. What time do you think clubs close? I know you're practically a nun, but for crying out loud, Kate—you can't have thought I'd be in bed by midnight."

"A text couldn't have hurt," I said. "It's late. It's dangerous for you to be traipsing across the city with God-knows-who in the middle of the night."

"Look, I don't know what bug crawled up your butt, but we already had this conversation." Jane squeezed past me. "You don't know anything about my job. It's important work."

"Being a waitress?"

Jane narrowed her eyes at me. "What's your problem?"

"I just wish..." I rubbed my hands across my forehead. "Forget it. It's not important."

"I know you think my job is stupid, but I happen to like it. Not everyone has to save lives in their careers, Kate."

"I didn't say that—"

"You were thinking it." Jane brushed passed me and went into the kitchen. She poured herself a glass of wine and didn't offer one to me, though I followed behind her. "I thought you'd be proud of me. Getting back on my feet."

"I meant a job like, I don't know, a receptionist or something. Helping mom at the bakery. Something with normal hours."

"I don't like working normal hours! What about nurses? They work overnights. You don't think they're nuts."

"They're saving lives. Someone has to do it."

"Again with the saving lives!" Jane set her glass on the counter. "You know, the people you work with are already dead. Sure, your job is important... but I think you do it because you don't like working with us living folks."

"Come on, Jane," I said. "I'm not trying to pick a fight. I was just worried about you."

"And I can take care of myself."

"Fine," I said, raising my hands. "Sweet dreams. I will stay out of your business."

"Good."

I had nothing left to say, since it seemed arguing with Jane was getting me nowhere. I headed upstairs and climbed into bed, but sleep was elusive.

Finally, an hour or so later, I heard Jane speaking into her phone. Another thirty minutes after that, the sound of a car stopping out front filtered through my window, followed closely by the opening and closing of my front door. Then one last, final click of the lock.

I rolled over in bed and wondered if Jane was right about my preference for working with the dead over the living. Since that was an unwelcome line of thought, I forfeited sleep as dawn peeked through the window. A quick shower, a fresh outfit, and a steaming cup of coffee later, and I was beginning to shake the fog of a sleepless night from my system.

I grabbed my keys, my gun, my bag, and just before I opened the door to head out for the day, I froze at a sound coming from my front yard. I leaned closer, listened. The repetitive *scrape, scrape, scrape* sounded like someone shoveling, but that was impossible. The only person I could think of who belonged at my house was Jane, and I could guarantee that shoveling my drive at seven in the morning was the absolute last item on her bucket list.

When I opened my door, however, I was even more surprised than if Jane had been out front with a snowsuit and an ice pick. Instead, there on my front walkway, stood Alastair Gem with a shovel in one hand, a bag of salt at his feet, and a grin that turned his tanned face into a work of art.

"Good morning," he said easily. "I imagined you had a late night and wouldn't have had time to clear your car out."

My first thought was to be grateful. Specifically, grateful of the fact I'd changed out of Russo's clothes. And more grateful that I wasn't carrying a bag of his shoes while coming face to face with Gem.

"Good morning," I returned as my mind buzzed on caffeine and confusion. "I did have a long night. How'd you know?"

He stared at me. "I think that's pretty obvious."

"Right. You, ah, dropped me at the hotel. Sorry—I haven't slept, and my single cup of coffee hasn't kicked in yet."

"Then it's a very good thing I've got an extra hot caramel latte with extra whip in the car with your name on it."

I looked up, spotted the limo. "And why would you do any of this for me?"

"You needed salt on your driveway. We couldn't have St. Paul's finest slipping and breaking a leg on this fine wintery morning." He winked. "Then, there's the fact I figured you might be a little tired after your case last night, so I thought I'd help out with a donation of caffeine. It's a little selfish on my part, anyway. The fresh air does a man good."

"Does it?" I retorted dryly.

"Can I tempt you into a coffee and a ride to the office?"

"I'm not going to the office. And where I'm going, I'd prefer to drive."

"Go ahead, then." There was a zip of humor in Gem's voice.

When I turned to look at my car, I saw why. Where my car had been the night before was now a snow fort. Most of the vehicle was buried. There was a good chance the doors were iced shut. In short, my vehicle wasn't moving for quite some time... and I had work to do.

"What do you get out of this?" I squinted at Gem. "And how'd you know I needed to be at work early this morning?"

"I thought you'd know me better than that by now."

"I met you yesterday. I don't know you at all."

"What can I say?" Gem spread his arms wide. "I'm an open book. I have money, resources, time, and I use them wisely. And when I see something I want, I go after it."

I scrunched up my nose. "I don't see how that's related to the case."

Gem expelled a breath. "Just get in the car. Otherwise you'll be half an hour late wherever you're going. And that's if you make it there without careening into a ditch. Word travels on your driving record, Rosetti."

I eyed him warily. "How will I get home if I catch a ride with you?"

"I'll leave that up to your partner."

I reached for my phone, felt my fingers ice up as I slipped a glove off to text Russo. I asked him to meet me at the address we'd been given for Leslie Rosehip's next of kin in half an hour.

"Fine." I flipped my phone around to show the address. "You're okay to drop me here?"

Gem didn't even look at my phone. He dumped the rest of his salt in a messy pile around my front walkway, then made his way to the door of the limo and held it open for me.

"I'll drop you anywhere you want to go."

I glanced over my shoulder at the thick layer of salt. "You don't do this kind of thing often, do you?"

"It's not in my blood," he said. "I'm British. We don't get this much snow."

"I'm sure that's it," I muttered, thinking it was probably his billions more than his English accent that kept him from shoveling the pavement.

Once Gem and I were situated in the backseat, he reached for a cupholder where two large lattes were waiting—one with my name on it and one with his. His name was circled with a heart. I raised an eyebrow.

"Admirer?" I asked with a smirk.

"Jealous?" He flashed me a quick grin. "I can't help that people fall fast for my charm. Or maybe it's the accent, or the dashing good looks? What do you think?"

"I think you should hand me my latte before it gets cold."

He laughed, handed it over. I took a sip and found that it was the most frothy, creamy, delicious thing I'd ever tasted. I closed my eyes and groaned in appreciation.

"I won't tell your mother."

My eyes flashed open. "Excuse me?"

"She runs a coffee shop, no?" His eyes glittered. "I won't tell her you're having an affair with my lattes."

"Where is this from?" I asked defensively.

"My private café."

"You have a private café?" I gulped down my hot beverage, then waved a hand. "Don't answer that. I'm sure you own many more things than a private café."

"Then I won't answer. Where to?"

"Oh, right." I flipped up my phone and read the address off so the driver could hear.

Then Gem raised the window between the two compartments, and we were thrown into peaceful silence. He flipped on the radio. "Music?"

"Whatever you like." I shifted uncomfortably in my seat. "It's your car. And frankly, I still don't know what I'm doing in it."

"You're going to work."

I lapsed into silence. I looked at my nails. Sipped my latte. Swallowed hard.

"You're in the clear, if that's what you're worried about," I said softly. "There was another body last night, but I'm sure you already know that. This time, there was no stamp. I don't have any reason to believe this victim was connected to your club. At least, not yet."

The light music Gem had turned on in the background thrummed around us. The only sounds were the two of us as we alternated sips of our lattes.

"Is that the only reason you think I showed up this morning?" Gem asked. "To get inside info on the case?"

"I already told you—I don't know why you're here."

"Do you think it might be simpler than that?" Gem raised an eyebrow. "Have you considered the fact that I might just like you, detective?"

"No, I hadn't considered that, actually."

He grinned again. "I enjoy your company. I thought it might be nice to get to know you better, but for some reason, I suspected you might turn my invitation to dinner down flat."

"You would be correct."

"I know you're not interested in me... yet." He raised his latte, exposing the heart. "But I can be quite persuasive."

"Sorry, I'm not interested."

"Is there someone else?"

"I don't have to answer that."

"No, I suppose you don't." Gem sat back. "You are a challenge, detective."

"So *that's* what this is about." I eyed him. "Is this one of your little games?"

"I've never been more serious. I just meant you're hard to impress." Gem smiled. "Normally, I have my assistant schedule dinner at The Four Seasons for a first date. With you, I had to shovel and salt your driveway to get you to accept a cup of coffee."

"This isn't a date."

"That's all you got from that?" Gem crooked an eyebrow. "That's fine. Maybe someday you'll change your mind."

"If you want my advice..." I leaned over and dropped my voice to a low murmur. "Don't get too close."

Gem leaned in too. "Why's that?"

I grinned, then sat back. "The last person to see me naked ended up with a broken nose and a black eye."

"Well, now I'm intrigued."

By the time our banter dulled to a quiet chit chat of surface news, we had arrived at our destination. I was impressed with how quickly the time had passed.

"It was lovely to see you this morning," Gem said. "It was a refreshing change of pace."

"If you like that sort of pace, feel free to shovel my drive anytime you want." I shifted closer to the door. At Gem's smirk, I shook my head. "And no, that's not an innuendo."

"Shame."

"This is the place." I pulled the door open once the car was stopped. "Thanks for the ride."

Gem reached for me, his cool hand landing on my wrist. It tingled where we touched, sending tendrils of an alluring sensation through my veins. "You didn't ask me for an alibi last night."

"I was your alibi last night."

Gem nodded. "And Wes?"

"I'm not there yet. I already told you—we don't have a tie to your club yet."

"I get the feeling this doesn't mean I'm off the hook yet." When I didn't respond, Gem's eyes grew serious. "I showed you our new security system. I'd be happy to walk you through last night's footage this afternoon if that would help clear any of my staff."

"I'm sure you would."

"I mean it, detective." Gem's hand slipped from my wrist as I stepped out of the car.

The wind whipped at me, bringing with it a gust of fluffy white particles that suctioned themselves to my clothes and found every bare inch of skin on my body. I shivered, hoping it was from the snow and not the absence of Gem's touch.

I turned to say goodbye to Gem and was surprised to find him halfway out of the car. He shrugged into his jacket and scanned the front lawn of the Rosehip residence.

"You know..." I raked my gaze over Gem. "You know you can't come inside. This is official police business."

"I just thought I'd say goodbye like a gentleman."

"A gentleman?"

But Gem was too distracted by something behind me to respond. His eyes narrowed as he studied whatever it was. Eventually, I turned, too, and found Russo standing less than a hundred feet away—leaning against his shiny black car as he watched our exchange with interest.

"Ah," Gem said, returning his gaze to mine. "I see."

"There's nothing to see."

"I didn't realize you were involved with someone."

"I'm not."

"You know, I think you lied to me."

"What are you talking about?"

"You said the last man to see you naked ended up with a broken nose and a black eye." Gem pursed his lips, nodded at Russo. "His nose isn't broken. It's just dented."

"Gem—" I fumed, but it was too late.

Alastair Gem was already inside the limo with the door halfway closed. He gave a cheeky wave, then said something to the driver, and the vehicle pulled away from the curb. A moment later, I felt a presence by my side.

"Now look what you've done." I wheeled to face Russo. "You pissed off the richest man in the state."

"Me?" Russo raised his hands in surrender. "I didn't do anything. Sorry if my presence caused a lover's quarrel."

"Shut up, Russo."

"I'm not sure what to think about the fact that Gem dropped you off last night... and this morning."

"Then maybe don't think about it so hard."

"He can't have liked seeing you come home in my clothes last night."

I gave a huge sigh. "You don't know what you're talking about."

"What a twisted web you weave, detective," Russo said as he joined me on the front porch. "I have to say—I underestimated you."

I raised a hand and knocked. Instead of engaging with Russo, I took time to study the expansive yard. The Rosehips's house was set back from the road by a long driveway—I hadn't realized it was so long while I was stomping up it, but I'd had fury on my side, propelling me over the icy surface.

The snow had already been shoveled and salt laid, leading me to think that either Alastair Gem had been very busy around the Twin Cities this morning, or the Rosehips had hired help that had been up at the crack of dawn preparing the residence to its owners' liking.

On either side of the doorway lounged a statue of a golden lion, guarding the front entrance in silence. Naked trees stretched branches high above the house, glittering white with the fresh snowfall. Hedges, bushes, and landscaping made for lumpy piles in the yard at this time of year, but I imagined in the summer this place would be plucked and pruned to perfection as it bloomed with beauty.

The door swung open, answered by a man in a suit. "Ah, detective."

I glanced at Russo, then back through the doorway. "That's me."

"We've been expecting you." The man smiled demurely, his hair matching the front lawn in its shocking whiteness. "Mr. and Mrs. Rosehip are waiting for you in the dining room. May I take your coat?"

Chapter 21

"I am wildly underdressed for this," I muttered to Russo. "I didn't know we'd be having tea with the Queen."

Russo leaned in close to me. "Speaking of underdressed, I'm not sure my black eye goes with the decor."

The inside of the Rosehip house indeed didn't look like a place where men got into fistfights... especially not fistfights with women. It was all paisleys and doilies and frilled edges that spelled old money and fragile china.

Huge mirrors with gold gilding hung on the walls, and the fireplace looked as if it'd been restored from its original brick and kept in good working order for the last hundred years. A lazy flame crackled in the hearth as we passed one living area, then a sitting area, then a library, before finally turning into a closed-off dining room that had a swinging door, presumably leading to a more functional kitchen.

"Mr. and Mrs. Rosehip, your guests have arrived."

I glanced at the butler, then peeked at my teal T-shirt, black slacks, and matching jacket. I felt more than a little out of place. Next to Russo, I felt like the janitor.

Russo fit in beautifully despite his obvious battle wounds. His suit was crisp and fresh—how he managed that while living out of a hotel and having a sleepless night was beyond me. He was freshly shaven and smelled expensive from a distance, and when he smiled, even Mrs. Rosehip's pinched lips turned into an involuntary curve upward.

"Do take a seat," Mr. Rosehip said easily. "My wife has prepared tea and scones."

"I'd hate to impose." I lifted my coffee cup to demonstrate I'd come prepared. "We're just here to discuss your daughter's case. We're so sorry for your loss."

At my offering of remorse, Mrs. Rosehip's expression slid downward, melting like a gooey marshmallow. Her carefully applied makeup suddenly looked cracked and dry, and she looked far older than her years. I could tell she'd been crying, despite the attempt to cover up all signs of distress.

"Thank you." Mr. Rosehip glanced at his wife, an expression of true pain aching in his eyes as he reached for her hand. "We understand you have a job to do. Whatever you need from us, of course we'll help. The detective who notified us last night—early this morning?—mentioned you'd be coming today."

I nodded to Russo, and we took our places on the side of the table opposite the Rosehips. A set of fine china sat before each of us. Lovely violet butterflies danced across my teacup while dainty ladybugs crawled in hand painted spirals over Russo's.

Mrs. Rosehip reached for a sterling silver teapot and began to serve me first, then Russo. She served her husband and herself with finesse, but as she reached for a raw sugar cube and dropped it into her cup, her hand shook. She attempted to stir her tea, but the spoon rattled against the bone china, and she gave up.

Russo politely ignored her obvious distress. "Mr. Rose-hip—"

"Nathan, please."

"Nathan," Russo continued. "Can you tell us a bit about your daughter?"

"We have two." Mrs. Rosehip looked up, as if surprised to find she'd spoken. "We have two daughters. You are talking about Leslie, I assume?"

"Yes, Leslie," Russo said. "Though we'd love to speak with your other daughter sometime about her sister."

"We'll discuss that later," Nathan said. "She's really in no state to do anything of the sort. She's upstairs in bed as we speak. She wanted to join us, to help in any way she could, but she's not well."

"Understandable," Russo murmured with sympathy. "Then let's start with Leslie. Just some background so we can better understand your daughter."

"Well, Leslie had..." Her father stopped, rubbed a hand across his chin. A smile crept over his face, one that appeared to be subconscious as he fondly remembered his daughter. "She had spunk, I'll give her that. She knew how to get what she wanted."

"She would have made someone a lovely wife someday," Mrs. Rosehip said. "She understood the nuances of high society. Of entertaining, fine dining, the like."

I wondered if Mrs. Rosehip knew that Leslie also knew the ins-and-outs of fine lingerie, like the skimpy red thong she'd worn yesterday, or the teensy tiny outfit she'd worn out for the evening. I wasn't fluent in fashion by any means, but Leslie's attire hadn't exactly spelled high society to me.

Certainly, it didn't hold a candle to Mrs. Rosehips's attire—a cream turtleneck with a purple cardigan draped over her shoulders, combined with simple pearl earrings. There wasn't a lick of skin showing outside of her face and fingertips.

"Did your daughter work?" I asked. "How old was she?"

"She was twenty-five, and no, she didn't work," Nathan said. "She had an allowance that she used for her pleasure activities, and she lived at home."

"She was engaged to be married, see," Mrs. Rosehip added. "It didn't make sense for her to go after a career when she was just going to leave it so soon."

"Why would she have to leave her job?"

Mrs. Rosehip stared dumbly at me. "I told you. She was getting married."

"I know, but—"

Russo stepped on my foot hard enough to make me grit my teeth in pain.

"Of course," he said aloud. "And her fiancé was...?"

"Richard Hanson," Nathan boomed. He looked proud to announce the name of his future son-in-law. "Hedge fund manager. Done quite well for himself."

"He's almost thirty," Mrs. Rosehip said. "Looking to settle down and have a family. Leslie was going to round out his life. The poor man."

"Has he been notified of his fiancé's death?"

Mrs. Rosehip nodded. "I had Nathan call him just as soon as we heard the news. Richard came right over. Unfortunately, he had to leave this morning just before you got here."

"You understand," Nathan continued, speaking directly to Russo. "He had to tidy up a few things at the office before taking off to grieve. He'll be helping us with funeral arrangements and the like, but he had to clear his desk so he could devote his full attention to it."

I didn't see how Richard having to go into the office made any sense, but it was becoming quite clear I didn't gel with the Rosehips at all.

"Do you know where your daughter was last night?" Russo asked. "Did she have plans with friends?"

"Oh, you know." Nathan waved his hand and chuckled. "Young women! So secretive these days. What do us men know?"

Russo chortled along good-naturedly while I fixed my gaze on Mrs. Rosehip. "Did your daughter tell you where she'd be?"

"Not exactly." Mrs. Rosehip shifted ever so slightly in her seat. "She enjoyed the nightlife around town. I imagine if you checked her date book or her phone, you might find reservations to a restaurant or something of the sort. Obviously it wasn't a *secret*."

I caught the glare Mrs. Rosehip sent her husband before her face morphed back into one of passive attentiveness.

"She was an adult," Nathan said quickly. "We didn't track her every movement. What sort of parents would we be if we didn't trust our daughter?"

"She was found near Lakeland Park," I said. "Do you know if her fiancé lives in the area by chance, or maybe a girl-friend of hers?"

"I don't know why she'd be over in that neck of the woods," Nathan said, his face reddening. "Didn't the cops tell me she was dumped there? So, she didn't choose to be there. The bastard—"

"That's absolutely correct." Russo extended a soothing hand toward Nathan. "We don't believe she was there by choice. The detective is just exploring all avenues at this time."

Nathan huffed out a breath, the red fading to a duller pink. He nodded gruffly. "Fine, then. And no—our boy lives over on Capitol Hill. He's got himself one of the Summit mansions, just a block from the mayor's place."

I gave a low whistle.

"I said he's successful," Nathan grunted, seemingly more and more annoyed at my very presence. He turned back to Russo. "Maybe ask him what Leslie was up to last night. I'm sure he'll know. Sometimes... they spent the night together."

Mrs. Rosehip's fingers went to the collar of her turtleneck. "They did not!"

"Margaret!" Nathan turned to his wife. "Our daughter was twenty-five years old and engaged to a wealthy man. You truly think they were waiting for marriage?"

Mrs. Rosehip—Margaret—sucked in her cheeks as if she'd tasted a raw lemon. "Nathan! We have company. Do not air family business in front of the detectives."

"Agent," I said, thumbing to Russo. "He's a federal agent, not a detective."

Nathan and Margaret were too busy facing off to notice my inopportune correction. Russo, however, was busy trying to hide a smirk behind his hand. Between my awkwardness, the cracks in the facade of the Rosehip family, and the sheer absurdness of the situation, it was a lot to handle.

"Surely it's nothing they haven't already assumed," Nathan said. "Never mind. Detective, you'll want to talk to Richard. He'll know more what our daughter was into these days. They spent a lot of time together. They were in love."

"Of course," I said. "Thank you so much for the information. I have a few last questions, and these might be difficult."

"And the rest of this is easy?" Nathan's face had passed red again and was leaning more toward purple.

Finally, I saw the cracks in the Rosehips' carefully crafted masks for what they were—intense, eye-watering, gut-churning grief. The Rosehips had lost a daughter, and no matter how polished they tried, or pretended, to be—or how much money they had—when it came down to it, these people bled and ached and hurt like the rest of us.

"Was there anyone who might have held a grudge against your daughter?" I asked. "Whether it was deserved or not?"

"Are you telling me that it wasn't some creep who snatched our daughter?" Nathan gaped at me. "You're telling me it might have been someone she knew?"

"Again, we're exploring all possibilities."

"Well, I, for one, can't think of a soul who might dislike Leslie," Nathan said. "And certainly not enough to murder her. She was a sweet girl. Innocent, naive maybe, but she was sweet through and through."

Mrs. Rosehip gave a nod of agreement. It appeared to be all that she could manage.

"What about her fiancé?" I asked. "How was their relationship?"

"Ideal," Nathan spluttered. "You're not insinuating it could have been Richard? That's preposterous. They were in love."

"What about Richard's businesses? Did he make any enemies in his work?"

"None that I know of," Nathan said, but his answer was decidedly less sure. "I don't know—he's been successful. Successful people make enemies."

"You're obviously successful," Russo said, laying his arms wide to incorporate the expansive home. "I hate to ask, but have you made any enemies throughout your career?"

"That's enough. It's none of your business," Nathan said. "I earned my money the hard way. Every penny. How dare you—"

Mrs. Rosehip pulled herself together, rested a hand on her husband's arm. "Nathan has been retired for seven years. Any enemies he might've made in the past have long since forgotten our name."

I nodded, pushed my chair back, and stood. "Thank you very much for your time."

"We might have a few more questions down the line." Russo joined me as he stood. "We will do everything we can to catch the man or woman who killed your daughter. You have my word."

We exchanged quick handshakes. Nathan's was thick and sweaty and Margaret's was dainty and limp. The butler magically appeared and led us back to our coats.

I shoved my arms into my jacket and waited for Russo to do the same. The door opened just as I was about to reach for the handle, and in walked a stunning replica of Leslie Rosehip.

This version was decidedly younger, dressed in a business suit and sky-high heels, her long hair straight as a board and platinum white. She wore over-sized glasses with thick black rims, but even those didn't hide her resemblance to the family.

"Oh! You're here?" The woman's lips turned into a frown. "You're the cops, right?"

"I'm Detective Rosetti, and this is—"

"Good, good," she said, flicking her wrist at the butler until he disappeared. "I was hoping to catch you here. I'm Leslie's sister, Prudence."

"Oh," I said, trying to match the image of the unwell girl her parents had described with the flourishing beauty before me. "We were, um, hoping to talk to you."

"Why did nobody tell me the cops were here?" Prudence yelled into the house. "I said I wanted to talk to them!"

"We'd be more than happy to talk to you now," I offered.

"Great. Because I've been trying to get ahold of you. I know who killed my sister."

Chapter 22

After an announcement like the one Prudence made in the entryway, it wasn't all that difficult to convince Leslie's sister to accompany us to the station for an official statement.

Prudence's parents had not been thrilled with the development. But their arguments against taking their second daughter to the station had come off as feeble at best. They'd obviously been caught in a lie and were in too deep to bow out gracefully.

I walked with Russo, carrying two cups of office coffee—or the brown liquid that passed for it—into the interview room. I slid one across the desk to Prudence. Russo plunked a handful of creamers and sugars onto the table, and both Prudence and I took a moment to doctor up our steaming beverages before speaking.

"This will be recorded, okay?" I rested a hand on a small device as I glanced at Prudence. When she nodded, I flicked it on and sat back, taking a gulp of coffee. I stated my name and Russo's, the date and time, and Prudence's information for the record before launching into the meat of the story. "Miss Rosehip, you say you have information regarding your sister's murder?"

"Absolutely." She nodded. "Her fiancé did it."

"Richard Hanson?" I raised an eyebrow. "Do you have any proof to back up your theory?"

"It's not a theory, I'm pretty sure it's a fact." Prudence reached for her coffee and made a face as she took a sip. She added another packet of sugar. "They had a huge fight right before she died."

"How do you know that?"

"Because she came home furious the night before last. She stormed into her room, and I went to see what all the fuss was about. I was hoping she wouldn't cancel her wedding because I had this great dress I was planning to wear for the ceremony."

"Assuming a lover's quarrel turned into murder is a bit of a stretch," I pointed out. "Unless you know something else?"

"I know Richard."

"What do you mean?"

"Richard Hanson is quite... intense," Prudence said. "He's rich and bossy and a stuck-up prick."

"I thought you wanted your sister to get married?"

"No, you misheard me." Prudence nibbled at one of her hot-pink fingernails. "I wanted to wear my smokin' hot dress to her wedding. I've never liked Richard. Then again, I'm not sure my sister did, either."

"Maybe this is me being a misguided male," Russo cut in, "but why would your sister agree to marry a man she didn't like?"

Prudence shrugged one shoulder. "Money."

"Your sister needed money?"

"Needed... yeah. That's the right word." Prudence studied us, waiting for the implication to hit. "My parents were funding her, but they cut her off recently."

"Why would they do that?"

"Because she was making a bad name for the family." Prudence paused for an eyeroll. "My sister spent her money on drinking and clothes—and not the sort of clothes my mother approved of. My family is big on looks. Big on reputation. My sister did what she wanted; she didn't play my parents' little games."

"Ah."

"But, in their defense, Leslie's spending—her whole life, actually—was getting a little out of control lately. Her newfound fame, if that's what you want to call it, was going to her head. She was terrified that she'd be thrust out of the spotlight any second. I mean, she got famous on Instagram! It's not like she has a talent or something, you know?"

I made a non-committal noise in my throat.

"So, she spent all this money on beauty products, hair and makeup. My parents wouldn't have cared, but then she started posting scandalous pictures of herself to get more and more 'likes' or 'hearts' or whatever stupid thing is on trend. My parents do not stand for new-money flashiness. It's pretty obvious if you've seen our house. Or my mother's turtlenecks."

I couldn't entirely hide my smile despite my best efforts. Prudence was candid, I'd give her that.

Prudence saw my smile and took it as encouragement. "My parents warned her several times that they'd cut up her credit cards if she continued down the same path. They had loud arguments and fought almost every night when she came home... or rather, morning. It would be five or six a.m., and my parents would be up having coffee. Leslie would gallivant into the room looking like a raccoon with her mascara streaked, sometimes still drunk, her skirt hiked up around her waist. My parents were not a fan. They tried everything."

"And the only thing that worked was to cut her off completely."

"Except even that didn't work," Prudence said. "I know the cops didn't say exactly how they found my sister, but she was probably out clubbing or something, right? I mean, how else would someone have snatched her?"

I didn't answer and neither did Russo, but Prudence wasn't stupid.

"What did your sister's fiancé think of her lifestyle?" I asked. "Did it bother him? Did he join her?"

"Oh, of course not. Richard runs in the same sort of circles as my father. They go to yacht clubs and wear over-priced polo shirts and believe women should work in the kitchen and be seen and not heard. He's old school all the way."

"Is it safe to say Leslie's habits bothered him?"

"I really don't know," Prudence confessed. "I imagine it did. He probably colluded with my dad to cut off Leslie's money supply at the knees. It was the only way to control her, really, and even then—like I said—it didn't work."

"And your mother was okay with all of this?"

"Probably not, but what was she going to do?" Prudence said. "She just wanted her daughter married off and out from under her roof. I think she wanted Leslie to get pregnant right away so she'd 'transform' overnight into the angelic daughter she never had. Become a mom, wear turtlenecks, that sort of thing."

"I am still not understanding how any of this ties Richard to your sister's murder."

"Check his bank accounts," Prudence suggested. "You can do that sort of thing, can't you? I've seen it on CSI. Maybe Richard didn't kill her himself—that doesn't seem like him, really—but he easily could have hired someone to do it. He was probably just sick of her, didn't want to marry her. He probably didn't like the way she acted."

"Why not just separate?"

"Do you know my family?" she asked. "My dad would freak. It was probably safer for Richard to kill Leslie just so he didn't have to marry her."

I jotted a note down on a piece of paper. No doubt Jimmy had already briefed Asha on the case, and she'd be on top of the background scopes—but it never hurt to double check.

"Miss Rosehip," I said, "do you know where your sister might have been last night?"

"I don't keep tabs on her, but I'm sure it's not hard to find out." At our blank stares, Prudence continued. "Have you looked at her Instagram? She posts every two seconds."

I glanced to Russo. "Do you have an Instagram?"

Russo met my blank gaze. "What do you think?"

Prudence let out a huge sigh. She pulled out her phone, clicked a few buttons as those hot-pink nails flashed. "Oh, duh. I should have guessed. She was at that new club. Something with diamonds in the name or whatever. No wait—that's not it. A gem or something."

My heart sank. "We checked her wrist for a stamp, but there was no sign she'd been admitted to a club."

Prudence rolled her eyes. "My sister was a VIP everywhere she went. They don't stamp VIPs. Do you recognize this place?"

Prudence spun her pink phone case around so I could see the last image Leslie had posted before her short life had come to an end. My heart continued to sink, delving into a freefall as it plummeted into oblivion.

"As a matter of fact," I said, "I do know that place."

"And the man who owns it," Russo added under his breath. "Very well."

"You know Alastair Gem?" Prudence's eyes widened. "That is way cool. My sister would've killed to be seen with him." She winced. "Bad choice of words. Anyway, that's probably why she was there—hoping for a glimpse of the billionaire. If she'd managed to hook Alastair Gem around her pointy little fingernail, she would have dumped Richard in a heartbeat."

We concluded our interview with Prudence after a few more questions led us in the same circles we'd already gone over. She didn't have much to add in the way of proof that Richard had killed his fiancée, but she had given us a lot to think about.

I walked Prudence outside and hitched her a ride home with a young officer who looked a little too greedily at Prudence's trim figure. Prudence didn't seem to mind in the slightest, and hurriedly waved me off when I asked if she'd like me to accompany them both back to her house.

Afterward, I met Russo outside of my mother's coffee shop. He opened the door to let me inside first, and a gust of wind pushed us toward one another. My mother's eyes didn't let up as we stepped apart and approached the counter. I spouted my order quickly and threw cash at the register before Russo could offer to buy my drink again.

Russo ordered in a distinctly more mature manner and made small talk with my mother for a few moments while Elizabeth made our drinks and shot me sly little looks over the espresso maker.

"Don't even start," I said as she handed me my drink. "It's just work."

"Sure," Elizabeth said. "But according to your mother, he's already browsing engagement rings."

I took my latte to a table in the corner and waited until Russo joined me. "You don't have to chat up my mother every time you come in here."

Russo's eyes widened. "I didn't realize small talk was a crime in Minnesota."

"You know what I mean. She's getting attached to you."

"Then it's a good thing I didn't tell her the truth about where my black eye came from."

"You're never going to let me live that down, are you?"

"I most certainly am not."

We lapsed into silence. The snow had stopped falling outside and left behind a glistening white world. It made for a beautiful Christmas ambiance, but the roads would be a mess for the rest of the week.

"I'm sorry," Russo said. "I know you didn't expect to hear that."

I narrowed my gaze on him. "Hear what?"

"About your friend."

"Alastair Gem is not my friend," I said. "He's a part of the case."

"A part of the case who drives you around in a limo and brings you coffee?"

"He's not a murderer."

"Maybe not."

"I know he's not," I said, then hesitated. "I'm his alibi. I was with him during the window of death last night. Unless Melinda finds something that changes her guestimate for TOD during the autopsy, then he's got an airtight alibi."

"Lucky for you."

"It doesn't matter one way or another to me." While I spoke the truth, it somehow felt like a lie. "I just met him. He's not anything to me, and you know what? I don't know why I'm explaining myself to you. We have to focus on finding the killer—and if it's not Gem, then we need to look elsewhere."

"His friend?"

"Remington?" I asked. "He might have an alibi. We saw him at Rubies last night just before the time of death window. Gem recently had security cameras installed. I'll meet with him this afternoon to go through security footage. If Remington's on there, he's out of the running, too."

"I assume you'll want to take this meeting alone?"

"Come on, Russo." I snapped. "If you've got something you want to say, then say it."

"I'm not saying anything." He sipped his latte and looked mildly miffed. "I'm working the case, too, if you haven't forgotten. I'd like to be kept in the loop with the security footage developments. That's all."

"Fine."

"And Richard?" Russo prompted. "What do you think about him?"

"It's hard to say without having met him, so your guess is as good as mine. We have an interview scheduled with him this afternoon."

"I'll go with you," Russo said firmly. "That's one visit I'd rather you not make by yourself."

"I'll get something scheduled—does one o'clock work?"

"You tell me a time, and I'll be there."

"Will you also be driving me?" I wheedled. "Because I happen to not have a car today."

Russo waited a beat, dragging out his victory a moment longer. "Of course. I'll drop you at Gem's after because I'm a gentleman, and I'd hate to make Gem dig his limo out of the snow for a second time today."

"I'm sure he keeps it in a garage," I growled.

Russo barked with laughter, then winked. "I am sure you're correct."

My fingers wrapped around my coffee mug as the door opened and another whoosh of wind whistled toward us, curling around all my extremities. "What do you think, Russo—really? Are we getting close?"

He gave me a tight smile. "We'll get him, Kate. This is the closest I've been to him. Between the two of us, he isn't getting away again."

"Am I early?" What I was about to say next was interrupted by the appearance of a bubbly blonde next to our table. Lassie pointed to my latte. "I thought you were going to buy my drink."

I tipped my chin toward the counter. "Get whatever you want and have my mother put it on my tab."

"I think this is my cue to take off." Russo stood. "I'm going to check in with Jimmy and Melinda."

"Do me a favor," I said as Lassie shuffled to the counter and Russo stood to leave. "Will you order a coffee for Melinda and bring it to her?"

"I thought that was your job."

"Yeah, but I've got to pay my mother with my hard-earned cash. You can expense your lattes."

"You still owe me for a busted shower curtain."

"And you owe me for the free show."

That settled our debate. Russo's cheeks turned a mild shade of tomato red as he sidled over to the counter and waited in line behind Lassie. By the time Lassie returned to the table, Russo had his collar turned up, a flat white in hand, and his body braced as he pushed the door open to the cold.

"He's so hot." Lassie gave a whimper the second the door clicked shut. "How do you keep your hands off him?"

I wrinkled my nose. "About that..."

She squealed. "You didn't?"

"It's not what you think," I said. "But I didn't exactly keep my hands off of him."

"Do tell."

"Did you see his black eye?"

"Oh, Kate—you *didn't*."

I gave an exaggerated wince.

"Poor guy," Lassie said. Then her face brightened. "But he stuck around, so maybe that's a sign there's hope after all?"

"No hope whatsoever. Anyway, speaking of special agents, I was hoping to talk to you about the case I'm working."

"You mean Leslie Rosehip? And the fact that she's dead?" Lassie met my gaze evenly. "Yeah, I heard about it. I'm basically a detective. Anyway, I know who did it. But I'm sure you already figured that out, right?"

"You do?"

"I do." Lassie sat back in her chair and smiled. "But you know if I dish, I get an exclusive."

"Whatever you want. If you're right." I raised my eyebrows. "Now, who do you think killed Leslie Rosehip?"

Chapter 23

"I imagine you have some sort of proof to explain how you know that Richard Hanson killed his fiancée?" I asked Lassie. "You wouldn't just be wildly guessing with such accusations, right?"

"I mean, I wouldn't exactly call it a guess," Lassie corrected. "More like an educated theory."

"Based on what?"

"Books." Lassie shrugged. "It's always the husband. I mean, technically Richard wasn't her husband yet... but he was well on his way. She bought her wedding dress. That basically means it's a done deal."

I expelled a huge breath. "You can't walk around accusing people of murder based on themes you've read in novels."

"Freedom of speech. I can accuse whoever I want. I mean, it's not like I wrote it on my blog—I just quickly mentioned it to you, my best friend and confidant. It's your job to figure out if I'm right or not."

"Okay, then let's talk about facts. Did you ever speak with Leslie?"

"I emailed her, but she never responded."

"What'd you email her about?"

Lassie's eyes lit up. "That's it! There's your proof."

"Where?"

"I emailed her because of the rumors."

"Hold my hand and walk me through this. What rumors?"

"The ones about her affair? You can't tell me you haven't heard."

"She was having an affair?"

"Supposedly. I just emailed her asking if it was true, and if she wanted to provide a statement for my blog either confirming or denying. She never responded. I didn't even get an auto reply from her publicity person."

"How rude," I said, sarcasm seeping out. "Someone didn't want to discuss their personal life for the entire world to see?"

"I know!" Lassie missed my dry tone completely. "So, what do you think? Was it true about an affair?"

"I didn't even know who she was until this morning. I don't have any information for you yet."

"But you will, right? You promised an exclusive."

"Yeah, if you gave me good information. All you've told me about are rumors."

"You wouldn't have known about the rumors if it weren't for me." Lassie shifted forward in her seat, her eyes flicking across the room as if whatever she wanted to say next was extremely private. "There is one more thing."

"Oh?"

"I'm not sure if you've noticed, but I'm pretty nosy."

"No," I drawled. "Get out of town."

She ignored my sarcasm again and lit up with a happy smile. "I really shouldn't be saying this because it's private, but I have a source—a good source—who saw Leslie leaving a club last night with a man."

"Does this source have a name?"

She narrowed her eyes at me. "She's trustworthy."

"Which club?"

"Rubies."

I struggled to keep my emotions under lock and key. "Okay, and do you have a time she was seen?"

"My source said it was around eleven p.m."

"Any description of the guy?"

"Tall and handsome, dark hair. I didn't recognize him."

"You?"

Lassie blushed. "Okay, so I don't have a source. I *am* the source."

"What? You were at Rubies last night?"

"I went to visit your sister," Lassie admitted, slumping in her seat. "She texted me and told me she got a new job at Alastair Gem's bar, and that she might have a story for me."

"Jane said she had a story for you? What sort of story?"

"I don't know. She wouldn't say anything when I got there. She said it was too early to tell, but she wanted me to come to Rubies and get a feel for the place and include a write up about it on my blog. I'm not really sure why."

My mind whirred. "Does the story have something to do with the club? Did she think something was wonky about the way it was being run? Why wouldn't she tell me about it?"

"To be honest, I just thought she'd spotted some B or C-list local celebs stopping by," Lassie said. "You wouldn't have cared about that, so maybe she wouldn't have told you."

"That's true, I guess."

"That wouldn't have been wrong, either. I mean, if I'd gotten a snap of Leslie as she left with her hunky mystery man, it would have driven traffic like crazy to my blog. She would have been forced to respond to my email about affair rumors with a photo like that tucked in my back pocket."

"I was at Rubies last night, too—undercover work," I added quickly. "I didn't see you there."

"I didn't see you either, but I didn't stay for very long. I found another blogger, and we ended up having a chat in the VIP section for a while. Maybe I missed you? I left right after Leslie, actually, around eleven. That's how I saw her."

"I didn't get to the VIP section," I said. "I was in the back discussing security footage."

"You're the only woman I know who goes to a club and is more interested in the security tapes than the hot single guys."

"It's my cross to bear."

"Do you think Richard might actually have killed Leslie?" Lassie asked. "I mean, if she *was* going off with random men, her fiancé couldn't have been happy about it. Plus, he's rich and powerful, and sometimes men like that are... you know... assholes."

"I've got nothing to tie Richard to the murder."

"Oh! Maybe it was the mystery man? I wish I'd gotten a good look at his face. I only saw him from behind. I was a few margaritas in by then, so I wouldn't exactly trust me with a sketch artist."

"I'm not going to pair you with an artist."

"You could at least pretend I'm being helpful."

"You are being helpful. This is the first confirmed sighting we have of Leslie leaving the club with someone just before her death."

"Wait a second..." Lassie mused. "If this mystery man was the last person to see her alive, why hasn't he come forward? He's got to have heard the news, especially if he spent the night—or part of it—with Leslie. She's a local celeb—her death is already in the news. Unless..."

I waited while Lassie pieced the puzzle together.

Finally, it clicked, and she glanced up at me, her lips pursed in surprise. "Do you think it could have been the mystery man?"

"As far as I'm concerned, it could have been anyone," I confirmed. "We need evidence. Speaking of, I have to get going. Autopsy's almost done."

"There's no chance I can sit in on the results, is there?"

"That's a negative. I'd get chewed out by Russo if any of this went public. It didn't go over so hot last time you started blogging about murder."

"That sucks."

"Hey, I already promised you an exclusive when it's all over."

"You and your sister, I swear," Lassie huffed. "So far, all I've seen for my efforts are a big fat latte. Actually, a skinny latte. I'm on a diet. You've been hanging out with all these hot dudes lately, and it's getting me ready to look for a boyfriend again. Maybe I'll meet someone at Rubies."

"That is an awful place to meet someone these days." I stood. "Take my advice and stay away from Gem's club."

"What about your sister? She works there."

I felt my lips straighten into a thin line. "Right."

"Sore spot. Sorry."

"I'll call you later, okay?" I paused before stepping away from the table. "On second thought, you want to run a story?"

"When do I not?"

"What about mentioning the fact that you've got an anonymous source who saw Leslie leaving with an unidentified male on the night she was killed?" I suggested. "Maybe someone else saw something and will come forward."

Lassie's eyes twinkled, and she pulled her handbag from underneath the table. "You got it, chica. I'll forward you any responses. Then again, if you'd just read my blog already, you'd see them for yourself."

"I'll take the SparkNotes version," I said. "You're a pal."

"Love you too," she said. "And by the way, if you decide not to have a go with that agent, pass my blog information along to him, will you? Or better yet, my phone number? Tell him I won't give him a black eye."

Chapter 24

Melinda sipped her flat white as she gathered me, Jimmy, and Russo into her office like a pack of little ducklings. She ushered us onto her couches and chairs and waited until we were completely still and silent before she spoke.

"I'll make this quick," Melinda said. "Overall, my analysis shows that the likelihood we are dealing with one killer for our last two victims—and more, if we include Russo's case files—is very high."

"We suspected that," I said. "But what makes you so sure?"

"Leslie was restrained at the wrists like the other girls. The markings are consistent. This man uses the same instrument to bind his girls."

"I'm guessing there wasn't any DNA evidence to help us out on this one?"

She shook her head. "Not yet. We're still running a few fibers in the lab, but he's careful—and getting more careful each time. He's learning."

"But everyone makes mistakes," I said. "And it turns out I have a source who saw Leslie Rosehip leaving Rubies with an unidentified man last night around eleven p.m."

"That's just before she was killed," Jimmy said. "I thought she didn't have a stamp showing that she was at the club?"

Melinda shook her head in agreement. "No stamp."

"She was led directly into the VIP section," I said. "They don't stamp for VIPs."

Russo snorted and gave a shake of his head. "I should've known."

"It's likely she met her killer there," I said. "I'm going to review security footage with Gem this afternoon. Hopefully he had a camera pointed at the main entrance. All we need is one shot of Leslie with this mystery man, and we might have our guy."

"What about the fiancé?" Jimmy asked. "Russo said he might be good for it."

"We can't rule him out," I agreed. "Russo and I are headed to interview him after this."

"It's also been suggested that the fiancé had the funds to hire a killer," Russo said. "Asha is checking into his financials to see if she can follow the money."

"Good," I said. "But that scenario still seems unlikely to me. What are the chances a hired killer would be smart enough to mimic a killer to throw us off his scent? Why would he need to do that? Especially since Melinda's saying we're dealing with one and the same murderer."

"I just said it's statistically likely the killer is the same across these cases," Melinda said. "There is room for error."

"Richard should be easy enough to alibi-out for the out-of-state murders," Russo said. "If we know he was in Minnesota during those times, it won't necessarily clear him of Leslie's murder, but it will rule out the theory that he could be our serial killer."

"I'm on it." Jimmy heaved himself to his feet. "I'll talk to Asha. Keep me posted with the Hanson and Gem interviews. I'm going to dig through the files Asha pulled on all the employees at Rubies."

"Anything else?" I stood. "Russo and I have an appointment with Richard at one. With the slick roads, it'll take us a good half hour to get to his place."

Russo stood. "Then let's get this party started."

THE DRIVE TO RICHARD Hanson's house wasn't a difficult one... on a normal day. To get from West Seventh to Capitol Hill was a jaunt I'd made many times in under ten minutes.

But the "hill" part of Capitol Hill was wildly slippery due to the recent precipitation, and the cars that had parked on either side of the narrow streets looked more like snow piles than vehicles. Russo skidded out of control more than once, and I kept a firm grip on the passenger's side handle.

By the time he pulled over onto the wide shoulder of Summit, I was more than a little sweaty. Russo exhaled a breath he appeared to have been holding during the entire commute.

"Why do you live here again?" he asked. "Please, do tell."

"It grows on you."

"Does it?"

"The cold keeps you young."

"Does it? Because I almost just died five times in the last twenty minutes. I must have aged twenty years on the drive over. I probably have gray hair."

"It's good to keep your blood pumping."

"I prefer other methods of getting my blood pumping."

"On that note," I said, pulling on the door handle. "Let's get going. What's our plan with Richard?"

"You can take the lead if you like," Russo said. "I don't think he did it."

"How generous of you."

"I didn't argue about you taking Gem alone this afternoon, did I? Gem feels far more reasonable to me for these murders than Hanson."

"Is that Russo-the-agent or Russo-the-person talking?"

"Can't it be both?" Russo kicked at a pile of snow and shook his head. "I think the man's an idiot."

"Why's Gem an idiot?"

"Because I don't like him."

"Ah. Makes total sense."

I raised a hand as we reached the front steps and knocked on the door of the old, stately mansion. When a figure pulled the door open, I greeted him with a thin smile. "Mr. Hanson? I'm Detective Rosetti, this is Agent Russo."

"You're a fed?" Richard's eyes were quick and cunning as he scanned Russo. "I thought the feds and local cops didn't like working together."

"What made you think that?" Russo asked.

Hanson smirked. "I watch TV. Can I help you?"

Richard Hanson wore a navy suit and a starched white shirt with gold cuff links and a thick watch that likely cost more than a month of my salary. He looked startlingly put together for a man who'd supposedly just lost the love of his life.

"We're here about your fiancé, Leslie Rosehip," I said. "We are so sorry for your loss."

"Thank you," he said in a clipped voice. "It's obviously a huge loss. In fact, I was just headed over to the Rosehip residence as we have a great deal of preparations to get started on for funeral arrangements. I hope we can keep this quick."

I glanced at Russo as Hanson stepped back from the door and gestured for us to follow him inside. Russo gave an exaggerated chomp of his gum and rolled his eyes to the ceiling as we stepped into the entryway. Distaste was barely disguised on his face.

Richard Hanson's house looked like it'd once been a model for the Parade of Homes. The outside was charmingly old but appropriately maintained while the inside, despite several exposed brick walls, was done up with modern appliances and decor. If I didn't know a man lived here, I'd think the house had been staged for sale.

We entered a small sitting room across from a neat-as-a-pin office and sat on chairs that crinkled from lack of use. A serving tray that I was certain had never been touched sat on the table before us.

"Do you need water?" Richard asked, looking around, as if he wouldn't know where to find a glass of the stuff if we said yes. "Or can we get started?"

"Let's get started," I said. "I'm going to start with a difficult question, Mr. Hanson. I know it's a sensitive subject, but—"

"You want to know my alibi," he interrupted. "Look, Ms.—"

"Detective," I said. "Detective Rosetti."

"Right. I'm obviously devastated by the loss of my fiancé, but I'm not a fragile vase—you do not have to handle me with child gloves. I understand this is a murder investigation."

I glanced at Russo who looked torn between the former distaste and a new sense of amusement.

"Of course it's a murder investigation," Richard continued. "What else would it be? My fiancé didn't exactly kill herself. And neither did I, which is what you've come here to find out. Leslie and I were in love."

"Thanks for that." I crossed my arms over my chest and leaned forward. "Then if I may... Where were you last night between the hours of ten p.m. and one a.m.?"

"Home." Richard gave a taunting smile. "Alone."

"I don't suppose you have anything or anyone to verify that," I said. "Internet activity, phone calls from your landline, a visitor stopping by?"

"No."

Richard was toying with us. My nerves were already frayed, and it took every last hint of self-restraint to not reach across the table and give him a good hard shake.

"Face it, detective," Richard said. "I'm guessing you're looking for a man who's killed more than once. The feds don't get involved for a simple murder case. You're from the East Coast?"

Richard looked to Russo, who snapped his gum in response.

"Originally, I'm from Texas," Russo eventually drawled. "But I don't tell everyone that."

I swiveled my head to look at him.

Russo winked. "You never asked," he said under his breath as he sat back in his seat. "The accent faded years ago."

I forced myself to pay attention to Richard, who watched our exchange with a less-than-amused smirk. "Mr. Hanson—"

"Is it a serial killer?" he asked. "Like I said, I watch TV. There's something about serial killers, murders crossing state lines, that sort of thing, before feds get involved, right? I mean, it's not because my fiancé was famous. She might have thought she was, but in reality, she was just popular on Instagram."

"That's not what I've heard recently," I said. "It appears your fiancé was gaining in popularity."

"I suppose that's what happens when she posts pictures of the breasts I bought her online."

"You didn't approve of Leslie's..." I struggled to call it a career. "Hobbies?"

"It was a lifestyle," Richard said. "And no, I wasn't a huge fan. But she would have settled down once we were married. Her father and I would have made sure of it."

I swallowed hard.

"Look, I cared for Leslie, I really did," Richard said. "But were we soulmates? Star crossed lovers? No. Could we have fallen in love down the line? Maybe."

"If that's the case, why did you propose to her?"

"Family ties." There was no hesitation in Richard's voice. "I get along well with her father. Leslie needed a husband and money, and I needed a young and beautiful wife who'd complete the picture for me. It was a win-win all around."

"Mr. Hanson, I apologize for the sensitive nature of the following question," I said. "But did you have any reason to suspect your fiancé was seeing another man?"

"Man?" He gave a short laugh. "Try men."

I blinked in surprise. "Oh?"

"I didn't know for sure, but I assumed. I expected it, even." Richard shifted back against the couch. "I work a lot. Long hours, extensive travel. You've seen Leslie's social media—at least, I assume you have if you're any sort of detective. You see the sorts of things she posts, the types of places she spends her time."

"That doesn't mean she was seeing other men necessarily."

"The texts, the late nights," he said. "It really didn't take a genius to figure it out. If you told me she'd had sex with someone consensually before she died, I wouldn't be surprised."

"Did the thought of Leslie with other men anger you?"

"Look, Miss—er, detective," Richard said, running a hand tiredly over his face. "I know another girl was found dead a few days back or so. Is there a link between them? If so, I didn't kill her. I was in New York at the time. I remember reading about it online."

"You didn't answer the question," I said, but he had a very good point. If we truly suspected Richard Hanson for the murder of his fiancé and the other women, all we'd need to do was wait for Asha to confirm his whereabouts and we'd have our answer. "Did it make you upset?"

"Mildly, at first," Richard admitted. "But I had a few frank conversations with her father. Nathan assured me her wandering ways would stop once we were married."

"How did he know?"

"He has ways of controlling his daughter."

"Like cutting off her money supply?"

He eyed me cautiously. "That'd be one way."

"And you planned to do the same thing once you were married?"

He smartly didn't answer. Which was answer enough.

"Right."

"You don't understand," Richard said. "Women like Leslie need a firm, guiding hand to show them down the right path. She'd have thanked me a few years from now."

I looked darkly at Richard. "Thank you for your time. We may have a few follow up questions. We'll also be checking into your alibi. I hope you understand."

Richard rose. "Of course."

"May I use your restroom before we leave?" I stood and thumbed over my shoulder.

Annoyance crossed Richard's face, but he gestured toward the hall. "Take a left. It's just through the kitchen."

Russo gave me a questioning glance, but I ignored it and took off down the hallway. I passed through a sparkling marble and stainless steel-covered kitchen to a small bathroom in the hallway.

I flushed the toilet a second later and washed my hands, though I hadn't used the spotless facilities. I'd just wanted a second alone in Richard Hanson's house. I needed to gather my thoughts, to calm the anger bubbling beneath the surface. A part of me wished Richard was responsible for the murders so I could arrest his smug face. But Jack Russo was correct—Richard didn't feel right.

When a sufficient amount of time had passed, and I was able to stop white-knuckling the counter, I made my way out of the bathroom and back through the kitchen. A glittering card on the fridge caught my eye, but the name on the front halted me in my tracks.

Alastair Gem.

I came to a dead stop, my heart pounding.

A quick scan told me it was a personal invitation to the Christmas party Gem had mentioned to me in his offices. The thick cardstock looked to be made of pure platinum and adorned with diamonds. I was sure they weren't real, but it did the trick of catching my eye.

Voices from the sitting area shook me back to reality. I rejoined Russo and Richard, finding them discussing the recent snowfall with a severe lack of enthusiasm.

I cleared my throat to alert them of my presence. "Richard, I have one more question. Do you know where your fiancé was last night?"

He shrugged. "Some club. She probably posted it on Instagram."

"She did," I said. "But had she told you beforehand?"

"Maybe, I don't know. We talked briefly in the afternoon, but if she told me, I forgot."

"Do you know Alastair Gem?"

Richard's gaze flicked between us. "What's this about?"

"I couldn't help but notice an invitation to a Christmas party on your refrigerator."

"That wasn't mine," he said. "It was Leslie's."

"Why'd she stick it on your fridge?"

"Because she wanted to show it off? She was obsessed with Gem." Richard shrugged. "Before you ask, no—I didn't care about him. Gem's unattainable. Leslie just... had this fantasy in her head that if she met him, he'd fall for her. You know, a celebrity crush. It was stupid. But the party was all she talked about for weeks."

"Were you going with her?"

"She didn't invite me," he said. "I would put a cramp in her ability to hook Gem with her manicured nails—that I also paid for."

"And that—"

"For God's sake, it didn't make me mad," Richard said. "I have better things to do than sit around at stupid holiday parties. I have a trip scheduled to meet with investors in Charlotte during that time, anyway."

"Thank you," I said. "Last thing—had your fiancé ever met Gem in person? Did she have a reason to fantasize about him aside from what she might have read on the news?"

"His wallet, I suppose," Richard said. "His fame didn't hurt. People like Leslie and me, we want the best. I was the best she could get; she was the best I could get. We know our limits, detective. The answer is no. She hadn't met him—at least not to my knowledge. If she had, she certainly would have left me for him. Frankly, I wouldn't have blamed her."

Richard quickly showed us out before I could pepper him with more questions. Russo and I made our way to the car and climbed in, each falling lost in our own thoughts until we were well on our way back to the precinct.

"He's a dick," Russo said.

"I wanted to slap cuffs on him." I gave a wry shake of my head. "Poor Leslie."

"I dunno," Russo said. "In a weird way, maybe the two deserved one another. Speaking of, do you need a ride to Gem's?"

"What's that supposed to mean?"

"I was just thinking about Leslie's fantasy about Gem."

"Sure you were."

"About that ride?"

"Yes," I said through gritted teeth. "I'm meeting him at his office downtown."

"I bet he can't wait."

"Would you like another black eye?"

Russo chuckled and flicked his blinker to turn down the on-ramp. The highways were sloshy but faster than the back-roads. It only took us twenty minutes to reach Gem Industries. Russo pulled up out front and parked in the same spot he had before, flashing his badge once again at the valet.

"I'll wait for you."

"That's not necessary," I said. "I'll call an Uber."

"You mean, you'll take Gem's limo?"

I shrugged.

Russo pinned me with his gaze. "Am I interrupting something by waiting?"

"Don't be ridiculous."

"Good," he said. "Then I'll wait."

I heaved a sigh and climbed out of the car. I stopped when Russo called after me.

"Kate," he said, catching my attention with my first name. "One more thing."

I popped my head back through the rolled-down window. "What is it?"

Russo tapped his fingers against the steering wheel and stared aimlessly through the windshield for so long I thought he'd forgotten my presence. I cleared my throat.

Eventually, he turned back toward me. "I don't know what you have going on with Gem, and frankly, I shouldn't care. But I just think it's worthwhile to point out his name keeps cropping up in the investigation."

I patted the window. "Right. Well, you have nothing to worry about."

"I'm just saying that in my experience, coincidences don't exist."

"You're forgetting that Gem has an alibi."

"Gem has a lot of money."

"Yeah, but he can't be in two places at once."

"No, but he can get to and from places quickly. Buy alibis. Eyewitnesses. He's smart. Probably smarter than both of us. Is there a chance he's playing with us? I don't know the answer to that, but I think it pays to mention it. Be careful."

"Russo, I—"

"I'm just thinking aloud," he continued. "The timeline is tight. Could he, after dropping you off at the hotel, somehow have managed to meet up with Leslie? Maybe he had someone else dispose of her body."

"It's a stretch."

"Just think about it. The timeline is tight. Time of death can be tricky to pinpoint, and maybe Gem's using it to his advantage. It's smart—using the lead detective as an alibi."

I considered Russo's theory. While I hated to admit it, he did bring up a valid point. A bit of doubt crept into my mind. After all, hadn't Gem been the one pursuing me from the start? *Why?* A nobody-detective and a billionaire-playboy didn't belong together in any world except fiction. He had shown up at my door last night and again this morning. For no reason whatsoever.

I didn't need to speak for Russo to see the reality clicking in my gaze. Before he could offer any more delightful insights, I left him sitting alone in the car with the window down while I stomped toward the illustrious building that belonged to Alastair Gem—one of the most complicated men I'd ever met.

The biggest question of all loomed in my head.

What was Gem's end game?

And more curiously, why had he roped me into it?

Chapter 25

Gem Industries was even more impressive the second time around. The Christmas lights and festive decor had exploded exponentially since I'd last been inside the lobby. Sparkles dripped from every surface. Candlelight set off an alluring ambiance as light flickered from every glittering surface. It felt like Santa's Workshop had met Breakfast at Tiffany's.

I made my way up to the front desk and leaned against the counter. It was the same woman as last time manning her post.

"Hi," I said, flipping my badge out. "You might remember me, I'm—"

"Hello, detective," Ms. Karp said crisply. "You may proceed upstairs."

"Um—" I glanced down at my badge. The receptionist hadn't even flicked her gaze at it. "Okay. Is Mr. Gem—"

"He's expecting you."

I made my way through the lobby to the tune of high heels clicking against marble floors as women and men shuffled through their busy days. While I didn't claim to be sentimental in the slightest, or even festive, I paused at the inner atrium to study the enormous Christmas tree display.

After I shook myself free from the mesmerizing holiday glitz, I completed my trek to the elevator. Feeling a bit stupid, I stepped inside and hesitated, wondering how I was supposed to find Gem. Surely the elevator wouldn't go up to the penthouse without special permissions. Gem had swiped something last time, and—

Mid-thought, my stomach lurched as the elevator ascended. When it stopped, the door inched open, and I found myself with a view of the magnificent city skyline in the distance. From this vantage point, it looked like someone had shaken the snow globe that was the Twin Cities and let the dust settle in a stunning, white blanket over the twisty roads and arching skyscrapers.

I watched for a long minute until the sound of my name startled me from the view. I spun around, finding Gem standing not three feet from me.

"How'd you know..." I hesitated as the monitor on the wall behind him flashed with security footage of his buildings. "I see you've got an eagle eye view."

"I like to know what happens in my facilities." Gem spread his hands wide, a smile perched on his lips. "Did you enjoy the tree downstairs?"

"It's impressive."

"Detective..." Gem studied me. "Are you here as Detective Rosetti, or are you here as Kate?"

I cleared my throat. "Detective Rosetti."

A look passed over Gem's face. "What can I do for St. Paul's finest?"

"I'd like to take you up on your offer to view the security footage from Rubies last night."

"Ah, of course. Would you prefer to look at the tapes here or have me send them over to your tech team?"

I reached out a hand and rested it on Gem's wrist. "Thank you."

Gem studied my hand, and I wondered if he felt the same warmth that I was feeling. I withdrew my hand with a snap, causing Gem to give an amused chuckle.

"Did you know Leslie Rosehip?" I asked.

"Back to business." Gem sighed, considered, and gave a small shake of his head. "I don't believe so."

My gut clenched. "I'm sorry, but I don't believe you."

"Oh?"

"She had a personalized invitation to your Christmas party."

Gem gave a knowing, relieved smile. "Ah, that."

"Yeah, that."

"Kate, you can't believe that I personalize those invitations. I have a PR firm who handles the logistics. They take a guest list from me and tag that onto the guest list they create for me."

"How long is this guest list?"

"My *personal* guest list was about four people long and included Wes Remington and yourself."

I grinned. "Yeah, right."

"I invited you, didn't I?"

"My invitation must have gotten lost in the mail."

"You don't need an invitation," he said with a wink. "Especially not if you come as my date?"

"Oh, no. No, no, Gem. You've got the wrong idea."

"I'm hoping persistence will pay off. Maybe once the case is closed?"

"How long was the guest list?"

"I don't know, Kate. A thousand? Maybe more? I didn't see the list, nor do I personally know everyone on it. If Leslie Rosehip was invited, I assure you I had nothing to do with it. It was just business."

"Like this meeting?"

"Excuse me?"

"It seems that you like to blur the lines between business and pleasure at times."

"I would've said I wished you'd let those lines blur a bit further, but that would obviously be too forward of me." Gem's voice had turned a tad frosty. "What's your question, detective?"

"I'm just trying to understand why your name keeps cropping up in my murder investigation."

"Again, your question?"

"No question, an observation."

Gem's eyes had lost all touches of amusement. He'd turned into a polished, hardened businessman. "If you're going to accuse me of something, detective, just do it."

"I'm not accusing you of anything."

"Do you think I had these women killed? Paid someone to do it? I'd ask you why, detective. What do I get out of it?"

I bit my tongue.

"Sex? No, I certainly don't need to pay for that... or kill for it. Thrill? Also no. I have enough of that in my daily life, especially now that I have the pleasure of you breathing down my neck every time a woman in this city is murdered." Gem turned, walked toward the once-again-empty receptionist's desk. "For fun? No. I prefer my fun to be with the living. So, detective, what's my motive?"

I didn't have a response prepared, mostly because Gem had a point. He was good at arguing—smart, cool, collected. It was equal parts frightening and impressive.

"I'm sorry to have taken up so much of your time," I said finally. "I'll be out of your hair shortly—if I could just peek at the security footage quickly?"

Gem rapped his fingers against the receptionist's desk and stared behind it, as if he wanted to call someone for help. At the last second, he turned away, muttering under his breath. He strode toward a door that blended into a wood paneled wall on the far side of the room.

"Well," he said, "Are you coming?"

I hurried after him, watching curiously as he rested his hand against a keypad on the wall and a hidden door slid open. Behind it was a spiral staircase that we climbed to another level.

This time, we reached an office that was far more personal. Three of the walls were windows, giving us a stunning eagle-eye view of the cities and suburbs beyond. A wet bar sparkling with crystal decanters and colorful liquors sat against the non-windowed wall, along with a sleek glass desk and no less than three oversized monitors.

Gem slid easily behind the desk and clicked a few times. His hands moved expertly over the keyboard, telling me he actually knew what he was doing on the computer. He wasn't just the talking head of the company, he was the blood, sweat, and tears behind it.

I tried to hide my impressed expression as his fingers flew and windows opened and shut on his computer. While he was busy, I studied the room beyond the desk. Though minimal and sleek, it contained a few telling personal elements.

Aside from the wet bar, Gem had a dartboard behind his computer with a clear lane to toss darts from across the room. On a shelf sat a photo of him and Wes. Next to it was an old, grainy wedding photo in black and white. It was the latter that drew my attention.

"Your parents?" I asked, nodding toward it.

"Here's the footage." Gem's eyes flicked to the photo, but his finger crooked for me to join his side. "What time stamp would you like me to start the tapes from?"

I moved to get a better view of the screen and let my eyes focus on the nine different squares that showed vantage points from a variety of cameras.

"Ten p.m.," I said. "But can you make it go... you know, a little faster? Not real time?"

"And here, I thought you'd want to sit next to me and watch security footage for the next four hours," he said dryly. A few clicks later, and the images progressed at a speed faster than reality.

We watched in silence. I focused on the cameras that had views of the front door and the back hallway. I saw myself and Gem enter the building, but I didn't see any sign of Leslie as the cameras rolled closer to eleven p.m.

"If someone's a VIP, what entrance do they go in?" I asked. "Is there a different one not covered by cameras?"

"No," Gem said. "They'd have come through the front door."

"Back up then, will you? To the opening."

"But we haven't finished through the ending."

"I need to see something."

Gem made it happen. I watched the steady stream of guests as they entered Rubies. I watched Bobby pick his nose, scratch at his privates, and stare too long at female guests with short dresses.

"You need new security," I told Gem.

"Find me a bouncer who behaves better, and I'll be happy to swap for you."

"There she is," I said finally, jabbing a finger at the screen. "Pause?"

Gem stopped the tape. He studied the woman on screen for a long moment.

"Do you recognize her?" I prompted.

He studied her for an even longer moment. "No," he said finally. "Not that I remember. The caveat is that I meet a lot of people. It's possible we've met, but it would've been nothing more than a fleeting handshake at best."

That matched what everyone else had told me about Leslie, so I nodded, gestured for him to play the tape. I saw Lassie approach the front of the line, trying and failing to engage Bobby in a round of small talk. She waved to a friend quickly after, and then got lost in the throng of people in the main room.

"Okay, back to where we left off," I said. "I want to see if we can catch who she left with."

Gem did as I asked and jumped forward in time. I watched as I confronted Jane at the bar. Then as Gem and I climbed the stairs. We disappeared from view when we entered the office.

While we were inside talking with Wes, I watched the front doors. Just as Lassie had said, she left a few minutes before eleven. I squinted closer, asked Gem to rewind a few times.

"What are you looking for?" he asked on the third run-through. "Can I zoom in somewhere?"

"I have a source who places Leslie as leaving the club around eleven."

"Maybe it's ten minutes later. Time can be... elusive in a place like Rubies."

I shook my head. "It would've been almost exact."

"Where's your source? Do you see her on the screen?"

"There she is!" I pointed toward a small, blurred figure that had to be Leslie Rosehip. "That's her! Who is that at her side?"

Gem hit pause and we both leaned in closer. I was aware of his breath grazing my hand, and his arm brushing against mine. If he noticed, however, he didn't acknowledge it.

"I can't recognize him," Gem said. "Even if I did know him. It's like..."

"It's like he knows where the cameras are," I said grimly. "Besides you and Wes, who knew there were cameras being installed?"

"Everyone who works for us," Gem said. "As well as the techs who installed the cameras. And, of course, anyone with two eyes who can see the camera head. It's not invisible."

"That narrows it down."

"I didn't know it was supposed to be a secret." Gem studied the image closer. "I'd say it's definitely a male."

The figure leaving with Leslie did appear to be a male. He was tall and bulky, though it was impossible to say if he had any other defining features. He wore a fedora tilted at just the right angle to shield his face from view and a puffy winter coat that interfered with our ability to guesstimate an approximate weight or physique.

"You don't recognize him?" I pressed, my voice taking on a desperate quality. "He must work for you, Gem. Take a look again."

"I would help you if I could, but I don't hire every employee at my club. That's what I have Wes for. He takes care of all the logistical details including keeping the doors open and the place staffed. I own hundreds of companies. I can barely keep the names of my personal staff straight."

"Can you get him on the phone?"

"Wes?" Gem muttered something under his breath, but a few seconds later, Wes's face appeared on the large computer screen.

I looked over Gem's shoulder and gave a wave. Wes didn't look thrilled to see me.

"What's she doing in your office?" Wes asked Gem. "I hope it's not about that case. Again."

"This is a business call. I'm going to share my screen," Gem said to Wes. "Tell me if you recognize anyone in this frame."

After a moment, Wes leaned forward and appeared to be studying his monitor. "I see Bobby in the corner there," he said finally. "The bouncer."

"Yes, we see Bobby too," I said exasperatedly. Unfortunately, Bobby didn't appear to be paying attention to anything except the leggy blonde he was chatting up at the doorway. I doubted he'd remember the man in the photo. "Anyone else?"

"That's a nice fedora," Wes said. "But it sort of blocks the guy's face. Is that who you're trying to find? If so, I'm sorry. I've got nothing for you."

"Do any of your employees wear a fedora?" I asked. "Or look to be about that size?"

"You mean a tall male with a thick winter coat?" he said. "Yeah. About ninety percent of the guys I hire fit that description. And I'm sorry, but I don't pay attention to headwear when my employees are off the clock."

I blew out a sigh. "How about the girl behind him?"

"The one where you can just make out a piece of her nose and a curl of her hair?" Wes shook his head. "Sorry. I don't recognize her either."

Gem disconnected, looked at me. "Happy?"

"I'd be happier if he had a different answer. Let's continue rolling the tapes."

Gem clicked *Play*. A few minutes later, we left Wes's office and headed outside. The next minute, however, caught my attention. There was movement in the hallway as Wes left his office, glanced around, then made his way downstairs. He disappeared through a door leading into the back alley.

"Where's he going?" I muttered. "Any ideas?"

"Smoke break?" Gem asked. "Fresh air? I don't know."

"Does he smoke?"

"No."

"Can you get him on the phone again?"

"I'll tell you what, detective. I'm not questioning my best friend and business partner. If you have an issue with him, take it up on your own time."

I straightened at the crispness in his tone.

"I think I've been very cooperative," Gem said. "You don't have a warrant, and yet we're here, reviewing my security footage."

"Thank you." I expelled a breath. "We'll take it from here. Do you mind sending these over to my colleague, Asha? We'll get the warrant to you as soon as it's finalized."

Gem rose from behind his desk without answering. He led me down the spiral staircase and into the lobby where the elevator doors magically opened before us. A woman had appeared behind the receptionist's desk and was chatting quietly into her headset as her fingers clicked rapidly against a keyboard.

"I suppose this is it for now," Gem said. "Thank you for stopping by."

"Gem—"

"Good evening, detective."

I took a deep breath, let it out slowly. Stepping into the elevator, I turned to face him. "I'll call you if anything else comes up."

The doors slid silently shut. And with it went any hope of a friendly working relationship with Alastair Gem.

"Nice work, detective," I muttered to myself.

I'd alienated one of the most powerful men in the cities, accused him of murder when I was his best hope of an alibi. My gut feeling told me he wasn't behind the killings, so why couldn't I let down my guard and be civil in our dealings?

The police chief, the mayor, and the rest of the TC Task Force would certainly be appreciative of a good working relationship with Gem Industries.

But no. I'd upset Gem, his best friend, my sister, and the agent who was supposed to have my back on the case. I made my way through the lobby downstairs, the Christmas tree now leering at me with its glittering branches.

As I stepped into the outside frost, I couldn't help but see Gem's face, etched with disappointment, as I'd walked away from him.

"How'd it go?" Russo asked.

"I don't want to talk about it," I said. "Can you take me home? There's something I need to do."

Chapter 26

Russo didn't know that the thing I needed to do was laundry.

Or make a cup of coffee and sit—alone—and think.

Or eat a stack of saltine crackers with peanut butter and strawberry jam standing over the kitchen sink.

The washing machine tumbled Russo's clothes in the background while I munched on crackers and sipped coffee. My caffeine levels would be through the roof, but after a day of no sleep and a killer on the loose, my only path forward was to push through and sleep when I was dead. Or, hopefully, not dead, considering the current circumstances.

Most of the afternoon had blown past between my interviews with Richard and Gem. As I switched my laundry to the dryer, I glanced outside and saw the fingers of darkness reaching down from the heavens, ready to cloak the world in blackness yet again.

I returned to the kitchen table and studied the files before me. Again. And again, and again. When I'd asked Russo to bring me home, I'd wanted to go back to the beginning. Take a look at the case with fresh eyes. I was more confident than ever that all the clues were there. All the pieces of the puzzle were waiting to be put together. I just couldn't find the missing piece.

Unfortunately, it hadn't helped as much as I'd hoped. After my work today, I had thought revisiting the case files would trigger something I hadn't noticed before. While reading through it all again had been interesting, none of the information had cracked anything wide open. It was there, I knew it. I just couldn't find it.

The more I lingered with my thoughts, however, the more anxious I felt. As the dryer thumped through Russo's sweats, I brushed the saltine crumbs from the counter into the sink and brought my cup of coffee to the kitchen table where I sat and pulled out my phone.

Before I could talk myself out of it, I dialed my sister's number. I wasn't surprised it went to voicemail, but I didn't hang up right away. I stared at the phone for a minute as if it'd tell me what to say. When I wasn't hit by any such bolt of inspiration, I hung up and typed an apology message to Jane. I signed off by asking her to call me when she got the chance.

Five minutes of staring at my phone didn't grant me a response, so I pushed it away. As I stood, however, it rang. I leapt for it and hit answer before I realized it wasn't Jane, but Asha.

"What are you doing?" I watched the screen on my phone as Asha's face popped up, exposing the shaved side of her head. "Why can't you call me like a normal person?"

"I am!"

"But I can see you. Can you see me?"

"I can," she said patiently. "It's called a *video* chat. Video is this newfangled thing where you can see live images—"

"I know what a video call is," I said roughly. "I meant... I'm at home. What if I was in the bathroom?"

"Trust me, sweetie, you're not my type. Also, why would you answer a video call naked?"

"I didn't know I was answering this one clothed! I thought it was a regular phone call. So, do you have something for me or what?"

"Something-s," she said. "Emphasis on the plural."

"Oh, finally. I need something."

"Aneta Bila," she said. "That's the name of Jane Doe."

"I take it she's not from around here?"

"Czech heritage," she said. "She bounced around Europe for a while before she came to America. I think she was in Russia before she came here—probably her link to the new country."

"Any way to tell if she was brought over voluntarily?"

"I don't know the answer to that, but I do know that she lived in a house around here." Asha rattled off an address. "When I researched that location, it pinged in our system. We've been over there a few times for investigations—seems to be a popular place for working girls to stay."

"You're a genius."

"I know," Asha said. "And you haven't heard it all. Bobby, you know, the bouncer?"

"What about him?"

"Two cash deposits hit his account lately. Five thousand dollars each time. They coincide to the mornings after the murders. One just hit a few hours ago and triggered my search."

"Someone's paying him off for something."

"That'd be my guess."

"Anything else?"

"That's not enough?"

"Thanks, Asha. I'll follow up and Jimmy and Russo can catch up later."

Asha's face disappeared from my phone as she disconnected the call. I putzed around the house for the next twenty minutes until the laundry buzzed. I quickly took the clothes out and folded them, dropped them in a bag, and poured the rest of my cup of coffee in a to-go mug.

My coffee was cold by the time I finished the arduous process of shoveling my car out of its snowy grave. When I eventually climbed inside, I cranked the heat up and clapped my hands together until feeling returned in my fingers. Then, I made quick phone calls to Russo and Jimmy.

I got Russo's voicemail and briefly wondered what he was so busy doing that he wouldn't take my call. Instead of dwelling on Russo's schedule, I moved on and got ahold of Jimmy to let him know where I was headed. I asked him to fill Russo in if he appeared at the precinct before I had a chance to connect with him.

The drive to the St. Paul address Asha had sent me was a quick one. I tried Russo again and got no answer. Jimmy had texted me to say he was on his way over, so I texted back letting him know I'd get started, and he could join when he arrived.

Climbing out of the car, I studied the snow-swept front yard of the rundown single-family home. The front porch was crumbling. The windows were old, and I could feel gusty air whistling through the house before I ever stepped foot inside. Climbing past an overgrown dead bush that had fallen across the pathway, I shivered. The only sign of life was a cigarette ashtray on the front porch that was filled to the brim, some of the butts still lit and smoking.

I raised a hand and knocked on a porch door that had more holes than screen. It was answered a moment later by a woman with a baby on her hip, a cigarette perched between her lips.

"Nicole?" Asha had sent over the details on the house title, and I relayed the name she'd given me. When she didn't answer, I spoke more clearly and slowed down. "Do you own the house? Are you Nicole?"

"Maybe," she drawled in a thick eastern European accent. "Why you ask?"

The infant in her arms reached for the cigarette, and she brushed his hand away. The poor kid only had one sock on, and he kicked in frustration and swiped again. Again, she brushed his hand away.

"Should we go inside?" I asked. "I don't want your little guy to get cold."

"We're fine. Who do you want?"

"I'm Detective Rosetti with the TC Task Force, and I'm looking for Aneta Bila—her last residence was listed to be here."

Recognition clicked in her eyes, then dulled. "I don't know her."

"Look, I'm not interested in your immigration status or any of your girls—I'm interested in Aneta and who she associated with."

"Aneta not here anymore," she said, expelling a breath that caused me to cough and wave smoke away. "She left a couple nights ago, never came back."

"That's why I'm here. Aneta was found dead a couple nights ago. I'm trying to find out what happened to her."

"Dead?" Nicole looked genuinely surprised. However, her surprise disintegrated into a dull expression that told me she'd had this news delivered to her before, and she'd grown numb to it. "I thought she'd met a man. She always talked about meeting someone."

"Was Aneta close to anyone here? Any of the other girls?"

"Just me."

I didn't believe Nicole, but I didn't want to push—not yet. "Then maybe you can tell me if she's been seeing anyone special lately?"

She shrugged. "Nobody special. At least, no paying customers. She was spending a few nights out and not pulling in any cash. So, maybe she was."

"Was what?"

"Seeing someone." Nicole shifted the child to her other hip. "What else would she be doing? She was going out but not coming back with any money. Maybe she discovered a friend."

"Where did Aneta like to go out?"

"Here and there," she said. "Bars, clubs. Wherever she could find work."

"She was at Rubies the night she died. Were you aware?"

"I don't care where they go, so long as they pay their rent."

"Of course." I rubbed at my forehead. "So, you don't have a name, or..."

"No names."

"Well, thanks for your help. If you think of anything else, please call me—"

"Why should I help you?" she interrupted. As she did, the baby nuzzled against her. She brushed hair out of his eyes in a sweetly tender gesture. "Aneta is already dead; she can't be helped. She needed help before, but your government didn't help us, so what can we do?"

"Aneta deserves closure. I'm trying to help her now—and girls like her. If we don't stop the killer, there will be more girls like her who end up dead."

Nicole sighed, still snuggling against the child. "Aneta did say one thing. There was a guy. I don't know anything about him, but I think he worked at a bar. Ruby? Something—I don't remember. I told her not to go back there but she didn't listen."

"I guess not."

"What can I say? It must have been love." A look darkened Nicole's expression. "We talked just before she died. I told her to come back with money or don't come back at all."

"I see. So, when she didn't come back, you thought she'd made her choice."

Nicole gave a firm nod. I didn't believe she'd have reported Aneta missing either way, but I did believe her story. It fit. And this confirmed that our pool of suspects had just shrunken to a finite number. If this man Aneta was seeing really did work at Rubies, we could find him. It would only be a matter of time.

The excitement in my gut grew. The caffeine buzzed, and my mind raced. We were getting close—I could feel it. A little more digging, and we'd get there. We just had to do it before he killed again.

"Thank you for your time. I appreciate you talking to me, and I know Aneta would be grateful. Do you know if she has any family in the area?"

"No family here." Nicole blew out smoke. "The girls who come through here have nothing."

"I'm sorry."

"Where will they bury her?"

"I'll find out and let you know. At the moment, her body is at the morgue if you'd like to see her..."

"No. Goodbye." Nicole must have decided the conversation was over because she blinked once, then closed the door in my face.

"Okay," I murmured under my breath. "Goodbye to you, too."

I glanced at my watch as I turned around. Neither Russo nor Jimmy had arrived. Pulling out my phone, I checked my messages hoping for a word from my sister.

There was nothing from Jane, but Russo had texted me that he'd talked to Jimmy and that they were on their way. I texted them both back telling them not to bother coming since I was done here. I told them to meet me at Rubies instead so we could poke around a bit more, put pressure on the fissures, get something—or someone—to talk.

I was so distracted after my conversation with Nicole that I didn't hear the footsteps approach. I didn't see the hooded figure beside me. I didn't notice that he was dressed in all black with a full winter mask pulled down over his face, obscuring his features, until it was too late.

I did, however, hear the click of a switchblade as the knife snapped to attention. By the time I swiveled around, the blade glinted against the soft glow of streetlights. My fist was ready, but he was faster.

He had the knife to my throat before I could call for help, and his other hand pressing against my windpipe so the only sound I could emit was a strangled, guttural groan.

Russo, I thought ironically. The man wedged himself into every aspect of the case, but the second I needed him, he wasn't around.

A low voice spoke in my ear. "A word, and you die."

The darkness of early evening blurred any identifying features. The masked man wore sunglasses to cover his eyes, along with a thick hat and gloves. His jacket was incredibly bulky. The only thing I knew for sure was that he was taller than me and weighed more. He was probably stronger than me, too, but he'd had the element of surprise on his side, so it wasn't exactly a fair fight.

"I can make this simple." He hissed. "Drop this case, and I'll leave town."

The man let up slightly on my windpipe, just enough to allow me to speak.

I swallowed, gasped for air. "Not a chance."

He threw me against my car hard enough so that my elbow cracked and pain shot up my arm. Nothing broke, but he'd rattled me good. I thought of Russo once more as my vision went blurry from lack of oxygen.

Finally, I managed another gasp of air which allowed my vision to return.

And somehow, in my desperation fueled by the images of two young, dead women, I found the strength to swing. The impact of my punch wasn't anything compared to how hard I'd hit Russo in the shower, but I caught my attacker off guard with a swipe to the ear. In this cold, it was certain to sting.

His grip let up on me as he flinched. Taking advantage of his pause, I edged in a second hit to his abdomen. He sucked in a painful-sounding breath which told me my placement had been admirable.

Unfortunately, that only served to anger him further. I spun around, clicked the lock on the car, and flung the door open. He lunged for me, and I sent my leg backward in a kick aimed at his groin.

I missed the sweet spot but connected with his knee, which worked just as well. He bent forward with another stifled groan.

I threw myself toward the front seat of the car, but I never made it. I first felt the man's fingers as they fisted in my hair. A jolt came next, followed closely by searing pain on my scalp.

The next thing I knew, I was face down on the ground, snow crunched into my nose. The man had tossed me from the car and thrown me to the ground. My face burned against the impact of cold and gravel against my cheeks. The corner of my eye had landed on a chunk of ice that would leave a mark. The only saving grace was that I hadn't blacked out at the impact.

I braced myself for the next blow, sensing the man's anger had grown. He'd expected an easy tussle, and he'd gotten a good fight. When the next blow didn't come, I opened my eyes to the sound of footsteps and saw a pair of pink tennis shoes on the other side of the car.

Their arrival coincided with a noise of surprise from the man, and then a strangled yelp along with the sound of some sort of air release. It took only a second to realize what was happening, then I buried my face in the snow and held my breath while the pink-shoed woman depressed a long stream of pepper spray at my attacker's face.

The sunglasses dropped, fell to the ground as the man reached for his eyes. He took a step backward, stumbled. I reached for his leg and pulled, sending him sailing into a heap as he tried to get away.

I moved to stand, felt a rush of dizziness, and steadied myself on my knees as I caught a blast of the lingering pepper spray floating through the air and scrunched my eyes shut.

I lunged after the man, but he was faster. He struggled down the street ahead of me, pulling ahead so that by the time I rounded the corner of the first block, he was gone down one of the several alleys that spiderwebbed through this part of town. Seeing as I was in no shape to sprint after him, I hesitated, caught my breath, and eventually made my way back to my car.

Nicole waited for me on the sidewalk, a cigarette still between her lips and a can of pepper spray in one hand. The baby was nowhere to be seen.

"Thank you for that," I said once I made it back. "Nice shot."

Nicole surveyed me. "I thought you were supposed to fight good."

"I do fight good! I was just surprised. But, I do appreciate it. You know, if you ever need a favor..."

"Sure."

"Why'd you do it?" I asked. "You could have stayed inside with your baby. I wouldn't have blamed you."

"Is not my baby," she said softly. "Is Aneta's."

I blinked. "You're caring for Aneta's baby?"

"What else to do? There is nowhere for baby to go. So, he's mine now."

"If you want to legally adopt—"

"Time for my favor," Nicole said. "Before you worry about baby, worry about Aneta. For her son. Find who killed his mother and make him stop."

Chapter 27

A car crunched to a stop as my conversation with Nicole ended. She took one look at Russo and blinked.

"I'm done here," Nicole said. "No more questions, and I'm not talking to a man."

"Of course. Thank you, again."

"Gee, nice of you to show up," I said as Russo came to a stop before me. "You missed the fun part."

"I wasn't even supposed to be here."

"So why are you here? I told you to meet me at the club."

"Sixth sense," Russo said, studying my face. "I take it I missed something? Something substantial judging by that shiner?"

I blinked rapidly to clear the pepper spray. "No, the black eye's just for kicks. I thought we could match."

"Who—"

"The killer—or the person I assume is the killer—paid a visit just now as I was finishing up with Nicole. He caught me by surprise, Nicole shot him with pepper spray, and he ran away. Cool story, now can we get a move on and find him?"

Russo's face hardened, but he tucked the sympathy away and went straight to business. "Did you see his face?"

"He was masked and wore sunglasses. Every inch of him was covered. I can't even guess a race or ethnicity. He spoke... Midwestern though."

"Midwestern?"

"You know, 'normal'. No accent to me."

"How long did the two of you chat that you got a feel for him?"

"He told me that if I backed off the case, he'd leave town."

"And you said...?"

"What do you think I said?"

"Ah, I see." Russo nodded. "It didn't occur to you to lie?"

"Nope."

"Now what?"

"We have to go to the bar. Nicole is certain that Aneta was seeing a guy who worked there."

"Our killer?"

"Only one way to find out."

"I'll drive."

"I'm driving myself," I said. "You can follow me."

Russo gave me another once over. It looked like he was on the verge of saying something—asking if I was okay, maybe—but he refrained at the last second and nodded instead.

"Fine," he said. "But I'm not letting you out of my sight until the case is over."

"Sure," I said, swinging my keys around my finger. "Then keep up."

"HE'S NOT HERE?" I RAISED an eyebrow as I faced off with Wes. "What do you mean he's not here?"

"I mean, Bobby didn't show up for work." Wes sat behind his desk and studied me. "I feel like I'm the one who should be upset about this, not you. Why do you care?"

"That's confidential." I ran a hand through my hair. "Do you have his home address? A phone number?"

"Sure." Wes typed something on his keyboard, pausing only to glance over my shoulder at Russo.

The FBI agent had turned his back on us to study the photos along the wall. He was staring extra hard at the one featuring Wes and Gem together.

"If you like the photo that much, you can have it," Wes said. "I've got another copy."

Russo spun around without missing a beat. "The address and phone number for your employee, please?"

Wes hit print, and the machine whirred behind his desk, spitting out a sheet of paper with Bobby's name and address on it. He handed it across. "He's not gonna be happy to see you."

"They never are," I said. "By the way, where did you go last night?"

"Go?"

"The security footage." I watched carefully for his reaction. "We requested it from Gem Industries, and I reviewed it today. You left via the back entrance last night. Where did you go?"

He didn't crack. "I went outside for a moment."

"I didn't see you coming back in on the security footage."

"I didn't," Wes said simply. "You're wondering if I have an alibi for the window of time in which the girl was killed, I'm assuming?"

My silence counted for an answer.

"I'm sorry, detective. I don't have a good answer for you," Wes said. "I went outside for a bit. Took a walk to clear my head. I was alone."

"Why don't I believe you?"

He shrugged. "Is there anything else I can help you with?"

"Yeah, is my sister supposed to be working tonight?"

"Unless this is related to the case, I don't think I should answer," Wes said. "Out of respect for your sister. You understand."

"Fine," I said through gritted teeth. "Then if you'd like to do me a personal favor, maybe tell her to call me back when you see her."

I didn't wait for a response before I spun on my heel and left the room, already reading over the computer printout and timing out the best route to Bobby's house in my head. Russo followed close behind, smartly choosing to let me stew in silence.

"You'll follow me?" I prompted.

Russo spun his keys around his finger and gave a short nod. "See you there."

Bobby lived in a duplex on the east side of St. Paul, not far from Lake Phalen. His residence was in an area of town that wasn't quite good and wasn't quite bad. It was a mix of low-income families doing their best, older couples who'd been in their homes since the turn of the century, and crappy rental places that had been popping up in the last few years to round the city out.

Russo and I made our way to the front door. I knocked. It took three more pounds to garner an, "I'm coming!" from inside. A few minutes later, the door swung open to reveal Bobby dressed in nothing but a pair of grey sweatpants with holes worn in the knees.

He didn't wear a shirt, and judging by the way he lazily scratched at his chest and yawned without flinching, the cold air didn't bother him. Neither did the sight of a female detective and a male FBI agent standing before him.

"Yeah?" he said in greeting.

"You probably remember us from the other night," I said. "I'm Detective Rosetti, and this is—"

"The FBI dude, right. Get down to business. My show's on, and I don't got that DVR thing to pause it."

"Why aren't you at work?" I asked.

"Um, why is that any of your business?"

"Wes was expecting you," I said. "We showed up at Rubies to speak with you, and yet here you are."

"Wes wasn't expecting me," Bobby said. "I got the night off."

Russo raised his eyebrows. "That's not what he said. He tried to call you."

"My phone's off," Bobby said. "I told you—my show's on. I don't like distractions."

"Okay, well, I suppose that's neither here nor there, but we did want to talk to you about—"

"Hang on a second," Bobby interrupted. "Are you really saying you just came from Rubies?"

"Yes. We thought you were scheduled to work."

"I *was*, but then I got a call saying they didn't need me this afternoon."

"Who called you?"

"I don't even remember. One of the girls."

"The girls?"

"You know, a server." Bobby shrugged. "I don't bother to remember their names. I'm not even sure she told me one. The chick just said she was calling from Rubies on behalf of Wes. Apparently, he hired a new bouncer and wanted to give me the night off. I've been working every frickin' day so far, so I didn't think twice about it. I deserve a night to myself."

"Are you sure this girl who called didn't give you a name?"

"I don't remember. Like I said, those girls are inter-changeable. Doesn't matter the venue, waitresses last a week usually, a month max. Only a few stay on long term."

A dark thought crossed my mind. I glanced over at Russo to see if he was thinking the same thing I was and surmised he'd come to the same conclusion by the tightness in his jaw.

"Bobby, I think someone is framing you," I said. "Or at least trying to throw us off the scent by using you."

"What the hell are you talking about, woman?"

"Detective," I said tersely. "And we know about the money."

"What money?"

"Five thousand bucks. Twice. Each deposited the night after one of our victims died."

Bobby scratched so hard at his bare chest that a patch of red bloomed on his skin. "Er, how do you know about that?"

"It doesn't matter. Who gave you that money?"

"I don't know," Bobby said, raising both hands. "Honest. I have no idea."

"Yeah, we're not buying it. You've already lied to us. Fool me once, Bobby..."

"I'm telling you the truth, honest. See, someone put a note in my pocket that told me if the cops came asking around about a girl, I was just supposed to say I hadn't seen her. I read the note and figured, what the hell? Why not give it a try?"

"It didn't say which girl?"

"No, nothing. That's all it said. So, when you came around asking about people, I just said I hadn't seen whoever you were talking about. I didn't think there'd be any harm in it. I mean, I didn't do anything wrong, and I really needed new brakes on my car."

"Nothing wrong? You mean, besides lying to the police, impeding a murder investigation, aiding and abetting..." I trailed off as Bobby's face went pink.

"Okay, okay, well I didn't actually do anything wrong besides that stuff," he said. "I'm not going to get in trouble, am I? I don't know anything, anyway. I didn't see who put the note in my pocket."

"Do you still have the note?"

"No," he said. "I tossed it. It said to get rid of it."

"So, we don't even know if you're telling the truth."

"You think I could make up a lie like that?" Bobby retorted. "C'mon, detective. I may not be brilliant, but you probably are. I can't lie to save my life."

"You already lied to us."

"Not really," he said. "I just didn't look at the picture you showed me, so it was easy to say I hadn't seen her. I just stared at the table really hard. I didn't actually lie about that."

My eyes rolled so hard they almost got stuck in the back of my head. I sensed Bobby was telling the truth this time around. I also got the feeling that we'd been played. The killer had sent us on a wild goose chase—he'd planted money in Bobby's account to direct our attention his way. Then, when we'd been ready to confront him, he'd thrown us for another loop by ensuring Bobby wasn't where he was supposed to be, casting further suspicion on him.

Worst of all, we'd fallen for it—hook, line, and sinker. We'd chased after Bobby who was, by all accounts, a dead end. The killer had been careful to keep Bobby at arm's length, a decoy and nothing more.

But, why? I realized I'd said the last question aloud when Russo cleared his throat and looked to me, waiting for an answer.

"Why now?" I asked. "Why send us after Bobby tonight? Unless..."

Russo's head snapped up, his gaze locking on mine.

"We've got to get back to Rubies," I said. "Now. He's going to kill again, and he wanted us out of the way."

"His grand finale. He'll leave town afterward. We're getting too close, and he knows it." Russo rested his hand on mine, gave it a squeeze. "We'll get him, Kate. I promise."

I nodded. "Meet you there."

We made our ways to our respective vehicles, got in, and fired up the engines. I had Jimmy on the line before I pulled on the street.

"Get over to Rubies," I said. "Now. Our man's going to kill again."

"Who is it?" Jimmy asked. "I'm on my way."

"I don't know that yet. But the target will be someone high profile," I said. "He's making a statement. It might be someone personal..."

"Kate?" Jimmy said after I'd fallen silent. "Is everything okay?"

"I've got to let you go, Jimmy," I said. "I'll meet you there. I've got someone on the other line. Call Russo if you need anything."

We disconnected. I didn't have anyone on the other line, but a thought had popped into my head that stole all of my attention. Things were getting personal for the killer. We'd had a hand-to-hand altercation this afternoon, and he hadn't bested me like he'd planned. We'd discovered the identity of his first Jane Doe. We'd peeled back the layers to Bobby. He wouldn't like any of it.

Russo was right—our guy was going to ditch town, but not without one last shebang. And I knew with an impending sense of dread, that it would be personal.

I dialed another number. "Jane, I'm not kidding—pick up the phone. You're in danger. Call me back. Please."

No sooner had I disconnected than my phone rang. The number wasn't in my contact list. I hit answer.

"Detective? This is Wes," the voice said. "Wes Remington from Rubies."

"What's up?"

"Your sister was supposed to work tonight," he said. "But she's an hour late, and I haven't been able to get ahold of her. I was wondering if you've heard from her."

"When's the last time you saw her?"

"This morning. I picked her up when she called last night, and she stayed with me. She was still there when I left for the office this morning."

"You haven't heard from her since the morning?"

"She texted me this afternoon saying she'd see me soon, and then... nothing."

"I've got to go," I said. "The cops are already on their way to Rubies."

"She's not here."

"I know that," I snapped. "But we've got to start somewhere."

"I'll call Gem. He'll know what to do."

"She's *my* sister," I said. "I'm going to find her."

Chapter 28

I sat in my car, stunned. My mind raced as puzzle pieces clicked into place. It wasn't Wes's fault my sister had been taken—if anything, it was my fault. I hadn't listened when he'd warned me. Now, Jane was most likely alone at the hands of a man who'd killed multiple women. And this time, it was personal.

I glanced at the clock. Russo and Jimmy would be on their way to Rubies. I had planned to meet them there, but the more I thought about it, the more I was convinced my help wasn't necessary at the club—the boys could handle it. I needed to find Jane. But who had taken her? And where would he be keeping her?

It was the coffee cup that did it. The spark of genius, the stroke of good fortune—whatever I wanted to call it. All it took was a glance at my mother's handwriting on the edge of my latte to point me in a direction that just might save my sister's life.

I dialed my mother and launched into my question the second she answered. "Do you still have that tracking app on Jane's phone?"

"It's on my phone," my mother said. "You mean, the one you specifically said was invasive and that you disapproved of, and *yada yada*?"

"Listen, Ma—you're a genius," I said. "Pull it up. Tell me where Jane is."

"Isn't that snooping? Don't you disapprove of snooping?"

"Mom."

My voice cracked, and my mother thankfully obliged. A few muffled sounds came across the line as my mother struggled to figure out how to use speaker phone and her screen at the same time. Finally, she muttered, "Gotcha!"

"Where is she?"

"Well, this doesn't make any sense," my mom said. "Why would she be all the way out in Stillwater?"

"Where in Stillwater?"

"I don't know. Someone's house, judging by the looks of it. Does she have a new boyfriend?"

"Do you have an address?"

"Well, of course. How else am I supposed to stalk my daughter?"

"Read it to me."

I punched in the numbers and street address as my mother rattled them off.

"You're brilliant," I said breathlessly. "Talk to you later. Love you."

"Kate."

"What?"

"You never say I love you. Not all flippantly, not like that. What's wrong?"

I hesitated. "I'm not sure yet."

I could sense my mother's frustration. She started to say something several times before settling on a simple "I love you" back.

"Be careful, Kate," she continued. "And tell your sister... I'm sorry. I love her, too. Dearly."

"She knows that," I said. "We both do. I'll call you later."

The time to the last address my mother had given me said twenty-seven minutes on my GPS. Which meant that with lights and a lead foot, I could make it in fifteen if I really flew.

I pointed my car toward Highway 36 and floored it the second I merged, sailing down the left lane at speeds I'd never dare travel for anyone but family. Once I was settled on the straightaway, I called Russo and breathlessly explained the situation.

"Wait for me at the location," he said promptly. "I'm turning around to join you. I'll be a few minutes behind. Don't go in without backup, Kate."

"Then get backup there. Fast."

"You didn't promise."

"No," I said. "I didn't. I've gotta let you go, Russo. Make the calls—get Jimmy, get a team. I don't know who we'll find out at this farm, but my sister'd better be alive."

I WAS RIGHT. IT WAS a farm.

The turnoff was north of Stillwater, past the well-known, quaint town on the river and well into farmland—where tractors drove on main thoroughfares and every other stretch of road smelled like manure. The homes here were spaced far enough apart to ensure privacy... and seclusion. A perfect place to keep someone hidden.

I pulled onto the dirt drive and turned off my main headlights, leaving only the daytime running lights to glow as I crunched over the freshly plowed road. Whoever had taken Jane had been prepared. They'd cleared a path in advance, which told me they'd planned her kidnapping. That didn't bode well for me... or for Jane. Our killer was smart and prepared, deceptive, and now cornered.

I pulled onto the side of the road the second a house came into view. One light burned inside and another glowed in the garage, but I didn't think anyone could see the car from the bend in the road.

I checked my gun. It was at my hip, loaded, ready for use. The fresh snow muffled my footsteps until I met a patch of ice.

All it took was one wrong step, and suddenly, a loud *crack* shot through the darkness as my heel plummeted through a patchy layer of ice. I paused, my heart racing as I glanced behind me, but my car was all but invisible against the tree line. It took a painstaking ten minutes and a near bout with severe frostbite, but I made it to the exterior of the garage without detection.

I hesitated near the stucco building in a low crouch and let my ears adjust to the utter silence. It was so quiet my ears pounded in the complete stillness. Blood rushed through my veins and adrenaline jolted my senses into high gear.

That's when I heard it.

A sound from the main house—a loud crash. Something heavy falling, and then a shrill scream.

Jane.

I took one glance at my phone, saw that Russo had texted me twice. The first time, he asked that I wait outside. The second, he demanded it. My phone trilled with a third vibration as he sent a message threatening some nasty consequences if I didn't respond to him in the next few minutes.

I silenced my phone. The decision was swift and final, and I was halfway to the house before I could rethink my choice. I might tick off Russo and Jimmy and the rest of the TC Task Force, but it was worth the risk when my sister's life was at stake.

The house itself was a single-family home—red paint lined the outside, the door sat bright against the exterior lighting in a shade of faded blue that had peeled from years without attention. White shutters hung on every window, giving the house a distinctly patriotic vibe.

I reached for the doorknob. *Locked.*

I crunched through a layer of crispy snow to the side where I found several basement windows. I tugged on each until I found one with a loose latch. I managed to wedge it open with just enough space to wiggle through.

I dropped through to the basement floor. The only casualty was a slight tear to the leg of my pants and a scratch to match. I didn't notice the blood until I was halfway across the basement, headed for a set of wooden steps leading one floor up to a closed door.

Soft lamplight seeped through the crack beneath the door. From the other side came the sound of a voice—one person spoke in low tones, seemingly asking questions, though it didn't sound like he was getting a response.

Good on you, Jane, I thought. The longer she could stall, the better.

I tested the lowest stair. The basement itself was near empty, save for a laundry room with rusted machines that looked like they hadn't been used this century. An old wash bin let out a steady drip from the faucet, and I ignored a scurrying sound as tiny nails scratched across the cement floor.

I ascended carefully. Despite the patchy construction job on the staircase, it seemed to be holding up well. Until I reached the third step from the top.

The creak came out of nowhere. My heart leapt into a race as panic set in. The voice on the other side of the door stopped its murmuring. The house fell still.

Then footsteps resumed, headed my way. I glanced down, but there was nowhere to hide, even if I could move fast enough to get out of sight, I was stuck. Once the door at the top of the stairs swung open, I'd be a sitting duck.

"You're not going to get away with this, you know," Jane chirped suddenly. "Hey, you—yes, I'm talking to you. My sister's gonna find you."

I exhaled a breath. It could've been a coincidence Jane had chosen this very moment to speak, but I suspected she'd heard my misstep and was trying to cover the noise with a distraction of her own.

The footsteps stopped. I closed my eyes for a brief second and breathed a sigh of relief. I listened carefully as the man responded, thinking his voice sounded somewhat familiar. Had I met him before? It was too muffled to say for certain from a distance. I needed to see his face.

"Why'd you do it, anyway?" Jane asked. "You've had me sitting here for hours. Obviously, you're going to kill me. You let me see your face, so I'm not getting away. Why wait?"

Come on, Jane, I urged her silently. *Say his name. Tell me who killed those girls.*

My throat closed up as I thought back through the investigation. I glanced down at my phone and the dark screen, seeing a new message there as I clicked the screen to life.

On it was a note from Asha. A name.

Asha: Reggie Woo.

As I watched, another message came through.

Asha: Bartender at Rubies—new to the area. Travel matches up with other murders. He last worked at a bar out east—one belonging to Alastair Gem. He transferred over here to help open the new club and killings resumed.

"Come on, Reggie," Jane pleaded. "Talk to me. I see the knife in your hand. But I thought you strangled those other girls. Why the knife?"

"Because you're special," the bartender said. "I have reserved special treatment for you. Thank your sister."

I cursed. I should have known, should have seen it. Tall, dark, handsome. Access to many young women who would be happy to spend alone time with a bartender employed by Gem Industries. He'd told us he was new to the area. And yet, we'd been a step behind this entire time. *Why?* I wondered. How had we missed him?

Because there were other options, better options, I thought. Gem himself, or Wes. And my theories hadn't been completely off base—there had been something off with Rubies, with Gem Industries. The only question left was whether anyone else had known what was happening, or if Reggie had acted on his own.

"This is your fault," Reggie said good-naturedly. "If you had listened to your sister and stayed away from Gem Industries, I wouldn't have known you existed."

"My job is important," Jane sassed back. "I wouldn't let you keep me away from it."

He snorted. "Waitressing?"

"I know you think that's all I'm doing, but it's so much more. My sister thinks that, too," Jane said. "You're both wrong. I was working for Alastair Gem himself."

"Yeah," Reggie agreed, "me too."

"He knows about you. Even if you kill me, it's over, Reggie. He's got your name. I texted him before I confronted you."

"That's bull," Reggie said. "You don't have his number. And it's an awful lie because I have your phone."

"Check it," Jane said. "It's there."

"Doesn't matter. It's over for you."

"If you hurt me, Kate is going to hunt you down. She won't let you get away with this."

"I wouldn't dream of anything else," Reggie said. "I'm sure we don't have long before she turns up here. They'll have figured out Bobby's nothing but a deterrent and will put the rest of it together. I'll take care of you first, then when your sister joins us, I'll take care of her next. If she gets here in time, she can watch."

"You vastly underestimate Kate."

"She was the one I wanted all along," Reggie said. "The bitch couldn't keep her nose out of my business. Poking and prodding around the case. She couldn't just leave it alone."

"Kate always catches the bad guy," Jane said. "She's the best there is."

"She thinks so. But there's always someone better. That's me."

Jane gave a bark of laughter. "I wouldn't put money on that. Even better, once she bests you—she's going to find out about what's happening at Gem Industries."

I stiffened at Jane's tone and wondered if she was trying to tell me something.

"What are you talking about?"

"Alastair knew something was going on in his company. He needed someone to go undercover to investigate."

"And he sent you," Reggie scoffed dryly. "Right."

"Who better?" Jane chirped. "Nobody would suspect it. Nobody expects anything from me. That's why there's no point to killing me; there's nobody to miss me."

"That's not true," I heard myself saying before I could stop to think. "That's not true at all."

Having blown my cover, I twisted the knob and burst through the doorway and into a threadbare kitchen. Before me, Jane sat tied to a chair with a gag dropped down around her neck like a piece of jewelry. Reggie stood behind her, a knife raised to her throat.

My breaths sounded heavy in the sudden silence. Reggie smiled and looked unsurprised to see me standing before him.

"Did you catch all that?" Reggie asked. "It's about time you joined the party."

"Jane," I said, directing my attention to her. "Are you hurt?"

"I'm fine! Don't worry about me."

"I hate to interrupt, detective," Reggie drawled, "but I'm going to need you to put your gun down."

"Why'd you do it?" I turned my attention from Jane to Reggie. I didn't drop the gun, just tilted it downward. I kept my mouth moving in hopes to distract him from my grip on the weapon. "Was the first one an accident? Then it all turned into a thrill? Why couldn't you stop? Those girls were innocent."

"Not as innocent as you'd think," Reggie said. "Those girls were grateful to me. I *helped* them."

"Yeah, right," Jane muttered. When I looked at her, she met my gaze evenly. "He was running a prostitution ring through the bar system."

"Reggie?"

Jane nodded to confirm. "I meant it, Kate—I wasn't just working at a bar to work at a bar. Mr. Gem asked me to personally investigate his own staff."

"Why wouldn't he have called the police?" I asked. "He should have told me."

"And then what?" she pressed. "Risk you guys shutting everything down? No offense, but he wasn't convinced there was anything wrong happening. He just wanted to know for sure."

"We could've—"

"He would have gone to you the second his suspicions were confirmed. Put yourself in his shoes, Kate. What *should* he have done? Called the cops to say he might have a corrupt employee, but he wasn't quite sure, and maybe they could peek around?"

"Yes."

"He was cooperating with your investigation while running his own," Jane said. "It didn't take me long to figure out what was happening once he hired me. Reggie here isn't exactly subtle."

"Luck," Reggie said. "You were lucky."

"I looked at all the recent transfers from one Gem bar to another," Jane said. "I knew if Gem suspected something, it probably wasn't just a one-off event that had him worried. Turns out, you're the only employee who has previously been employed by Gem Industries besides Wes, and I knew it wasn't him."

"Nice work," I said. "We caught that tonight, but we were behind."

"I had an advantage," Jane admitted. "I'm working for Gem himself, and he lets me have lots of help and even some money to look into stuff. I just ask him a question, and he gets me the answer. After the info pointed me toward Reggie, I only had to watch for one night to know he was the one behind everything."

Reggie tensed, the knife coming to touch Jane's skin. "Oh?"

"You're friendly to everyone... except for your girls," Jane said. "Two women came in late last night, and you didn't look happy to be talking to them. I approached the first one and she bolted. The second one talked. She told me all about your little arrangement."

Jane's eyes turned toward me. Her eyes flicked toward the gun, then back to my face. I understood she was stalling, giving me time to think. But all the thinking time in the world didn't solve the tiny problem of how to make my move without Reggie harming Jane in the process.

"He meets girls at bars and clubs, sometimes where he works—other times not," Jane continued. "You're good at finding the ones that need help, aren't you, Reggie? The high-risk ones. The immigrants, the poor ones, the heartbroken and desperate."

"It's a skill," Reggie said. "And you should know that you've just signed Andrea's death warrant. She talked, she's dead."

"Her real name's not Andrea," Jane bit out, her eyes flicking toward me. "It's Shelly Crows. And she's already gone. I told her to go to the police, but she wouldn't. So, she left. You won't find her."

"Leslie Rosehip," I said. "She doesn't fit the pattern."

"No, but talk about easy." Reggie's eyes held a gleam in them as he stared into the distance. "You were getting close, and I needed something to throw you off. Leslie fit the bill."

"She came into the bar and what?" I asked. "How'd you get her to leave with you?"

"I offered her a job. Rich little lady like her can fetch a high price for the right buyer."

"Her parents had just cut her off financially, and she needed money."

"Perfect timing." Reggie smiled. "She seemed interested, but at the last second, she decided she didn't want to go through with it. So, I had no use for her."

Jane looked sick, and I felt bile build in my throat. "The other girls, did they want out? Is that why you killed them?"

"They overstayed their welcome."

"You gave them their passports, told them they were free to leave," I said. "Then you kidnapped and killed them."

"I didn't intend to add your sister to my resume, but she made it too easy. Confronted me without backup like an idiot. If she'd told you, then you'd be here, and she'd be safe at home."

"It doesn't work like that. We've always been a team," I said. "Ever since we could play games together. You remember our favorite game, Jane?"

I looked carefully at Jane, hoping she understood.

"You know the one," I said slowly. "Grey duck."

"Right." Jane nodded. She shifted slightly in her seat, gave me time to subtly adjust my grip on the gun. "I remember. Duck... Duck..."

Before she could utter the final phrase, Jane launched herself away from the knife. The chair clattered to the floor in sync with the sound of a gunshot.

Blood spurted From Reggie's shoulder as he lurched backward, reeling with the impact from the bullet. My eyes flicked to Jane who was covered in blood—hers or his, I couldn't say.

"Jane!" I called, but there was no response.

Every instinct told me to rush toward her, but my training kicked in and reminded me there was a killer who needed to be restrained. I turned my attention to Reggie who was already hauling himself to his feet. His left arm swung uselessly like a club at his side.

I rushed at his legs, dipping beneath the knife as he slashed at me. We fell together, crashing to the ground. He landed hard on my wrist, and I yelped in pain as my gun skittered across the floor toward Jane.

I went for Reggie's arms to pin him down, but the movement was enough to give Reggie the opportunity to shift his bulk upward. He tossed me to one side, and the air crashed out of me when I hit the wall. My head struck something hard, rattled my consciousness. When I opened my eyes, I realized I'd blacked out for a moment because Reggie was standing above me, the knife returned to his hand.

He held the shining blade over me, the thrill of murder in his eyes as he plunged it downward. I rolled, but I couldn't get past his legs. The blade screeched closer, aimed at my stomach. I rolled out of the way with a second to spare as the knife chopped into the wooden floor.

The room spun. I pushed myself to my feet and launched myself at Reggie before he could straighten. I landed one solid kick to his groin, and he went down in a huff, crumpling to one side in an automatic response. I took advantage and slammed my foot to his back, pressing him face first into the floor.

"Reggie Woo," I said, still somewhat out of breath. "You're under arrest."

"I think you're looking for these?" Agent Russo appeared from a hallway before I could continue. He pulled out a set of handcuffs and tossed them to me while simultaneously crossing the room and releasing Jane from her bindings.

I finished the reading of rights while snapping on the cuffs. When I finished, I looked up at Russo. "Nice of you to show up."

"I didn't want to take the credit for your hard work," he said with a thin smile. "Who's hurt? Tell me that's his blood."

I felt a jolt of surprise as I caught sight of the gigantic pool of blood on the floor. "Jane? Are you... Did he get you?"

"I'm fine," Jane said, but her face was white.

Not two seconds later, she slumped onto the floor. I moved toward her, listened for her breathing and found it coming in shallow gasps.

"She needs medical attention," I called. "She's injured."

"She'll be okay." Russo was already by my side. "It's a shallow cut; it just looks bad. Most of that blood belongs to him."

I nodded but couldn't speak.

"Ambulances are on their way. They'll be here in a few minutes."

"We got our confession," I choked out. "It's not recorded, but—"

"You and Jane both heard it. We have another witness who's just come forward... Shelly Crows? She's willing to testify. There will be others."

"So, it's over," I said. "It's really over?"

Russo leaned over, brushed a hair back from my face. "It's over."

EPILOGUE

Christmas Eve bloomed bright with sparkling lights, glittery red tinsel, and dripping chandeliers of light as the driver pulled up in front of Gem Industries.

"How'd you ladies get an invite to the Christmas party?" The driver of the limo sent by Gem craned his head backward to look at me. "Any chance either of you need a date? I've heard it's the biggest event of the year within five hundred miles."

"We have dates," I said with a smile at Jane. "Thanks, anyway."

"Ah." The driver focused on me. "Wait a minute... you're not... are you the gal who's dating Mr. Gem? I heard he'd invited someone for the first time in ages, and she's supposed to look sorta like you."

"Have a great night," I said shortly, opening the door. "Thanks for the ride."

"Anytime," the driver said. "And if you don't mind, tell him Sal Hanson wouldn't mind an invitation next year."

"I'll let him know."

I stepped into the now-familiar Gem Industries building with Jane following close behind. It dazzled with Christmas wonder. The actual gala was located on one of the uppermost floors of the building, but that hadn't stopped the Gem Industries employees from going all out on the entrance.

293

A trail of golden lights lined a red carpet over which fake snow flurried about our ankles. Real evergreen trees stood guard on either side of the walk, decorated with strands of tinsel and garlands of silver streamers, topped by diamond angel figurines.

Jane and I followed the path to the elevator and took it up to the necessary floor, watching the city lights until the doors opened to reveal the main event. The room glittered under dim, lush lights with twinkling patches of fake snow glinting off every surface.

"You'll do great." Jane rested a hand on my wrist. "Don't worry. Just breathe and try to have fun."

"Easier said than done," I grumbled. "I hate parties."

"With that attitude, of course." Jane gave me a playful wink. "You look stunning."

I thumbed the fabric of my dress subconsciously as I stepped out of the elevator and tucked my clutch under my elbow. I hitched my gown so I didn't stumble over my heels as I puttered into a sea of beautifully dressed women and men.

I'd opted for a simple black dress with an open back and a V-neck front. The only accessories I'd selected were a swipe of red lipstick and tiny diamond studs in my ears. My hair had been swept back in an updo courtesy of Lassie, and my shoes had been borrowed from Melinda's collection.

"Ma'am," a voice called before I could catch my breath. "You're Ms. Rosetti, yes?"

I looked at Jane. "Er, yeah. We both are."

"Detective?"

Jane pointed at me. "That'd be her."

"Wonderful." The woman smiled as she raised a phone to her ear. "Mr. Gem wanted to know when you'd arrived. He'll greet you inside."

"That's really not necessary."

"I'm just doing my job," she said, hand over the receiver. Then she removed her fingers and spoke louder. "Mr. Gem? Yes, she's here."

Like magic, Gem appeared across the room from behind a hidden door. He looked like the billionaire he was in a suit and bowtie, his curls tamed in a side part that made him look like a dashing financier until he smiled, and that boyish glint turned him into a mischievous playboy.

By the time he reached my side, both Gem's assistant and my sister had vanished into the crowded party.

Gem came to a stop before me. "Glad to see you made it, detective."

"Thanks for the warm welcome. Does everyone else get such personalized greetings?"

"Only the guests who've received a personalized invitation." Gem winked and reached for my hand. "May I grab you a drink?"

I hesitated. "You know you're not my date, right?"

"Yes, well... I think your date is occupied."

I followed Gem's gaze and located Jane in the middle of the dance floor. Two minutes into the party, and she was already whirling around the dance floor with Wes Remington—beaming like the star atop the tree.

"I don't know," I said. "I guess—"

"A cabernet?" he guessed. "You're off duty, detective. And it's Christmas Eve. My driver will take you home when you're ready."

I looked down, found Gem had secured my hand in his while I'd been distracted by my sister. "Actually, I'd like that."

Gem grabbed us both glasses of wine, offered one to me. He clinked glasses with mine. "I don't suppose you'd grant me a Christmas wish and join me on the dance floor?"

"Do your cheesy lines work on anyone?"

Gem laughed. "You'll have to let me know. I haven't tried it on anyone else."

I grinned back. "It's not working tonight. I don't dance."

"I beg to differ." Gem waited until I took a few deep sips of my wine. "One dance."

"I'm going to need a little more of this." I wiggled my wine glass. "I'm an awful dancer."

"That's not true at all." One of Gem's hands came up and clasped mine, the other looping around my back. His palm rested against the bare skin on my lower back. "This isn't so bad, is it?"

I shivered as Gem's breath brushed against my forehead.

"I've experienced worse," I admitted. "But I work with savage killers, so the bar's pretty low."

Gem's chuckle was soft as he pulled me closer. He smelled like Christmas and money and fresh snow. Before I knew it, my head rested against his chest as we moved in meditative circles around the dance floor.

"Thank you," Gem said, breaking the silence.

"For?"

"Coming to the party," he said. "Taking a chance on me. Putting yourself in danger to solve the case. Not looking at the easiest solution, despite pressure from the department to get things wrapped up."

"You don't have to thank me for any of that. Except the showing up tonight part," I added. "The rest of it was just me doing my job."

"I employ thousands of workers. Not one of them has the work ethic that you do. Or the natural talent and nose for their jobs. You're something special, detective."

"Don't get sappy on me, or I'm out of here."

"Your sister—"

"Thank you," I said. When Gem looked surprised at my interruption, I continued. "You believed in her. You trusted her to do a big job."

"I didn't expect to be thanked for that," Gem said. "I thought you'd blame me for putting her in harm's way."

"I'm not pleased about that, but she's an adult. She can make her own choices. And she was trying to help. If nothing else, I can understand that."

"Well, if that's the case, I'll consider your debt absolved if you dance one more song with me."

Gem winked, and I glanced up, surprised to find that the song had ended. Another eased forth from the speakers, and I let myself be pulled into Gem's arms all over again.

As it turned out, I didn't hate dancing as much as I thought. Not with Gem.

We spiraled around the dance floor, no longer speaking, as the music grew louder and swept us into a tiny world that belonged exclusively to the two of us. When Gem's gaze landed on me, I tilted my face upward to find a complex expression on his face.

"You look beautiful tonight, Kate," he said, his gaze flicking toward my lips. "I'm glad you're here."

"I'm glad I'm here, too." I murmured it without thinking. "I would never have..."

Gem distracted me from finishing my sentence as he leaned in and tilted his head closer. He waited for me to meet him halfway. I did, inching inward, until his lips brushed against mine.

"Kate!"

I jerked backward, my hands leaping off Gem's chest like he was on fire. My fingers went to my bottom lip where a whisper of Gem's kiss had left my skin scorching.

"Jane," I muttered. "You startled me."

Jane had one arm hooked through Wes's. Both of them had the happy-in-love glow of a new relationship. It was amplified by the free-flowing fine wine and the full emotions of the holidays.

"I'm sorry, I know I'm here as your date and whatnot," Jane said. "But maybe you can hang out with Mr. Gem for a bit? Wes and I are going to... well, he's going to show me the view from upstairs."

"Yeah..." I wiped a hand across my forehead. "Have fun, kids."

Once they disappeared, I turned to Gem.

"They're going to get in some trouble," I said. "I hope you know that."

"It's Christmas Eve," Gem said evenly. "There's magic in the air. Who knows what can happen?"

Unfortunately—or fortunately—the moment had been broken before I'd done something stupid. Dancing with Gem was one thing, but full-on kissing him was another thing entirely. I wasn't in any sort of place to get involved with a man. Not with my career leaping into overdrive.

"It's not like that," Gem said quietly, as if reading my mind. "I like you, detective."

"It's not the right time for anything serious," I said. "I'm really sorry."

He nodded. "Can I tempt you in some finger food, at least? Maybe you'd like to come to my office? I can have dinner sent up."

"I think—" I hesitated. "I need some fresh air. I'm going to step outside."

"Will you come back?"

My fingers played with my clutch, giving away my nerves. "I don't know, Gem. I think I'm going to call it a night."

He could have argued that I'd just arrived, that I hadn't eaten, that I'd taken the time to dress up for what—five minutes of a gala? Instead, he just nodded. As if he understood.

"I'll let my driver know you're ready to go home," he said. "I hope, detective, that I'll see you again soon."

"Let's hope it's not related to a case next time," I said, then colored as I realized what I'd said. "I mean—I just hope..." I frowned. "Stay out of trouble, alright?"

Gem laughed. "I most certainly will. Can I walk you out?"

"It's your party," I said, seeing a man approaching Gem and standing off to the side. "I'll just duck out. I'll—uh—"

"I'll call you." Gem nodded to the man at his side, then rested his hand on my back and steered me toward the front entrance. When we reached the elevator, he brushed the softest of kisses against my forehead. "Good night, detective. And Merry Christmas."

The doors closed, and I watched as Gem disappeared, leaving me alone with my reflection and the thump of music that followed me twenty floors down.

"What the hell is your problem?" I muttered to my reflection when I reached the ground floor and stepped out into the Christmas wonderland of Gem Industries.

I stared upward as if I could see through forty levels of floors to the party happening without me. I could have stayed. I could have dined on gourmet food, sipped imported wine, circled the dance floor in Gem's arms. And yet here I was, leaving early on Christmas Eve to go home alone. To a dark house. For no reason at all.

Except, there was a reason, I realized as I stepped outside and felt the flurries land on my cheeks and sweep over my eyelashes. I looked up and saw Gem's limo waiting for me.

Behind his car sat another vehicle. A black rental parked with its hazards on. A man leaned against the shiny exterior, his arms folded across his chest.

"Merry Christmas, detective," Russo said with a grin. "Can I drive you home?"

"Russo," I said, glancing around warily. "What are you doing here?"

"I didn't think this sort of party was your thing," he said with a shrug. "So, I grabbed a pizza. Thought you might need a bite after whatever happened up there."

I considered for a moment, feeling something soften inside of me. Whether it was Christmas magic, or the realization that Russo had been a friend all along, or the slight scent of steaming hot pepperoni pizza, I couldn't say. But I knew when faced with the choice between a dark house and saltine crackers or a warm car and conversation with Russo, there was only one right choice.

"Um, if you could tell Mr. Gem that I won't be needing your services tonight," I said to his driver. "I've got a ride with Agent—er, with a friend."

The driver nodded, then disappeared as quickly as he'd appeared.

"I hope you know this doesn't mean anything," I said as my heels clicked through the snow. "I'm just starving."

Russo laughed. "I figured as much. That's why I didn't get you a present. Except for this one."

My eyes widened in surprise that quickly turned to humor as Russo flung the car door open. He proudly displayed a pizza box tied with a big, fat red ribbon on the front seat.

"I thought you'd have ditched town already." I eased closer and rested a hand on the warmth of the cardboard. "Wasn't your flight this afternoon?"

"It's tomorrow morning now," he said. "I changed it."

"Dare I ask why?"

"I don't think you actually want to know the answer." Russo's eyes landed on me. "Don't worry, I won't change that flight."

"So, you're really leaving?"

"I am," he said, pressing a finger tenderly against the green-ish skin around his eye. "DC is a safer distance from your fist."

I raised a hand, skimmed my thumb over his bruise. "I'm really sorry about that."

"Don't be. I deserved it," Russo said with a grin. "I'm not sorry it happened, truth be told. I'm glad I met you."

"Shut up," I said, "and get me a slice of pizza."

"Yes, ma'am," he said. "So, what *did* happen upstairs?"

"I don't want to talk about it."

"Are you and Gem—"

"I'm not looking for anything serious right now," I said. "With *anyone*."

"I see," Russo said. "Then it's a good thing I'm not, either. Hop in, detective."

Russo drove me home. We finished the pizza while sitting curled up on opposite ends of the couch. We talked until the sun rose. For the first time in a long while, I didn't welcome Christmas morning alone.

"Well," Russo said finally, glancing at his watch. "I should get to the airport, now that everything's wrapped up."

"Did you notify the other victims' families?"

"Where we could. With your help, and Jane's undercover work... along with some singing from Reggie, we're about as closed up on this case as we can hope to ever be."

"Well, I'm glad to hear that," I said. "Thank you, Russo. For this. For everything."

"Anytime, partner," Russo said. "Maybe I can call you sometime?"

I walked him to the front door and smiled back. "Maybe you can."

THE END

Author's Note

Thank you for reading! I hope you enjoyed meeting Detective Kate Rosetti and team. The second and third books in the series are currently available to be ordered on Amazon. And, if you enjoyed the book, please consider taking the time to leave a review at your retailer of choice! It is much appreciated and helps other readers to find books they are sure to love.

Thank you for reading!

Gina

List of Gina's Books![1]

Gina LaManna is the USA TODAY bestselling author of the Magic & Mixology series, the Lacey Luzzi Mafia Mysteries, The Little Things romantic suspense series, and the Misty Newman books.

List of Gina LaManna's other books:

Women's Fiction:
Pretty Guilty Women
Three Single Wives
Detective Kate Rosetti Mysteries:
Shoot the Breeze
Riddle Me This
Follow the Money
Murder in Style:
Secrets and Stilettos
Lipstick and Lies
The Hex Files:
Wicked Never Sleeps
Wicked Long Nights
Wicked State of Mind
Wicked Moon Rising
Wicked All The Way
Lola Pink Mystery Series:
Shades of Pink
Shades of Stars
Shades of Sunshine
Magic & Mixology Mysteries:
Hex on the Beach
Witchy Sour
Jinx & Tonic

1. http://www.amazon.com/Gina-LaManna/e/
B00RPQDNPG/?tag=ginlamaut-20

Long Isle Iced Tea
Amuletto Kiss
Spelldriver
MAGIC, Inc. Mysteries:
The Undercover Witch
Spellbooks & Spies (short story)
Reading Order for Lacey Luzzi:
Lacey Luzzi: Scooped
Lacey Luzzi: Sprinkled
Lacey Luzzi: Sparkled
Lacey Luzzi: Salted
Lacey Luzzi: Sauced
Lacey Luzzi: S'mored
Lacey Luzzi: Spooked
Lacey Luzzi: Seasoned
Lacey Luzzi: Spiced
Lacey Luzzi: Suckered
Lacey Luzzi: Sprouted
Lacey Luzzi: Shaved
The Little Things Mystery Series:
One Little Wish
Two Little Lies
Misty Newman:
Teased to Death
Short Story in Killer Beach Reads
Chick Lit:
Girl Tripping
Gina also writes books for kids under the Pen Name Libby LaManna:
Mini Pie the Spy!

Printed in Great Britain
by Amazon